The Welfare

The Welfare

R. J. Harrison

Kennedy & Boyd,
an imprint of
Zeticula Ltd,
Unit 13,
44-46 Morningside Road,
Edinburgh,
EH10 4BF,
Scotland.

http://www.kennedyandboyd.co.uk
admin@kennedyandboyd.co.uk

First published in 2025
Copyright © Esme Risner 2025

Paperback ISBN 978-1-84921-260-1

This novel is entirely a work of fiction. The names, characters and incidents portrayed in it are the work of the author's imagination. Any resemblance to actual persons, living or dead, events or localities is entirely coincidental.

All rights reserved. No part of this publication may be reproduced, stored in a retrieval system, or transmitted in any form or by any means, electronic, mechanical, photocopying, recording or otherwise, without the prior permission of the publishers.

Foreword

This is a novel inspired by stories of field work in the 1970s in London. It is fiction. Readers who believe they recognise characters or incidents should bear in mind these tales are from over 40 years ago. I did not set out to write a memoir. I changed just about everything. Even historically correct newsworthy incidents have been changed in the service of fiction.

I discovered from feedback from my wonderful writers' group that what I invented often sounds true, and what remains that is factual is mostly unbelievable.

R. J. Harrison, 2023

Acknowledgements

The greatest acknowledgement must go to all those public service workers who did then, and do now, put their work first, often at cost to their health, sanity or family. They have been poorly served by their political masters and reduced, too often, to doing only the best they can with poor resources and little appreciation.

Towards the end of writing this book, I became seriously ill, and without the extraordinary people in the NHS I would not be here to write this. We must not lose the NHS. I beg you to fight for its revival at every opportunity.

Writers of Whitstable have been supporting me on a writing journey of discovery. Without them I might never have started this novel, let alone finished it. Indeed, they finished this novel for me. I owe Richard White, Duarte Figueira, Nick Sweeney, Lin White and Jo Bartley, huge thanks.

R. J. Harrison

Contents

Foreword v
Acknowledgements vii

1	The Basement	1
2	Eating out	14
3	Gregory and the blue vase	21
4	Breaking, entering, and the Big Bang	27
5	The last tenant of Coxhall Mansions	35
6	Eric on the corner	43
7	Swimming out of darkness	52
8	The flicks	69
9	Intermediate treatment	82
10	That thing I said	88
11	Down and dirty	98
12	The other side of the road	107
13	Outflanked	117
14	Market forces	128
15	Winklers and wood panelling	140
16	The red dress	151
17	Inside out	160
18	Leviathans	171
19	C'mon Inn	180
20	Trouble in Tottenham	185
21	Home visit	190
22	Shadows	197
23	Grand Union	209
24	The wrong horse	219
25	Subnormal	230
26	The annexe	240
27	Aftercare	250

Afterword: a note from the author: 261
About the Author 263

x

1
The Basement

When my battered 2CV Citroen spluttered to the top of that hill for the first time, the sunlit carpet of London's landscape astonished me. I fell for the luminous clouds scudding over bleached domes, warehouses, and in one corner the glimpse of a glistening river snaking east to the sea.

How simple things seemed then.

Before I account for how I came to work for the Welfare down here, fell in love on that very first day and lost my job and friends, I should say I'd been down to this dirty town long ago. Came alone, as a boy, when railway engines were black beasts wreathed in steam and smelling of sulphurous coal.

I must have been blind then. I never saw the homeless, coiled beneath blankets, or the women down Goods Way selling sex. Never saw children with hunger in their furtive faces, or the angry men shouting at walls. I was drawn instead to the torrents of traffic and giant film posters for *The Great Escape* and *The Italian Job*.

* * *

There was ordinary companionship in my childhood village, the roads teeming with workers from engineering factories, the sweet smell of the maltings, and down Slash Lane the stench of the tannery. It was a safe, industrial community, surrounded by soft woodland and meadowlarks soaring.

Escaping the village streets, I took stolen railway rides south in the goods-van, rattling down to the centre of Old Smoke, sliding like a needle between banks of shrub and back yards to penetrate the fat of the city.

We slipped into the platforms of the grand St Pancras terminus among great clouds of steam hanging beneath the vaulted glass canopies. The impression of grandeur stayed with me like a glamorous secret, but I never really knew London then. Much later, it drew me to it when I was lost.

* * *

I trained, and first worked for the welfare, in the countryside and grew accustomed to night-duty, but in unexpected details I found the horror. In farmer Frank's case, it was how he'd placed his chair where cobbled gutters converged, carrying the rain and the urine of his beasts, a shotgun leaning between his splayed legs and blood trickling into the iron grating.

Old Frank, who liked a beer or two in the village pub, got tired of following the shepherd's lamp of his collie's white tail across the midnight fields, took to whisky, avoided people, and lost his dog to rat poison. To the end, he was considerate of others, his suicide cleansed by the relentless downpour.

Regardless of how many people I visited, I would always be alone. 'Do-gooder,' they would sneer, and spit on the soil.

So, I ran. Ran to London, with no idea it would be from the ashes of despair into a city on fire, with unemployment, riots and bombs.

Hopeful of a new job and gazing out at the shimmering city, I had no clue that I was still an innocent in a town where unfamiliar cruelties lay in wait.

* * *

I swept down Highgate Hill and parked up, lost in some back street, thumbing through a dog-eared A-Z street map, minutes before my appointment. My last chance of work after everything that had happened caught up with me.

A small, elderly man dressed in black, with tufts of white hair escaping his hat, leaned in with a gust of traffic fumes and a severe scent of cologne.

'You lost?'

'I can't find the Welfare. An interview.'

'Over there,' he pointed. 'Number thirteen. Unlucky for some, you say. Ring the bell.'

'Thank you.'

'Good luck. I am Doctor Hoffnung, and my surgery is there.' He nodded towards the adjoining road.

I climbed out of the Citroen, but the doctor had already turned the corner.

Number thirteen was like no council building I had seen. Georgian windows and fan-shaped glass over the door. Curtains fluttered at open windows, typewriters clattered, and telephones rang unanswered.

The door opened as I reached over to a porcelain bell push. All I saw was a woman walking backwards, waving her hands, shouting, 'Five minutes for a fag.'

Her heel caught a flagstone. We collided, and thinking she was falling, I grabbed her.

'Get off,' she yelled, pushing my hands away.

'I'm sorry,' I said. 'I thought...'

'Are you Jack?'

'Yes.'

Her eyes were smiling, cobalt blue.

'Hah! My fault. Wasn't looking.'

A shrill voice. 'Maddy. Shut the bloody door.'

'That's our receptionist. Let's go inside.'

I followed Maddy into a dark hallway. A trace of tropical perfume, then a flash of her blond curls in the shadows as she leaned forward. A hatch slid open and a pale beam of electric light framed her face in the gloom. Moments to go, and it hit me. I not only needed this job, but now I wanted it too.

'Rose,' she said. 'It's Jack Wilson for the interview. Watch him. He's handsy.'

Rose snorted with distaste, but Maddy's grin was so broad, I was surprised she got through the office door. Rose, pointing through a slit of a window, instructed me to sit in the empty waiting room, filled around the edges with a haphazard collection of old chairs. A pile of grubby toys sat in a torn cardboard box on the floor. I felt giddy and unhinged in this drab place. Nerves, I told myself, and stared at the Laura Ashley wallpaper, following the green tendrils of a leafy pattern.

Maddy came back with two steaming mugs. 'Coffee? This is black. Ask Rose if you want sugar or milk. I'm covering duty so won't be at the interview. They'll call you down soon.'

'They?'

'Didn't they tell you?'

'Tell me what?'

'We run team interviews. Everyone gets to meet you, and everybody can ask questions. Afterwards, you ask anything you want, and then it's all over.'

'How many of them?'

'Jack,' shouted Rose. 'They're ready for you now.'

'There you go,' said Maddy. 'I'll take you down.'

'How many?'

'Around thirteen. Room's full. Here, take this,' she said, holding out the mug as we went down steps, straight into a noisy and crowded basement room.

A giant of a man in a collarless shirt sat on the arm of an old sofa. Others, in silhouettes before a high, barred window, were chatting and laughing. A young woman in dungarees with a shock of black hair sat cross-legged on the floor.

'Afternoon, Jack,' said a small, smartly dressed woman with round spectacles. She had a Scot's accent, hands folded in her lap as she nodded to an empty chair. 'I'm Moira. We've saved a seat for you.'

She carried authority in every considered movement. Maddy left me to my fate and closed the door. The room was quiet now. I felt my heart thumping and put my mug on the floor before I dropped it. All eyes were on me with a mixture of smiles and boredom. An old man with severely cropped grey hair and orange socks snoozed, his chin on his chest. I waited.

At the top of the window opposite, a sudden parade of shoes, just feet and ankles, scuffed and skipped along on the pavement above. A school must have turned out for the day. Nobody else noticed. Perhaps they lived in this basement.

'Kate, give Nigel a nudge, will you?' said Moira.

'I'm awake,' said the man in orange socks. 'Listening with my eyes closed.'

His crumpled mohair suit shimmered. At a guess, he was once a skinhead.

'Do you want me to start?' he said.

'You might as well, Nigel, but first, let's welcome Jack,' suggested Moira. A scattered murmur of assent and one or two thumbs up. 'No time to introduce everybody, so we'll start now.'

'I want to ask what experience you have had with mentally ill people,' said Nigel, who stared out the window.

'I've been working for seven years since I left school. First with prisoners, trying to find work for them on release. Many had mental health problems. I did a spell in High Royds hospital on Ilkley Moor while training. For the last two years I've been dealing with mental health emergencies most days, and on night duty. I followed the duty psychiatrist around.'

Nigel swivelled round and fixed me with a ferocious stare. I sat back.

'So, tell me, Jack. Why do we need a Mental Health Act?'

I tried to meet his eyes. Bristles poked from every crevice in his face.

'Mostly to protect patients from hurting themselves, and others,' I guessed. 'People can only bear so much sadness and fear.'

'Think about it, Jack. Plenty of criminal law to stop people doing things, eh? Against assault, theft, causing affray. Why do we have to control people's private lives with another layer of law? Let the police do it. Why not?'

I guessed he was the team's resident mental health expert, and took a reckless gamble.

'Well, you'd be out of a job for a start.'

There was a scattering of chuckles. The large man loafing on one side of the sofa guffawed with a deep snort, so I pressed on. 'If I needed help and kindness, and I was fearful of the state, the last people I'd want to see would be the police.'

Nigel sat back and stretched his legs out. 'I'm done.'

'I'm Kate,' said a woman with one elbow on the man-mountain's thigh.

'Who is Erin Pizzey, Jack?'

'She founded Women's Aid, the first women's refuge in Chiswick, six or seven years ago?'

'Domestic violence?' said Nigel. 'Sounds like a bloody Hoover. Violence in the home. I call it that.'

'Shut up, Nigel,' suggested Kate. 'You've had your chance.'

I picked up my coffee with a steady hand. The interrogation was overwhelming, but I was beginning to like this disorderly process.

'How would you help a woman facing domestic violence, Jack?'

Nigel gave Kate a sour glance. She shook her shaggy blond perm in dismay and smiled at me.

'I had a little training,' I said. 'Learning to recognise the problem and gain the trust of the woman. Clarity about the options they have, which aren't many. Women I worked with were trapped in the villages. I got thumped by a husband for visiting a family home whilst he was at work.'

'I tell women to keep a cricket bat under the bed,' said Nigel.

This is over the top, I thought, and Kate's knuckles went white. Nigel continued.

'When he's asleep. Because they must sleep. I say to them, "You hit him as hard as you can, round the head. When he wakes up, you tell him. You've got to sleep, so if you ever touch me again, next time, it'll be an iron bar." That usually sorts it.'

The door opened, and Rose the receptionist surveyed the room.

'You've had ages. My turn, and someone needs to cover reception while I'm down here.'

Moira stared over her glasses at Nigel and glanced at the door. He jumped to his feet unsteadily, gripping his spindly legs, nodded, gave a wavering thumbs-up to the boss, then loped out of the room.

Rose took his seat.

'Was he going on about cricket bats under the bed again?' she said. 'Someone will get killed.'

'Rose,' said Moira.

'Yes. Jack,' she said, reminded of her mission. 'What do you do before you go off on your visits?'

'Tell someone where I'm going?' I suggested. She appeared unsatisfied. 'In case something happens to me?' She nodded but remained quiet. 'Tell you, Rose?'

'You tell me, Jack. I will keep a record, and if you don't come back, they will come and get you.'

Thirteen heads nodded solemnly.

'Thank you,' she said, and as she left the room, Maddy came in.

'All's quiet upstairs. Can I sit in?'

Moira nodded. From the corner, I heard a voice.

'Can you cook?'

'Me?' I said, unsure of what was going on.

A woman in a navy suit jacket and a cream blouse leaned forward. 'I said, can you cook?'

'I'm sorry, do I need to?'

'Yes. On Tuesday evenings we run the cooking club for mums. We take turns to teach recipes and eat together.'

'I can do spaghetti.'

'That'll do,' she said, still leaning forward, looking at me from under a sharp fringe of dark hair. She hesitated, as if searching for the right words.

'How old are you, Jack?'

'Twenty-five.'

'I must ask you. Are you ready for this job? It's tough round here. Crime, drugs, and lots of poverty. You must know what you're doing.'

'Am I ready for this?' Playing for time. Irritated. Gazing around the room.

'Some of the team look about the same age as me,' I said, fixing on the young woman sprawled on the floor. I glanced at Maddy.

'I've had a caseload of fifty for two years. I've removed babies from nursing mothers, worked years in a rough old remand home and taken a few punches along the way. Do you know what? I did most of it on my own.'

I couldn't stop myself. The sun slanted across the basement. I shielded my eyes for a moment and continued.

'You don't think of the countryside like that. You think it's all *Cider with ruddy Rosie*. Well, it's not. I had no back-up, worked a seventy-hour week and my manager knew bugger-all. The last job he did was to run a chocolate factory.

'I've done court work, hospital work, delivered a baby in a garage and found four dead bodies. A farmer in his yard shot himself, an old man set himself on fire with his fags, and two of them were smackheads who overdosed on stronger stuff. I had to stop, or I would have gone mad. I want to work for a team. I want to be part of a team. I am good at my job. I'm bloody good at this job, but I can't do it alone anymore. And that is the reason I've come here.'

'Thanks,' said the woman in the corner with a diplomatic smile. I was breathing a little too heavily. It went on like that. Questions from all sides. I needed a cricket bat to fend them off.

'Did you go mad?'

'No.'

'Are you a trades union member?'

'Yes.'

'Are you married?'

'No.'
'How would you get a wheelchair down these stairs?'
'Why?' I said.
'Because on Thursdays we have the disabled club down here,' said Moira.
'People with disabilities club,' said Kate.
Maddy lifted an arm as if asking permission to speak and turned towards me.
'How would you sum it up, Jack? This work that we do. What's different to family and friends helping people out?'
I didn't know where to start. I said what had been turning over in my mind all the way down the motorway to London. Readying myself for this interview.
'We have to ask the questions nobody wants to ask. We say to people things no-one wants to say, and we must search for things that no-one wants to find. Most of all, we have to hear what nobody wants to listen to.'
For the first time that afternoon, the team was silent. It was hard to read the room, to guess how my answer had gone down. I cared what Maddy thought, whether I got the job or not. She held my gaze for a moment.
'Can you give me one example, Jack? To show us what you mean.'
I shifted a little in my seat, the memory uncomfortable.
'Last month I had a call from the hospital about a teenager on my caseload. He had some brushes with the police. They didn't want to arrest him. The call was about his mum. She had just had a baby, and because of a rare genetic abnormality, the child was unlikely to survive more than a year.'
'Oh. How awful,' said Moira.
'What has that got to do with what you said, Jack?'
It was the woman with dark hair, a suit, and sharp features, leaning out from the corner again so I could see her. She had a penetrating stare. A fear deep inside flooded through me. I realised in that instant; she was the team leader, not Moira.

'Because no one else would ask the necessary question. Not the hospital, nor the police, or the family GP. I had to ask the boy because his mum refused to talk to us. I had to ask him if his mum made him have sex with her. Incest is the only cause of the baby's disorder.'

She sat back and asked the question I expected.

'Did she? Was the father of her baby her own son?'

'You asked me about questions we must ask. The rest is confidential.'

She nodded. It had been a trap to see how loose I was with personal information.

After an hour, it was over. Moira turned to me and said, 'Your turn, Jack. You can ask us anything.'

'Why do you have a cooking club? I've never heard of that before.'

'Because,' said the big guy with a Yorkshire accent, 'if we said it was a group for depressed parents who had no idea how to care for children, no one would come, would they?'

He had an amiable smile. I thought of the coal miners and steelworkers I knew in the north.

Moira called time, walked me back upstairs and Rose levelled her jewelled spectacles at me.

'You'll be okay, Jack. You're the last candidate, so they'll be deciding now.'

'Who decides, Moira?'

'All of them. They take a vote. Usually after a long argument. I expect you could do with another coffee?'

A cup was in her hand already. I lit a cigarette and Rose slipped her window shut as I went over all the earnest and idiotic things I had said. The sound of raised voices filtered through the floorboards, and then a thundering of feet as the basement emptied up two flights of wooden stairs.

Moira came into the room with the manager.

'This is Nina, our team leader. She wants a quick word.'

She turned to go.

'Moira. Can I ask? What do you do? I thought *you* were the manager.'

'What? Oh, aye,' she chuckled. 'I look after the administration. The money and the files. That sort of thing. We all take turns to run meetings.'

Nina eyed me from head to toe. An unsettling stare that could stop a goods train.

'They want you, Jack. You've got the job. You can start next week.'

'Do *you* want me to work here?'

'Doesn't matter what I think. We decide together. I'll say one thing. If you decide to take the job, we don't do favours here. Do you understand?'

Nina was standing, smoking, leaning with one hand on the wall.

'We don't do favours for the council. We don't do favours for the police, and we don't do favours for doctors, lawyers, and listen to me, Jack, you don't do favours for any of us here. You got that?'

'No favours. I think I got that.'

'Another thing you need to realise before you sign up. There are elections coming soon. Everything might change. The Tories have been making headway. They're talking about selling council houses off at a discount and that's a vote winner. If they get in, our team is finished.'

'So, there might not be a job for me.'

'The future is uncertain. All I can say.'

'Okay with me.'

'Good. We're going to a Moroccan restaurant in Highgate tonight. Kate and Rick will give you a lift.'

'I'm invited?'

'Of course. We've been interviewing for most of two weeks.'

'Maybe not. I'm short this week.'

'The team pays for you.'

'I don't need a lift.'

'You do. You got a job today. I expect you'll want to have a few beers.'

'Who's Rick?'

'The one built like a shit-house door.'

Nina stubbed out her cigarette in a bin.

'Congratulations, Jack. You did well. Enough to sway the team, despite your reference.'

'My reference?'

'You think we'd take you without a reference?'

'I've not had one before. What did it say?'

'It was the worst reference I ever read. It was so bad it made us laugh. What a pompous arsehole. By the way, I meant to ask. He wrote "aside from a certain unpleasant incident." What did he mean?'

'I hit him.'

'Yes. He said that when I rang him. Why did you do that? He wouldn't tell me.'

'He was selling case-file information to divorce lawyers at twenty pounds a pop and I reported him to County Hall.'

'Why punch him?'

'He had a mate in the police on the take. Between them, they put the blame on me.'

'So, they framed you for dishonesty?'

'Yep. So, I nutted him when he laughed in my face.'

'He said you punched him.'

'Not my style.'

'Don't do it here, Jack,' said Nina with a grin.

'I won't.'

'Not once. Not ever. You get this one chance with me.'

'Thanks, Nina.'

'Not me,' she said. 'You are too risky for my taste. The team decided.'

She let it sink in. It felt good.

'Nina,' I said. 'What you said, about favours. It's what we

do, isn't it? Don't they call us the do-gooders?'

She drummed her nails on the door frame. 'You work for the people who live round here, Jack. Nobody else.'

2
Eating out

'Do you like the meze?' said Kate. She had a combination of a tan and freckles and looked Californian. Rick said she came from Dulwich.

'It's tasty. But what's this bit of privet doing in it?' I said, holding up a leaf.

'Bay-leaf,' whispered Rick. 'Want another beer?'

'Please.'

Rick wandered off with his rolling sailor's gait. Kate was looking at the menu.

'I love London. Fabulous food from all over the world.'

She had a show-business smile. Big lips and dazzling teeth.

'I like Rick,' I said, 'he reminds me of some lads I knew up north.'

'He was a miner,' she said, 'until he killed a man. Some chap ran over his border collie with a milk float. Rick thought he did it on purpose and beat him to death with a metal crate.'

'No.'

'Oh yes. Served eight years for it. Studied criminology in the nick and trained for probation. Joined us instead.'

A shadow swept across the table.

'Did she say I killed a man in Ripon, just to watch him die?'

Rick set down two pints. He was grinning at Kate. 'Kate likes making up stories. I was no bloody good as a miner. It was boring. I studied at night school and did a diploma at Teesside.'

'You believed me. That Rick killed a man,' Kate said.

'I did.'

'Truth and lies, Jack,' she went on. 'Lots more to this job than kindness and the rough stuff. Working here, you find out who you really are.'

'Kate,' said Rick. I saw a look that said, *not now*.

'Oops,' she said with those huge, darting eyes. 'Rick tells me I go over the top. Wonderful to have you on the team. Maddy spoke up for you.'

'Did she?'

'She likes you. I can see you like her.'

Rick, holding his beer in both hands, looked at the ceiling. Kate ploughed on.

'Let's say Maddy made an impact on you as well. I *see* these things.'

Maddy was at the end of the long table. She saw me looking at her and raised a glass.

Rick shrugged and said, 'Bit much, isn't it? Like a family. Full on. Listen. Maddy has a partner, Tim. Been an item for years. Forever. So, take my advice. Keep your love life outside of work.'

'But you and Kate—'

'I know,' he said, and drained his glass. 'I speak from experience.'

'You're right, of course,' I said, although I found it hard to take my eyes off Maddy. 'I'm not ready for a new relationship yet.'

'Oh?' said Kate. Globs of mascara on her lashes, quivering as she blinked.

I needed to change the subject or invent a failed romance.

'What's it like,' I said quickly, 'working at Cossington Street?'

Rick looked at Kate, but she was still arranging my affairs in her mind.

'Tell the truth, Jack, it's a bit of a roller-coaster. Always has been. The idea of these field work teams is to be part of the neighbourhood. You must own it. Think of it as your *manor*.'

'Manor?'

'Yep. Like the gangs but different. It goes back a long way, to ideas like the Settlement Movement in Dickens' time.

Working alongside the community. Our complaints procedure is a brick through the window.'

'But we work for the council. We're not a charity.'

'Right,' continued Rick, but Kate interrupted.

'We are in, *and against* the state,' she said. 'Look it up at the library. It's a book.'

'Give him a break,' said a voice behind me. Maddy put her hands on my shoulders. Kate saw, and smiled, Mona Lisa style. Between plates of food appearing from the kitchens, everyone moved around the table. The chatter seemed louder. Rick held out his palms to Maddy, who pulled up a chair.

'Jack asked about Cossington Street,' he said.

'It's different from what *you're* used to,' said Kate. 'Driving across the countryside all the time.'

I think she was going to tell me more, about me, but Maddy explained.

'The plan is that nobody who needs us should be more than a four-penny bus fare from our door.'

'But you haven't even got a sign on the office. How on earth do they find you?'

Rick laughed. He wore a gold chain round his thick neck. I was thinking he'd make a good wrestler on television, when he said 'It's based on the probation service. It's hard for some people just to walk through our door. Especially with a big sign outside saying "The Welfare".'

'We're not *The Welfare*,' I said. 'That went out years ago. I'm not new to this, you know. I've been a professional for five years.'

'Professional?' said Kate, more sober now. Unsmiling. Like a light had gone out.

'I don't think,' I said, ignoring her, 'that it's any different here. You make it sound grand with "settlement" and books about it, but these people are the same everywhere. Even this posh place. Is it Hampstead? These people that we help; the mad, the sad, and the frankly very bad. The ones that batter their kids. These people are the same everywhere you go. We just do our job, and no one says thanks, do they?'

'Sometimes they do,' said Kate. She seemed disappointed. In a rush, I realised the beer was talking. The table was quieter. I saw Nina watching me.

'I'm sorry,' I said. 'I got worked up a bit. Nigel asked where I was from and I said Nottingham. He said "Oh, just a roundabout on the M1?" Where is he, anyway?'

'Why? Do you want to nut him too?' said Rick, who was still grinning. 'He works at night. He's a drummer in a jazz band.'

'I don't understand jazz.'

'Nigel doesn't have to,' said Maddy. 'He's on another planet.'

More dishes of food arrived and changed the mood. Chairs were shifted to the table, and I found Maddy next to me. As she began to talk, I understood that the team was pulling me in. Maddy's soft hands on my shoulder. Kate's mysterious disappointment. They were showing me the ropes, and I was in a huff. A boozy, self-righteous huff.

'You said you're not new to this,' said Maddy quietly. 'But *we* are. Always. Every day. We are always learning. From each other, and the people we help. It's a good way to work, Jack.'

'I didn't mean—'

'But this is important to us. What you said about "these people." I saw Kate's face when you said something about being a "professional". That's not how we think about Cossington Street. When we train, they say we should call people clients. Like patients for psychiatrists? We don't say that. The people we work with are not *cases* or *clients*. Any one of us could be "these people". You talk like it was them and us, and when you start thinking like that, you start doing things *to* people. Not *for* people.'

'You can't be in and against the state!' I said.

'You say that. Come on. Kings Cross police station is full of Nazis.'

'National Front,' added Kate, leaning over behind Rick's gigantic shoulders. 'It's practically their headquarters. They wear the little NF badge inside their mackintoshes. You can always tell. The ones who wear caps. You look next time. They razor the peaks, so they point down like the SS uniform hats. Filth.'

And then, a kind of war seemed to break out. A plate sailed through the air and, with a crack, was in pieces in the fireplace. I ducked as another flew past.

'It's for the tourists,' said Maddy. 'It's a Greek tradition for joy and happiness.'

'Greek? I thought it was a North African restaurant. Nina said it was.'

'Didn't you look at the menu? We had to come here instead because the Moroccan restaurant was shut after an arson attack. I bet that was the NF thugs too.'

My plate was empty, so I grabbed it, and flung it at the fireplace. To my astonishment, it bounced, ricocheted back towards the table, took out the flower arrangement, three wine glasses and landed in a large salad bowl. A long silence. Then the clapping started. A round of applause, and more plates hurtling round the room. Waiters protested that only *they* could throw plates, made of soft plaster, but it was too late. The fireplace was a heap of broken crockery. Maddy introduced me to Retsina wine, puddings arrived with glasses of Metaxa brandy and Kate consoled an anxious-looking waiter about the Turkish invasion of Cyprus.

Rick lifted a glass and pulled at his beard, nodding at Kate. 'She prefers the Latin type, but she settles for a rough diamond in the end.'

He grinned, relaxed. I laughed. I laughed so much that it hurt. A relief, and anticipation of something new like the start of a film. Lights down. Swelling strings and drums beating. The promise of excitement and yet, a lurking sense that it is ephemeral. That sometime soon, after you've lost yourself in those tides of fear and joy, it always comes to an end. The lamps come up and you leave, popcorn underfoot and spilled ashtrays everywhere.

Outside, it was raining, again. Iridescent rivulets down the midnight street. We huddled under the awning outside the restaurant, Kate on Rick's arm. Nina snapped up an umbrella, waved goodnight and headed up the hill. Maddy gripped my shoulders, stood on tiptoe and kissed my cheek.

'Goodnight.'

'Thanks for asking me along. It was great.'

'I hope so. It was *your* evening, Jack. In your honour. Tonight's meal was to celebrate you joining our team.' She squeezed my arm and then strode off down the road. I wanted to follow her, but everything Rick said, and understanding too late that this fabulous evening had been for me, left me incoherent. Maddy hailed a cab. Then she was gone.

Kate grabbed my elbow. 'You can sleep at ours tonight if you like, Jack.'

I shook my head. 'Thanks, but I need to get to my new place. I want to put my head down there.'

'When did you get here?'

'This morning. Drove down overnight. I'm knackered.'

'Nae mind,' said Rick, 'we'll see you home,' and together we strode up the shimmering monochrome pavement and across a zebra crossing. The traffic had eased, but half-way across the road, a lean, purple car lurched to a halt, the engine grumbling, then growling as the driver prodded the throttle.

Rick slowed to a halt and turned to look at the driver. I think he might have forgiven the hacking exhaust, but the driver was standing on the horn. Rick jumped, brought his legs up as if launching into a deep pool, then twisted and landed square on the broad and thin metal of the car's sleek bonnet, his arms and legs splayed.

'He plays rugby,' said Kate, as if it explained anything. The dent in the plum-coloured bonnet was considerable. Rick rubbed his backside as he strode round to the driver. 'You nearly killed me,' he roared as the driver, with a look of fear, refused to wind his window down.

'Never mind,' continued Rick, bellowing for the street to hear, 'my arse seems okay, so I won't report you.'

With the horn blaring continuously, the car swerved round Rick and shot up the hill, an arm energetically waving two fingers out of the now-opened window.

'I wish Rick wouldn't do that,' said Kate.

'He's done it before?'

'Only once, but the man saw him go into a pub, found a phone box, and called the police on him.'

'Was he arrested?'

'No. The other bloke was, for running into him on a pelican crossing. I told him. You won't get away with it twice, Rick. And here we are. Done it again. For all I know, he's been doing it for years. I said to him. One day, there'll be cameras about. On the streets. Do you know, near Cossington Street, they're always filming *The Sweeney*?'

'I had no idea.'

'He only needs to do this stunt again in the wrong place and it'll be all over the *Evening Standard*. I don't read that rag, though. Prefer the *Evening News*.'

'Maybe they'll give him a job, Kate?'

'What?'

'On *The Sweeney*. A stunt man or something.'

Kate smothered a giggle as Rick rejoined us. His car was a Renault Four and leaned over when he got in. Rain beat on the roof and swirled across the windscreen. Streetlights and the glare from shop windows seemed to smear across the glass. It was like the last hallucinatory thing I remembered before I fell asleep: the opening scene of a new film I'd just watched. *Taxi Driver*.

3
Gregory and the blue vase

After he tried to break my arm and made for a knife, I managed to shrug him off and stared him down. I did that long, deliberate look. Slowly, from head to toe. It works sometimes. Learned the trick from a copper. We were in our office basement kitchen.

Greg, a lump of a boy, loomed over me, his arms loose at his side. Rick had passed the care of Greg to me at this key point in the boy's life, leaving our care system.

'Give me the knife,' he said, unaware how illogical that sounded. I put the carving knife in the kitchen drawer but left my hand close enough to keep it shut. Greg stood between me and the door.

'Gregory. Not your knife, is it? Cutlery belongs in the drawer.'

'You're not going to give me any fucking money, are you?'

'No. You've had all that I can offer and a bit more. You're all set up now. Let's go and get some lunch at the café.'

At the offer of food, Gregory brightened and followed me upstairs. The office was spread over adjoining town houses close to the market. As we went out, I stooped to whisper in our receptionist's ear.

'Rose. The kitchen, downstairs. Can you please take all the sharp stuff out of the drawers?'

She beckoned me back. Gregory shifting from foot to foot close to the front door, leapt aside when the postman blundered in without ringing the bell.

'What about making my sandwiches?' whispered Rose.

'Bring sliced bread,' I suggested and waited whilst she thought it over. Sometimes better not to explain. She nodded but needed a concession in return.

'Tell him to get a bath,' was all she came up with.

Outside, we felt the unseasonable heat radiating from the road and pavement. Near the bookies, young men lit cigarettes and anxiously waited for their horses to come home. Laundered by Ladbrokes, they had a haunted look and rubbed their groins for comfort, as if a scintilla of extra masculinity might help win the day.

Gregory loped alongside me as we headed towards Church Market.

'Just a few quid for some bits and bobs for the flat.'

'There's none to give you. We have limits.'

The case notes had taken hours to read. Detailed narratives, more like essays than case files.

Gregory had been in children's homes and eight or nine foster homes for as long as he could remember. His mum, Trish, had left him, when a baby, wrapped warm and comfortable inside a cardboard carton at St Pancras Station. The box lettering announced 'STORK – Table Margarine'.

Trish worked the nearby road named Wagon Way and told us back then that she preferred St Pancras Station because it felt so much nicer. Someone might take a fancy to infant Gregory and take him away from London. To Leicester or Nottingham perhaps.

Gregory's identity was not Afro-Caribbean like his father, or Irish like his mother, or London British. He didn't run with gangs, steal cars to impress girls or hang around garage bands. I never noticed him listen to music. His culture, like thousands of other youths in London, was the culture of care. Young people who had grown up in care, shared the same problems, longings, outlook, and experiences. Many had been abused by the same people. All they had was each other. Except one day, they left the system. At eighteen, with half a dozen photographs and a bin bag of clothing and books, they became care-leavers, installed in a bed sitter and left to sink or swim.

* * *

I was enjoying my escalope and spaghetti in the Dolomites Café down the market with Greg, so I misheard him when he asked if I'd visit him.

'Of course, but I'd prefer it if you stayed out of prison in the first place.'

He sucked his teeth in disapproval. They all did, that year. Two months earlier there were two days of riots in Brixton and every young person wanted to be an urban desperado.

'I still want to see you,' he went on, immune to my low expectations, 'in my flat.'

He was eating a mixed grill with extra sausages because I'd said he could have what he wanted, although it came out of my wallet and not the office budget. Still bruised by his angry attack in the office kitchen, I suggested he might have all manner of knives at home.

'Nah, I wouldn't really stick you.'

Gregory held a piece of egg on the end of his fork. His elbows tucked in. Impeccable table manners. He must have had a spell with McDougal at Handle Rise residential. Everyone left that dreary place with manners. Dougie was a stickler for good behaviour. He ran the tightest of the twenty or children's homes in the borough.

'You understand why I want ten quid, don't you?'

'You want bits and pieces, Greg, but we sorted all the kit. We got it together. We made all the choices together. The black sheets and pillowcases, washing up bowl. We spent the lot.'

Gregory sliced his last sausage. Always hungry. I did want him to have the best start, but I'd already been given two new cases to replace his closed file.

'This thing I want,' was all he said, nodding. It took a while to encourage him to explain and then it all came out.

'You don't understand,' he began. 'All my life I've been here, and there, with him and her, and *them*.'

I knew what he was referring to. Everybody did, but no-one wanted to believe it. That loving care could become a different sort of loving. He pushed the plate to one side, empty already. A sleight of hand to mouth. I still had a mountain of spaghetti to deal with. A woman next to us, stirring her speckled café marocchino, twitched her nose slightly. Gregory's personal fragrance had landed.

'Everything I have ever had, was for something. Coats in the winter, shoes for school. Books for college. Been the same all morning. Mops and pans and fucking cutlery. Except when I was little, the Welfare bought me toys, but do you see? Educational toys. Jigsaws about geography. Kits to build electric clocks. All the time, everything is...'

He gazed down at his can of Tango. Both hands tightened. Then he looked me in the eye and shouted, 'FUNCTIONAL!'

The marocchino woman spilled her hot froth and grated chocolate. Ilaria, the waitress, took the glass and wiped the table in one swift movement whilst calling out, '*Un altro marocchino qua.*'

Gregory's gaze remained steady. Unblinking. Huge, deep brown eyes. At times he could be captivating, even with his t-shirt loose around his throat, borrowed from someone else a year ago.

'Different for you,' he continued. 'I bet you got stuff from your mum and dad, right?'

'What sort of things?'

'Stuff,' then, confiding his magic word, 'ornaments.'

He was right. I had an attic full of knick-knacks from my mum, after she died. I didn't like them, but I couldn't throw them away. A prisoner of sentimentality. I still wore my dad's waistcoat.

It was obvious the Marocchino had overcome her distaste for the smell of Gregory and was pretending to appreciate a fresco of a railway station in Alessandria. She leant closer.

'I want a blue vase,' he said, 'with a willow pattern. It cost £9.99 in Bones Brothers. I want something beautiful.'

For children in care, everything had to be bought from

Bones Brothers store. The council had a plan should we survive nuclear bombs: requisition blankets from Bones Brothers.

It had been an odd day. Half an hour ago I was struggling with him on the floor thinking 'I'm too old for this,' and now he wanted a blue vase. I was about to say that the idea of Moira authorising ten pounds for a vase was preposterous, when the Marocchino turned to me as if Gregory didn't exist and softly remarked, 'What a lovely idea your son has. Shall I tell you the story of the Willow Pattern? The lovers on the island?'

To my surprise, Gregory, who had the neglected appearance of a derelict, addressed her in kindly tones.

'Thank you, but the story of Chang and Kwang-se has fascinated me for years. That they escaped together, forever in love, as turtle doves, has always touched me.' And like a ragged prince, he put his hand to his heart. Without a word, the Marocchino returned her empty glass to the counter and left in a drift of lavender talcum.

Gregory whispered to me, 'She's a bit whiffy, eh?' and giggled.

It was the same giggle I saw when he was briefly with the Walkers. They had loved him, and cared for him, made him happy but also uncomfortable. He could not recognise love so he shat in their top-loading washing machine and had to leave.

I gave Gregory ten pounds before I finished my pasta. Two five-pound notes. It was my weekly cigarette money. He promised to bring me the receipt in case I could charm Moira with his story, and he left the Dolomites Café bound for Bones Brothers. It occurred to me, knowing Gregory, he would probably drop the thing on his way home.

I had two meetings, two home visits and a last-minute call out to an old man from Warsaw whose benefit had been stopped because he couldn't read letters in English. He had taken to snaring pigeons with rum-soaked raisins as bait on the end of a fishing line. I took him a box of food, answered the benefit letter surrounded by bird feathers and mollified the neighbours. He carried on though. It was a kind of sport for him.

On my way home I swung by Gregory's new flat. He had his own entrance up a flight of brick stairs outside. In the gloaming of a city spring evening, the harsh landscape softened a little. Gregory sat at the top. He didn't try to hide the joint in his hand and exhaled slowly.

'Gregory,' was all I said and he grinned.

'Ten quid a bag. Only grass. I only smoke grass. I'm not stupid.'

'I know,' I said. And I meant it. His mum Trish had crashed out of this world on heroin.

His story was a perfect con.

'Great, eh? Got the story off Hayley. Works every time. She was at Dougie's home with me.'

'I thought the hand on heart was a bit over the top.'

'Yeah, man. Do you want some?'

I thought for a moment, or two. He had a broad smile.

'Okay. Why not?' I sat down next to him.

4
Breaking, entering, and the Big Bang

Unless someone told you, you would never know that the dishevelled old house at number 13 was our busy local base. Nothing but a bell and a number on the door. Neighbours called us *The Welfare*. Fridays were often chaotic and unpredictable, needing two of us on duty.

Maddy sat opposite me, the olive-green duty-phone at one ear and another handset cradled on her shoulder as she tipped cigarette ash into a tin ashtray. It was a quiet moment before the office and the outside phone lines opened at nine. I stared out the window. The haunting, dark, and rain-swept nights of a desperate winter had given way to a blustery early spring.

Dr Hoffnung shuffled along the street in his oversized greatcoat, a homburg hat pulled down against his ears. Katy said he had all but abandoned his patients.

'Most of them were born in the nineteenth century anyway,' she added.

Rose, our reluctant receptionist, appeared in the doorway panting, having clambered up the stairs. She waved a note she found pushed under the front door. It read: *Brown at No.73 has fallen. Hope.*

Maddy stared at the ragged lines and said simply, 'Why does he do this?'

'Hope? What's "Hope" about?'

'Hoffnung. It means Hope. People round here call him Dr Hope,' she said.

The index cards, by address and surname, revealed the location of the emergency.

'That will be Edna in Cloudman Rd, half-way down on the right. Will you come with me?'

It was impossible to say no to Maddy. I followed her on our way out to visit Edna.

'That doctor is a menace,' announced Rose through the reception window. 'Shouldn't drive. I'm going to put sugar in his petrol tank. That'll teach him a lesson.'

'He doesn't have a car now,' said Maddy. 'They stopped him driving.' She suggested Rose call an ambulance.

'Every day something new.' Maddy grinned.

We had to pull the door shut against the wind, the street a canyon of Georgian terraced houses and an ice-blue sky with clumps of cloud scudding high above the rooftops. Maddy's tangled mass of fair, curling hair flew out behind her as we leaned into the gusts on our way to Edna's ground floor flat.

She told me Edna could remember the First World War and had survived the Blitz, but was defeated by a threadbare carpet in the hall. Edna was younger than Doctor Hope.

*　*　*

We could see her through the letterbox, up against the door. Even if we had a key, it would be impossible to enter that way.

'Edna,' called Maddy. 'Did you speak to Dr Hope?'

'Who are you?' bellowed Edna, resolute still.

'The Welfare. This is Maddy, Mrs Brown. I ring you every Monday for a chat. Remember me?'

'I can't get up,' explained Edna.

Seeing a pair of hard-backed novels wedging the sash window open, I volunteered to climb in, but Maddy would have none of it.

'My turn,' she told me, handing me her satchel. It was complicated. Black spear-tipped railings skirted a narrow ten-foot drop to the basement level. If she fell, and survived, there was no way out except through cellar windows nailed shut against thieves. My coat went over the iron spears, I lifted her up, she gripped the railings and twisted out of my grasp to land with her toes on the stone ledge, her face inches from mine. She beamed at me, triumphant.

'Glad I left the high heels at home.'

I could not escape those blue eyes.

'The hard bit over,' she said.

'Amazing,' I said.

'Hah! I could do with a cigarette,' she said, but instead she turned and stepped over the void, one leg each side.

'Let's hope it will open.'

A muffled shout came from Edna. 'Maddy!' she was yelling. 'Are you all right, my dear?'

At this, Maddy began to laugh uncontrollably, one hand grabbing the window frame, the other arm flailing about as she hooted at the irony of Edna, having lain in the hall all night, checking if *we* were okay. If the stove was to hand, she'd have put the kettle on.

Fortunately, the window slid up and the finest output of Agatha Christie tumbled into the abyss. *Murder at the Vicarage* and *The Secret Adversary* lay sprawled across the damp mulch of crisp packets and torn shopping bags.

Maddy was able to move Edna enough to open the door. She complained only of slight pain but had probably broken her hip. The ambulance arrived as we were putting blankets around her. Maddy, sucking on a Silk Cut cigarette, went with her to hospital.

'Can you cover this morning's duty for me?' were her parting words and I had no idea what was to come.

When I got back to the office, Rose slid open her window. 'Where's Maddy? Liza's covering phones for *you* lot. She's trying to get hold of you.'

'Maddy's in hospital, with Edna.'

'Edna Brown went through the Blitz.'

Rose pushed back her oversized, glittering spectacles with a middle finger, nodding deliberately to remind me that she had unreserved respect for a special breed of Londoner.

I went through the crowded waiting room and past the kitchen where Gregory had fought with me. Weeks later he left a tiny blue vase on my desk and insisted on buying me lunch at the Dolomites Café.

Upstairs, Liza beckoned me over. The youngest in our team, Liza supported local childminders but took her turn on duty and was covering the phones for us whilst we visited Edna.

'Busy downstairs, but I can take care of them. You need to get round the corner to the offices of that African liberation movement quickly. Something about a young man they are really worried about.'

The office housed the country's opposition party in exile.

I understood. *Really worried* about someone usually meant a mental health emergency. It was my job to help decide whether compulsory treatment was necessary.

'Has a GP or psychiatrist been round?'

'He won't listen to anybody and we can't get hold of Dr Hope. The police have arrived. Apparently, he has a gun.'

When non-British nationals experienced a mental health breakdown, it always left us with a dilemma. Hospitalisation was grounds for the Home Office to repatriate patients. I checked for my identification card, pulled on my winter jacket again and headed out. As I passed Rose's reception window, I heard Liza calling down the stairs.

'It's a toy gun. A plastic gun.'

The said offices were in a nearby street, behind our building. The party's leader was in prison. One of its most prominent leaders in exile lived along the road from Maddy in Muswell Hill. His wife threw joyful parties, according to Maddy.

As I hurried down Panton Street, two coppers holding on to their hats in the breeze stood outside the building, with a doctor in tow. The office was nameless, like ours.

'What's up?'

'Young man, excitable. Around twenty-three. All dressed up and nowhere to go.'

'The report said he has a gun.'

'Looks like a plastic one from down the market.'

'Is he threatening anybody?'

'Only us. The gentlemen inside say he's been anxious. Thinks the place is under attack.'

'Have you called an ambulance?'

'No.'

'Good, but if you do, tell 'em to turn the siren off, please. It'll only panic him.'

A researcher, Amadi Jacobs, came out and shook hands with us all.

'Don't worry, I think he will listen to you. If you can talk to him. I have told him we are welcome in this country, but he believes we are under siege by his home country's police. He may agree to meet a doctor. He is just a frightened boy.'

'He knows he is unwell?'

'I think so. Come, I will take you inside.'

'Hold on,' interrupted a copper, holding up his hand, snug in a black leather glove. 'Do you know a Maddy Cooper?'

I nodded.

'We're partners on duty. What's the message?'

'She said wait for her. She'll be half an hour.'

Amadi was impatient. He rocked from foot to foot and gazed around like an athlete waiting for the gun. Behind me, the policeman continued. 'Miss Cooper says an Edna Brown sends her love.'

'Let's go,' I said to Amadi.

The office was much like our own. A slightly dilapidated old Georgian family home with a thin, wooden staircase, and a window on the first landing, rattling in the brewing gale. Somewhere, something delicious was being cooked. I was hungry.

Amadi called up the stairs in friendly tones.

'Femi. Come now. I have a friend for you. He is a good man.'

Instantly, a young man sprang across the landing above. I couldn't make out his shadowed face, but it was clear he was prepared. A toy M16 rifle was tightly slung round his shoulders. He wore a beret and jungle fatigues and insisted I go away. We debated for a while whether he should come down to meet me, but he preferred the high ground.

'I just want to talk,' I offered, which, looking back, may have been somewhat disingenuous, and began to approach him up the stairs.

Hands open towards him, attempting my best practised calm conversation, I ducked when Femi threw his rifle and it clattered lightly down the stairs. Amadi called out in vain for him to be gentle and as I reached the top of the stairs, Femi seemed to retreat a little. I remember he was smiling.

Then he lunged forward and swung a beautiful punch, following through with his shoulder. Even as I admired his technique, I realised I was in trouble again. I toppled backwards, arms waving, and slid down the stairs on my back, thankfully riding a thickly padded coat.

Amadi caught me as I reached the bottom. As he cradled me, I stared up into his worried face. The second time that morning I had gazed into someone's eyes.

'Tell the police to call an ambulance,' I told him.

'Are you hurt?' he asked. He sounded scared.

'Not for me. It's for him,' I said.

With a show of force of two ambulance medics with the two coppers, Femi went safely to hospital. I visited later that afternoon to sign the papers and hoped he wouldn't be repatriated to his home country. I realised too late that if he were sent back, he might be killed.

Afterwards I met Maddy at the Butcher's Arms to put the day to bed.

'You're lucky you're not in a wheelchair.' It was as close to comforting as I could expect. 'You should have waited for me.'

'I was not controlling or ordering him about.'

'No, but he was a frightened boy and you're a big bloke.'

She had a point. I was looking at her face, trying to work out if she was cross. I mentioned that moment outside Edna's when, for a fraction of a second, I'd wanted to kiss her as she clung to the railings.

'That's us, isn't it? Other sides of the fence. So close and yet, um, so far apart?'

She spluttered over another Silk Cut, hooting with laughter, and in mock sincerity leaned forward.

'If I'd let go, for a moment, I'd have fallen too.'

She was right. We had responsibilities, I said. 'Thing is, when we've had a day like today. Difficult, isn't it? Difficult to go home to people who've had a normal day?'

'Maybe for *you*. For *me*,' Maddy answered softly, 'this *is* a normal day.'

I supposed it was. She had a point.

* * *

The next Friday we were on duty again. I was half an hour late for work and slipped into the corner newsagents for a chocolate bar. Ahmed, behind the counter, was neat in his brown work-coat and black tie. He smiled but never spoke. I assumed he had no English conversation.

The weather had been so erratic, and violent, that I didn't for a second realise what the visceral crack and shuddering thump was. The air rippled, we heard screams in the distance and Ahmed, marching to the door, said: 'What the fuck?'

I just stared at Ahmed for an instant, then ran across the road as Maddy stormed out of the office and caught my eye. We both understood something awful had happened.

On Panton Street, cars had slewed across the road and there was a cloud of dust, whipped away by the breeze. You could still hear panes of glass collapsing into the streets. Sirens. Car alarms.

'The office,' said Maddy. 'There was supposed to be a liberation march downtown today.'

Amadi sat on the step, his tracksuit bottoms wet with blood.

'I'm OK. There's nobody else here. I was sleeping. How are you?'

Stunned, I didn't answer. Behind him, the movement's offices were in tatters, the roof gone, a wall sagging and a desk perched on the remaining five feet of an upstairs floor. Much later, we learned that the regime's secret police had placed a large bomb against the back wall of the building, with orders *not to endanger white people*.

Detectives were in the windowless Bricklayers Arms, questioning the landlady, lifting complimentary halves of bitter and pushing slivers of glass around with their boots. There was nothing we could do.

* * *

Three months later, Edna Brown was out of hospital and Maddy came back to the office after settling her back into her apartment.

There were no doors between the warren of rooms in our office. Maddy stood in the doorway.

'There is someone to meet you.'

She stood aside, and Femi appeared and approached hesitantly, holding out his hand. I stood and shook it, holding on to him.

'So, you *were* under attack, but not from *me*. I'm glad they did not send you back.'

'I am so sorry,' he said, so slowly I had time to look at Maddy over his shoulder. She was smiling. I laughed. Femi laughed. He was smart in a well-cut suit, dazzling shirt, and a thin, red silk tie. Maddy and Liza began laughing too.

'Amadi sends greetings. He is well.'

'Good punch,' I said and rubbed my chin. He pursed his lips and then grinned.

'Best in my township.'

Rose shouted up the stairs. 'Maddy! Doctor Hope is on the phone.'

'There's a first time for everything,' Maddy said, her head to one side, and picked up the heavy green handset on the duty desk.

5
The last tenant of Coxhall Mansions

We listened to Dr Hope's voice, encased in a vice-like German accent. Maddy held the telephone at some distance from her ear. When he finished, she turned to us all.

'The last tenant in Coxhall Mansions is refusing to leave.'

'So what?' asked Liza.

'Hope said that Raymond is holding out on the top floor and needs to be in hospital. He thinks the man may be psychotic. Paranoid and not coping.'

Moira, skimming through address index cards said:

'Raymond Hunter. Olympic wrestler, several admissions to hospital and cared for…'

She paused, gnarled fingers whisking through another index drawer.

'…by his mother, Amelie.' She looked up at us. 'Who died last year.'

Coxhall Mansions, slated for demolition for years, would be turned into a park, residents moved to modern flats and houses. Good news, except for Raymond. Maddy glanced at her notes.

'Dr Hope did not assess Raymond. No lift and Raymond's flat is on the top. The thirteenth floor.'

Maddy went on, regardless of the room falling silent. 'The gas is off. No electricity. Raymond must be freezing.'

Until that moment, I must confess, I'd been gazing at Maddy. She wore a thick Guernsey sweater and her hair tumbled over her shoulders.

People looked at me.

'I think this is mine,' I offered, hoping that shouldering the job would impress Maddy.

'Let's line up a visit with Dr Hope, the police as backup and an ambulance for…' I checked my digital watch. 'Six thirty?'

I was proud of my black plastic wristwatch. Maddy said I'd found it in a cornflakes box, but I knew the future was digital.

* * *

Already dark outside, rain slanting across the glare of sodium streetlamps, Maddy first offered to join me but then admitted she had a meal planned.

'Something special for me and Tim,' she said.

Police officers and ambulance medics were standing by. I thought I would not need Maddy. Wrong again.

A police van sat in the shadows at the side of the dark tower. Coxhall Mansions was a hulk, ugly, and scattered with abandoned debris. I sat in my Citroen grateful I'd splashed £35 on a heater. Next would be a Sinclair Microquartz clock for the dashboard, or a heated rear window instead. Maddy said I should buy a radio. I listened happily to the rain, pattering on the canvas roof.

Dr Hope appeared around the brick gate pillars, clutching one to wheel him round off the pavement and into the yard. His black greatcoat collar up and his hat jammed down against the weather. In the half-light he reminded me of a Lowry stick figure. Dr Hope shouted at people who smoked cigarettes, so I threw mine out of the side window that flapped up and down.

'Doctor Hoffnung,' I said. 'Or is it Dr Hope?'

'It's all the same. You can call me Hope if you like.'

I took his thin hand into mine and realised how cold he was, how soft his skin. At five feet his hat brim was lower than my shoulder. Maddy sometimes said she chatted with Hope's hat. His face glowed child-like and kind, with eyes bluer than bird's eggs.

Assuming the ambulance was coming, and the police already on the top floor, we made for the stairs. Alongside signs declaring the building dangerous and entry forbidden, someone had used a paintbrush and tarry paint to scrawl *Fuck Enoch* on the curved brick wall of the stairwell.

'I would rather not,' said Dr Hope in clipped tones. 'He should have been shot.' He was smiling. 'Facking Nazi.'

His accent added a certain panache to his outburst. I began to wonder if he was capable of a credible mental health assessment of the frightened wrestler.

'You realise I cannot climb thirteen floors,' he said.

I had forgotten. Wordless, I quickly thought how Maddy and I might have used a three-handed lift.

'Use the fireman's lift,' he said, looking up at me again. 'I weigh nothing. Let's go!'

All kind of things went through my mind at break-neck speed. Wouldn't his hat come off? What if I dropped him? I bent down, took his frail right wrist, and as I ducked down to gather his legs and sling him over my shoulder, he gripped his hat with his left hand. He's done this before, I thought.

I made seven floors before I set him down. We stood on the balcony and took in the sights. Street lights hosing down the road with jewelled spray.

'You've done this before,' I said, taking his hand again and sweeping him up over my shoulder.

'Many times,' he answered from behind me. He smelt clean, as if scrubbed with liniment.

'The first time, a big British Tommy carried me out of Bergen Belsen concentration camp. Typhus. I almost died, being quite old and starving.'

In the darkness, I saw his startling eyes again.

'So, you understand,' he continued, 'I quite like being carried by you Britishers. Maddy is excellent. She is soft.'

'*She* carried you upstairs?'

'She carried me up *my* stairs,' he laughed, with something close to a cackle.

'Let's see about Raymond, shall we?' We clambered up to the thirteenth level.

Two young policemen approached. They wore crisp gabardine raincoats. Some policemen made a habit of polishing their black gloves using cream. One officer had used shoe polish instead, for as he wiped raindrops from under his nose with one finger, a black wonky moustache appeared.

Dr Hope hooted but was interrupted by the copper's colleague who stepped forward.

'And who are you, sir?'

'I am Josef Hoffnung and Raymond's GP,' said Dr Hope, pulling himself up to his entire five feet.

'He is Raymond's GP,' I assured the police. 'One minute, Josef!' I called, hoping to stop Dr Hope rushing in. 'Before we go in, can I be clear how I want this to happen?'

The officers, having been briefed by their sergeant to let the Welfare lead the visit, seemed resentful.

'Can one of you stand at the end of the balcony please and tell us when the ambulance arrives?'

The young man nodded. Dr Hope, who'd made thousands of such visits in endless decades of practice, stood with his hands at his side. He didn't look up and I understood why. The officer sporting a deranged boot-black moustache appeared so comical, we would not be able to stop laughing once started.

'I want you,' I said, looking at the door and averting my gaze from his priceless face, 'to stand here, and after we go in, remain outside but with your boot *inside* the door frame.'

He nodded.

'Important,' I said. 'Foot in the doorway.'

He nodded again. 'Do you want my torch?' he said.

'No, I don't want to scare Raymond. He's been in darkness for weeks. Thank you, officer. If you hear a ruck, please come in quick. Dr Hope, he's over ninety.'

The copper grimaced, incredulous, and Dr Hope snapped, 'I am not!'

I'd been given a master key and after calling and knocking I followed Hope in. The door opened into a living room in which a lumpy bed dominated. A window sat on the opposite side and a fireplace at the right. Although dark outside, this was darker. I thought, he's gone, no-one here. I can sense nothing. I hope to God he's not in the bathroom, not dead, please.

I repeated, 'Raymond. Mr. Hunter. I'm here with Dr Hope.'

Gradually my eyes adjusted. Tangled sheets on the bed but no body. Dr Hope edged forward. In front of the window, a giant heap of stale laundry loomed. I stared back at the shaft of light from outside. The policeman's shiny boot inside the doorframe and all so quiet, I heard the moustached one talking to the other.

'I got the torch this week. A new kind of bulb. Halogen. Fucking bright. I'll show you.'

I said 'No!' too late as he stepped over to the balcony to show off his torch. The laundry bundle erupted, and Raymond came straight past Dr Hope, heading for me. I dodged to one side, slipped on a sheet, and turned in time to watch Raymond shouldering the door shut and turning the latch. Futile thumps landed on the solid door.

Only a blue cast from a weak moon crawled through the window and then surrendered. I sensed where Raymond crouched from his breathing. Then a glint. Something chrome or steel.

'I think Raymond has a knife,' I whispered with forced calmness.

'Not a knife. A facking kukri!' said Hope. 'I saw one before on his mantelpiece.'

'Help me Lord,' begged Raymond. Calmer than I felt, *he* had the small, razor-sharp sword. Even then, I realised the situation had become a terrifying farce.

Raymond lunged forwards, and to be honest, I ran, and so did Dr Hope, although there was nowhere to run. So we ran around the small room. This required us to leap on the bed, stumble across, off it and around the horrifying circuit again.

Dr Hope began galloping with one hand on his hat and a leather bag in the other. The whole episode was accompanied by relentless hammering on the door and Doctor Hope regressing to Hoffnung and yelling '*Hilfe!*'

Overtaking me again, Hope whispered: 'When you grab him, I will deal with him,' and showed me a syringe in his fist.

I recalled my struggle with Gregory underneath the table at the office. He had a kitchen knife, but I never thought he'd stab me. I was not so comfortable with Raymond. Raymond was talking to God, and then abruptly fell over.

He slipped down like a heap of heavy luggage and I jumped on him. I had his wrist in as tight a grip as I could muster and sprawled across his giant frame, hoping to pin him down long enough. I shook with fear. Raymond began to heave against me, twisting his arm as Dr Hope struck. Hypnotised by the syringe impaled in Raymond's considerable buttock and regaining some composure, I asked what it was.

'Morphine,' he replied with triumph, 'worked in the trenches.'

'What trenches?'

'The German facking trenches,' shouted Hope, pulling himself to his feet.

Two things occurred to me. Dr Hope had served in the German Army in the First World War and later was sent to an extermination camp in the Second World War for being a blue-eyed Jew. The second thing was Raymond the wrestler, also stumbling to his feet, wasn't now just talking to God. He thought he *was* God, and said so.

I sprang to the door and turned the lock before Raymond realised what was happening. Two policemen and two ambulance men barrelled in and laid him struggling on the bed. One turned to Doctor Hope.

'How much did you give him, Dr Hope?'

'I don't recall,' he answered, adopting a kind of sang-froid attitude. 'Too much, I expect.'

It wasn't and he knew. Raymond was his patient. The ambulance crew realised too, being only the latest of generations of paramedics getting to grips with Dr Hope.

'And you!' he barked at the unfortunate copper who had taken his boot out of the door to show off his torch.

'You are a facking Nazi. See in the mirror. You have the same moustache as Adolf. Little Austrian piece of shit.'

We left to complete the papers by the light of the halogen torch.

'A bit unfair,' I suggested. 'I doubt they were born when you came to England.'

'I hate uniforms,' was all he would say.

'So you were a medic in the trenches?' I had to have the story right for Maddy.

'I was a soldier. Shooting you Britishers.'

I stared down at him and he mistook my confusion.

'I had a ladder, Jack, to shoot at you from the trenches.'

'You were in Belsen concentration camp?'

'In the second war. I qualified as a doctor. I tried to save lives, but could not save my own.'

We stepped with care down thirteen flights. At the bottom he took both my hands in his. At last, they were warm.

'Let me explain, Jack. My name was Haube. It means Hood like your Robin Hood, but I needed a new life. A new name. I chose the name Hope for myself because that's who I had become. Hope was all I had left when I was dying of the typhus. It is why I am still working. I can never repay you Britishers.'

He turned and walked down the road. I hadn't thought to offer him a lift. I wanted a cigarette anyway and stood on the pavement waiting for the ambulance to leave. I needed to follow the van to hospital and help to admit Raymond.

A car pulled up and the Director of our Service wound down the window.

'Hello, Jack.' I saw his deputy next to him. I guessed they'd spent the evening at a long Council meeting.

'What are you doing here at this time of night?'

'Being chased around a flat at the top of Coxhall Mansions by a patient with a machete.'

'Is he OK?'

'Sure, he's off to hospital now. *Very* happy.'

'Dr Hope, then?'

'Yes.' I smiled. 'What was the meeting about?'

'The local offices.'

He paused for dramatic effect.

'They're going to close them down.'

6
Eric on the corner

I think my love of epic films grew even more from the view from my bedroom window just off the Harrovale Road. Across the backstreet loomed a vast, sand coloured brick wall on which a monumental film poster sprawled, lit at night with an array of steel lamps on thin brackets.

I preferred the scene at night, in the rain, imagining the story unfolding. I never spotted the posters being pasted up. The enjoyment of them *appearing* was enduring.

The Regal Cinema closed. Red velour seating was pulled out to make way for a shopping experience. No-one bothered about the vast side of the building at the back. For almost a year, while builders tossed out mahogany bannisters and lumps of plaster in the shape of sphinxes, the lamps remained on and shreds of Woody and Annie Hall still fluttered in the breeze.

Leaving the cramped flat each morning, the ride to work was a joy. The old 2CV sailed along backstreets and turned onto Hamford Way, a long straight and empty road past pubs and a maze of a playground we helped squatters build for families.

Everyone helped. The council offloaded timber and gravel, pubs raised money for tools and hardware. The Hamford Way Adventure Playground was the pride of the neighbourhood.

Maddy met me as I started up the stairs with Rose shouting behind me.

'You're supposed to sign in, Jack.'

'I've got a stack of work from night-duty,' said Maddy. 'Can you pick up a part three job down the road?'

Part three was always a gentle piece of work. Part three of the National Assistance Act, drafted in the midst of war to sweep away 'Want, Disease, Ignorance, Squalor and Idleness', referred to help with retirement and nursing homes.

An older person, who had no friends or family to help them with their last move, often made the journey with me to a council retirement home. The journey was always threaded with mixed feelings. Sometimes sadness and despair, but very often, surprisingly joyful. Now and again the car ride was riven with terror at the idea of the workhouse, remembered as hated institutions.

Young people like Gregory always complained about my 'stupid' car, but older people didn't. They told me stories, adventures of war and often tales of romance. Grandmothers loved shocking me with lurid accounts of sex with strangers during the Blitz. Others were wracked with guilt about infidelities.

None would wear a seatbelt.

'Soon,' I would say, 'you'll have to, it'll be the law.'

Old soldiers would say, 'Fack orf.'

Maddy handed me the papers.

'Eric on the corner,' she said, as if I knew him.

'You must have seen him, high up on Richard's Road? Everyone knows Eric. Well, we all *see* him. That ghostly face at the window over Fennel's Pharmacy?'

The pharmacy was one of the last chemist shops to make their own medicines. Cedric Fennel was a dab hand with Gardner's wooden *Sifter and Mixer Machine,* before pressing his own pills in front of oak drawers with faded green labels. One said *Opium.* His brother Claude had a talent for tincture. Their cough mixture was to die for and worth the price of a bottle just to follow the mortar and pestle action.

I looked at the sheaf of papers, then at Maddy, and wondered if I should ask her out to the pub again.

'Eric lives over the shop,' continued Maddy. 'Has done for years and years. Family has all gone now. Claude takes up his food, but Eric can't get out at all now.'

'Does Eric understand I'm coming?'

'I had a chat with him this morning. He's on the ring-around-list and this morning he said he was ready. I told Eric you'd do an introductory visit today. He can check out Don's place.'

'Great. Don will sort him out. How old is Eric?'

'Nearly ninety.'

'A good life.'

'Younger than his GP.'

'Dr Hope? I had to carry him up the stairs at Coxhall Mansions and he said you carried him upstairs at home.'

'I did,' said Maddy with a broad smile. 'He's only little. Don't worry, Eric told me he can manage the stairs. You had better get going.'

'When am I supposed to take him?'

'Nine thirty.'

'Almost nine now.'

'I know,' she said over her shoulder as she went back upstairs. I heard her yell, 'Fancy a drink tonight?'

'Perhaps.'

I shut the door behind me and thought. *You bet.* I had to find out what Maddy was doing upstairs round old Dr Hope's house.

***

Fennel's Pharmacy was the thinnest shop I had ever seen. Triangular and sitting at the join of two roads merging into one, it overlooked the adventure playground and did a steady trade in sticking plasters.

Less than six feet across inside the door, the shop broadened to a counter about ten feet wide at the back. Claude was busy with the whole theatre of coloured glass jars and bottles, smelling of Limoncello and camphor.

'I'm Jack.'

'You've come for Eric? I'll show you.' He took me through a door at the back into a tiled hallway to one side.

'Top floor,' he said.

I was still looking at the shimmering tiles, deep green paint, and brown, polished oak panels, when he closed the door again. I was alone in the nineteen forties. A green enamel sign proclaimed *National Insurance Chemist*.

At each turn of the scrubbed pine stairs, a window gave out onto Richard's Road, rooftops, and a London panorama of streets, chimneys, and, glistening in the morning sunshine, the dome of St. Paul's.

For all the great city bustling out there, here, on this empty landing, all was quiet except for a creaking floorboard. Eric must have heard me. A door swung open and for a moment I gripped the bannister.

Weeks earlier, Femi had punched me down the stairs at the offices of his country's liberation movement in exile, but this was different. Eric had the smile of someone staring out from an old black and white photograph. A slight, wise grin in a pale, youthful face.

'Jack?'

'Yes. Did Maddy tell you I was coming?'

'She rings me every Monday morning. She has a lovely voice.'

'She's Welsh,' I said. Did everyone love Maddy?

'Come in.'

He gestured to me to walk into his neat, sunlit room overlooking the road junction. There were flowers blooming red and gold amongst wet indigo pots inside a low parapet.

'How do you get out there?'

'Through the window.'

A sash window was half open and dark puddles dribbled around the geraniums. Eric had been watering them this morning.

He was tall man, holding himself straight and moving easily for his age. It was hard to work out why he needed any care, let alone leave his home for an institution.

There *was* something. Something about the sideways look he gave me. I think he understood, for at that moment, he turned his head. There was a flash. More of a glint in the sunshine and a realisation. Eric had a polished metal plate over his left temple the size of a coffee saucer.

'I'm sorry,' was all he said.

'Why? Why are you sorry?'

'Some people are revolted. They recoil.'

'To be honest, Eric, it looks beautiful. Is it engraved? You should see what punk kids are sticking through their noses.'

His slight smile returned.

'Made of silver,' he continued. 'I had it engraved before they screwed it in. They used silver screws too,' and he leant forward so I could follow the delicate, engraved tendrils and read one elegantly etched word. *Tom.*

'Tom?'

'He was…' Eric paused, as if reading my expression first.

'How do you say it now? He was my…' He faltered again.

'My partner. He's always with me now.' Tapping his skull.

'Here.'

'What happened?'

'He bought it and I didn't. They saved me with wadding and a bit of biscuit tin with screws from a bent rifle.'

I examined the fine mirror polish of the plate. At an angle I caught a reflected glimpse of blue sky.

'Biscuit tin?'

He nodded. A full smile now.

'Huntley and Palmers, I think. With the moustache and medals of King George. When I got home, they put this one in. Old King George saved my life. Bless him.'

'When was this, Eric?'

'Nineteen sixteen. Battle of the Somme. The big push. They got Tom with machine gun fire. I watched him ripped apart and jumped after him into a hole, then a shell burst got me. Knocked me out.'

He gripped the back of a chair, as if in pain.

'I can't forgive myself.'

'Why?' I said, aghast at the thought of his pain and loss.

'I don't know why I'm telling you this, Jack. I don't. I've not told anyone. Not Cedric or Claude downstairs, even though they would understand.'

'No problem, Eric. We've got plenty of time.'

'It was an argument. He was cross with me. The last thing, before we were to go over the top. He had wanted to visit a brothel. He wanted *both* of us to visit a French brothel, but I couldn't. Didn't want to. I only loved him.'

'Of course. But why? Why a brothel?'

'He saved up for it. For us both. You had to pay extra for VD.'

'For what?'

'The clap. Gonorrhoea. Anything. We'd miss the offensive. We'd be sent behind lines to the hospital. Tom would have been alive. I wouldn't have had this *thing* on my head. It is a curse, but the only thing I have of him. All I have. I wanted a tattoo, but I'm afraid of needles.'

I had started by meeting his gaze as he talked. It's what you do. But I was looking down now at patterns in his Persian carpet. Listening to the emotion in his voice. When I looked up, there were tears in rivulets down his cheeks and to my surprise, my eyes were wet as well.

'We should go,' I said. 'If you're ready, Eric.'

He took out a silk handkerchief to dab his eyes. 'I am,' he said. 'I really am, Jack. I'm ready.'

'When did you last go out?'

He stood on the landing for a minute, thinking. He wore a smooth, lemon, v-neck pullover and a smart tweed jacket. His brogues looked handmade.

'November, nineteen eighteen. Victory Day.'

'Well, yes, Eric. But I mean, you know? To the shops. To the pub?'

He just looked at me. It sank in. He had never been out. He had never left the flat since Victory Day. For over sixty years.

'I didn't need to go out. I didn't want to. Didn't have to. So, I stayed here. Bernard, my brother, brought me everything I needed. Cedric fixed me up with painkillers and Claude got me off them.'

I had to grip the bannister again for a second time and went in front of him. He didn't seem to need my help, but if he stumbled, at least I could break his fall. I stopped every now and again to check each careful step until we reached the bottom.

'That is new!' he said, nodding at the chipped National Insurance sign.

'Nineteen forty-eight,' I said. 'They started charging for prescriptions later.'

'Thirty years ago? I've had free medicine for sixty years. Dr Hope told me so.'

Before I knew it, I'd said it.

'He's German, you know. Was probably shooting at you from the other trenches.'

'He was. We talk about it often. He's a kind old man, but he can't come see me anymore. Claude can't lift him up the stairs nowadays.'

'He probably paid for your drugs. And Bernard?'

'My younger brother? He died in the spring. Dr Hope said it was the flu. He just stopped breathing one night.'

Somehow, the broad expanse of Richard's Road helped change the subject. The Council had just planted forty thousand trees to *green* the borough. Saplings with stakes were everywhere, adding to older trees dug in as part of *Plant A Tree for Seventy-Three*.

I watched Eric drink in the fresh air, the green canopy softening the imperial Georgian architecture, then noticed he was leaning on a walking stick, the handle carved in the shape of a sheepdog.

He realised I was puzzled. He hadn't used it on the stairs.

'It *is* mine. Bernard showed me a picture. He bought it for my sixtieth birthday. Said I was an old man. He told me it was by the downstairs door. I could use it if I ever went out.'

'He was encouraging you to go out.'

'Yes.'

'Tempting you to go downstairs, but you never did.'

'No.'

'Well, here we are. You'd better get in.'

I snatched the towel from the passenger seat before he saw it. I doubted Eric would have an *accident* like so many of my passengers.

'I've seen these on the telly,' he said, looking around him and clipping on his seatbelt. 'Can we roll the roof back?'

'Of course, Eric. It is a bit nippy, you know.'

'I don't mind,' he said, examining everything. 'Whilst I was waiting for you, I realised what a silly old man I am. I never thought I was old until today. I sleep a lot and I dream all the time, but I'm never old in my dreams. Never. Perhaps nobody is old in their dreams.'

All the way to Don's establishment, Eric sat up and gazed about him like minor royalty of the kind whose names you can never quite remember.

'I've seen most stuff on the TV,' he explained, 'but you miss lots.'

Somehow, through his eyes, I began to see my familiar haunts anew.

'What are those signs everywhere?' he said, pointing.

'Road signs?'

'Yes. Red circles on posts.'

'I think it started in the sixties, Eric. Helps to keep the traffic flowing. Tells you when to stop and give way.'

'Cobbles,' he said. 'We used the pattern of the cobbles. If the cobbles were with you, you had right of way. If the pattern changed, you had to give way.'

I tried to imagine it. Keeping track of the road surface. It must have been just as crowded.

'Subtle,' I pointed out. 'Very subtle, Eric.'

'For you, maybe,' he laughed, and we arrived at Don's still chuckling.

Don met us outside and took Eric's arm kindly.

'Do you fancy a cuppa, Eric?'

'I do,' said Eric. 'Oh, Jack?'

I turned, and he dropped a half crown into my hand.

'Keep the change.'

'I can't spend that. We went decimal years ago.'

'I know,' he grinned, and went inside.

* * *

That evening in the Butchers, Maddy and I were imagining sixty years of looking out over the junction on Richard's Road. Staring at the traffic, the changing styles of cars and fashion.

She lifted a pint with obvious anticipation.

'I'd miss my pint,' I suggested. 'When I brought him home, he was happy as a sand-boy. He wants to stay at Don's and starts next week so I offered him a beer, but he said *no*.'

'I think Claude takes him a jug up,' she said.

'I've been meaning to ask,' I continued. 'Why did you carry Dr Hope up the stairs at his house?'

'Because he asked.' She smiled. 'He wanted to show me some photographs. He hadn't been upstairs in years.'

'There's a good view from my window,' I said. 'You can come and watch TV with me.'

'I've heard that one before,' she replied and did that funny, snorting laugh that you hated, or loved. I loved it. I really did.

7
Swimming out of darkness

I watched the rain falling against the window pane next to my desk. It was miserably cold and wet outside. Nearly a year had flown by since my arrival and I felt almost part of the furniture. Where had the time gone?

I heard soft footsteps on the stairs, and looked up to see Dr Hope's face peering around the doorway.

'I surprised you,' he said, laughing.

He gripped the door frame with one pale, bruised hand and took off his homburg hat with the other. Maddy pulled a chair across for him and he sat quickly, looking around, taking his time. I saw his hand fluttering beneath the hat on his knee. A tremor. He held it briefly, like a captive bird.

'You're hurt, Dr Hope.'

'I'm not. Just old,' he said, and changing the subject, went on. 'I saw Raymond at the hospital. Our friend from the top of Coxhall Mansions. He is much better and wants to see you. I think perhaps he wants to go home.'

'Is he ready?'

'No. And he has no home to go to.'

'I'll drop by and have a chat.'

'Good. Thank you, Jack.'

'Was there anything else?'

'Yes.'

Maddy leaned forward. Dr Hope fumbled in his coat pocket and brought out a small leather notebook, wetted his finger and leafed through the pages. When he looked up, we sat back quickly. A trace of Maddy's perfume lingered in the air.

'Chanel, Maddy?' said Hope.

She nodded with a fondness for him I wanted for myself. His notebook slipped to the floor and she retrieved it, handed it to Hope and glanced at me.

'I need to talk to Jack,' he said. 'Do you mind, Maddy?'

As she left the room, I told Hope I had visited 'Eric on the Corner' at his room in Don's residential home.

'When I arrived, he was surrounded by women residents chuckling and clapping their hands at his stories. He seemed happy.'

'Eric was a popular man, Jack. He had many friends, you know.'

'He never went out, for sixty years.'

'But the world came to him, and I am glad he is no longer in that apartment at his age. I will talk to Don about Eric's medication.'

I wondered at Hope's age. Well over eighty. Ninety?

'I want to ask you to see a boy for me, Jack. I am worried for him, and February is not a good time for young men afraid to go out.'

'Afraid to go out?'

'Not like Eric. He *chose* not to go out and he was told it was dangerous for him. Theo is different. I think he is depressed.'

'Then he needs to see a psychiatrist.'

'For what? For pills?'

'For an assessment?'

'You are right. But he will not go, and I do not think he needs his head examining. I can give him pills, but I don't believe he will ever get better that way. I want you to talk to him, Jack.'

'I'm not a therapist.'

'Good. He does not need a facking therapist.' Hope shifted in his chair and looked about the empty room, a trace of embarrassment in his eyes.

'I am sorry. I do not trust those psycho-donkeys. In Germany I was taken to Belsen camp and was terrified. Then you British bring me to London and send me to see a German psychoanalyst in Maida Vale. For what? And for six weeks he asked me about my mother and my father and what I like for sex.'

'Did he?'

'Yes. Well. Not the sex bit. But he wanted to.'

'Not a fan, then?'

'Excuse me?'

'You don't want analysis or psychotherapy for Theo.'

'Just kindness. He needs people. And all he has is his fack...' A pause.

'His?'

'Mother.'

'So, *she* is stopping him from going out?'

'Not exactly. But she makes him ashamed. So ashamed, he is full of fear. At twenty-five? Of what?'

'Why do *you* think he's ashamed?'

'Because, like Eric, he is a homosexual.'

I reached for my cigarettes whilst I wondered what to say, began to pull one out then pushed the packet away at Hope's angry stare.

'Sorry.'

'Not for me, Jack. Sorry for you. Have you seen the lungs of smokers?' He stroked the nap of his hat on the desk as if preparing for dissection.

'Yes. At the smoking clinic in Drayton Park. There's a chest-cutter surgeon there who keeps a pair in a jar to frighten us.'

'Is that so?' Hope seemed impressed. 'Will you see Theo?'

'Has he asked to see us?'

'Of course not. I am asking *you* to see him. I have told his mother you are coming tonight.'

I wished he had not done that.

'Does *she* want us to visit her son?'

'No.'

'Then I cannot visit him, Dr Hope. He doesn't want to see me, and his mother won't let me in.'

I expected Hope to argue, but using the desk to help him up, he shrieked 'Maddy' so loud that she, and others, came running.

'All I am asking is for this man to help me,' he complained whilst theatrically tapping his hat on the desk, glancing severely at me, and explaining about Theo to Maddy.

'Is Theo a risk to himself or anyone else?' she asked.

'To others, no. Perhaps his mother, but I do not think so. He may kill himself.'

There was a moment of silence in which Hope looked at me. I looked at Maddy and she looked at Hope. I reached for my cigarettes again and Hope surprisingly nodded. I lit up quickly, before he changed his mind.

'You said he was depressed?' I asked Hope.

'No. He is in despair. It is different.'

'Perhaps he needs to be in hospital,' said Maddy.

'No, let's see him first before we even think about that,' I said a little too quickly. Maddy stared at me.

'Good,' said Hope. 'We are agreed. Six-thirty tonight. Good luck.'

He turned to Maddy, took her hand in both of his, then picked up his hat and made for the stairs. Maddy followed him and when she returned, stood hands on hip.

'Why not the duty psychiatrist? Hope said he might be a suicide risk.'

'I think he just said that to get me to visit. If we tell them his GP believes Theo is a risk to himself, then they will take him in, to cover themselves. They'll say he needs assessment.'

'He does.'

'But not in the Towers. Not yet anyway.'

'Jack, what's on your mind?'

'Nothing.'

We were standing by the kettle, waiting for it to boil, my hand casually on top of a tall filing cabinet, inches from her soft shoulder.

'Just...' I hesitated.

'What?'

'I was in a mental hospital for three months, on placement when I was training.'

'And?'

It tumbled out.

'I should have said something, but I never did. I saw a man being treated for being gay. Electrocuted. He was sat on a dining chair in a big broom cupboard under the stairs with bare feet on chicken wire, and this psychiatrist was showing him slides of nude men and naked women. Every time a man appeared, he gave him a jolt. I felt sick.'

'Jack, that's terrible. Aversion therapy.'

'I know. I feel awful,' I said, conscious of my feet shifting about.

'Did you do anything about it?'

'That's just it. I saw the man afterwards. I was writing an essay. I asked him how he was, and he said he was fine. He said he was desperate and now he had hope. He said he wanted to be fixed and he trusted the doctor, so I thought it was all right. I was only twenty-two, Maddy. I didn't know what to do. The man was married and desperate.'

I thought she was going to put her arm around my shoulder but instead she put an arm round my waist. She looked up. I could feel her warmth.

'It's OK,' she said. 'We've all done stuff, or wished we'd done something differently. I can see why you want to meet Theo.'

We went into the outside yard for a smoke. Her arms were crossed against the cold. Jewelled beads of ice nestled in the leaves of weeds.

'Don't get on a mission,' she said. 'Don't rescue him, Jack. That's not what it's about.'

'I know. I'd ask *you* to do it, but I think Dr Hope came to me for a reason. If you're in the Butcher's Arms later, I'll tell you how it goes.'

She turned, half-way up the steps that led to the back door.

'Leave a note about where you're going. If you don't turn up at the Butchers, I'll know it's gone tits up and I'll come and get you out.'

'I'd do the same,' I said, as the door closed.

I gazed around. The outside-lavatory door of thin planks was splintered next to the latch. Someone had slipped over the back wall and jemmied open a toilet door with no lock. The boys were getting braver, but no brighter. Our team had agreed to run a group for local gang members, and I'd said I would organise it. It was next on the list.

* * *

At six-thirty it was dark, the pavement shimmering with rainwater as I rang Theo's bell. The door opened instantly and a tall woman with oiled hair wrenched back into a tight bun looked down at me.

'You've come to see Theo.'

'I have.'

'Do you have papers, identification?'

I showed her my card, noticed her broad shoulders and a wedding ring.

'Is Theo's father about?'

'He's dead,' she said in tones suggesting she had no regrets.

'I'm sorry.'

'Why do you want to see Theo?'

'Dr Hope asked me to.'

'I see. Come in out of the rain. Take your shoes off.'

I padded down the corridor behind her. To the right, two men watched the credits of a TV drama series. *Kung Fu*. I thought it odd they did not turn as I passed the lounge doorway.

At the end of the passage, to one side, a green door stood open and a slight young man said hello, trying to meet my eyes with his own and shyly beckoning me down some wooden stairs to a basement. I heard the door shut above us.

'Thank you,' he said, 'for coming.'
'Dr Hope said you didn't want to see me.'
'My mother said that. I had to say it when she was there. Are you from the Welfare?'
'I am.'
'I think I'm going mad.'
He was talking fast, his thoughts pouring out already.
'Going mad?'
'I don't know. I don't go out. I'm afraid to go out. I can't sleep. I have bad dreams.'
'Dreams?'
'About men. About boys like me.'
'You're twenty-five.'
'Yes.'
'About boys like you?'
'Yes.'
'What sort of bad dreams?'
'About sex. I think about it all the time.'
'Is that bad?'
'Don't you think so?'
His eyes met mine for the first time.
'No. I don't think so, at all.'
I thought about Maddy, her hug and scent. How she laid her head against my shoulder. Intoxicating.
Theo sat back on his chair, smoothing his legs with his palms. Behind him, a poster of Sylvester, a black disco singer. Theo saw me looking around.
'My mum thinks Sylvester is a woman.'
'Sylvester's a man?'
'Yes. Don't you know?'
'Sorry Theo. I can see he's an interesting person.'
I just waited for him to say more. That's the knack. Avoid the desire to fill the silent void. I heard an odd kind of drumming outside his window. Rain from a broken gutter was slapping onto a bin. Focused on that. Waiting.

'Can you help me?'

'I don't know. You seem unhappy. Is that right?'

He nodded, staring at the floor, then at me. Tears slipping down his cheeks.

'Theo. I need to know. Have you had ideas about harming yourself?'

He put a hand to his chest, fingers spread apart, a small smile emerging.

'Sometimes.'

I waited again, the silence broken by hammering on the green door.

'Mama,' shouted Theo. 'I'm OK, Mama.'

'Sometimes?'

'I don't know. I don't know how to do it. I just want it to end.'

'Can you tell me what it is that has to end? I want to find out if I can help you.'

The clattering of water from the broken drain seemed louder with scattered thuds of rain against the window. Theo was a handsome boy with big, glistening eyes that met mine again.

'I just want to be happy.'

'What *has to end*, Theo?'

'Darkness. The darkness has to go,' he said.

'Has anyone hurt you?'

'No. But I'm trapped here,' he said, rapping his head with a fist. 'I want to go to a party. I want to go to a pub. I want to go to the shops. My mum does all my shopping. She buys me these,' he said, pulling at his slacks and jumper. 'I hate it all. It's not me.'

'I saw some men upstairs.'

'My uncles. They are always here.'

'Brothers of your mum?'

'My dad.'

'Are you afraid of them?'

'No.'

I watched as he picked at the stuffing on his chair. Pulled at the threads. Perhaps he was lying about his uncles.

'Then you can go to a pub or party anytime. Nobody stops you?'

'Just me.'

'Then maybe we can help. Dr Hope can give you some medication that will make a difference.'

'No. No pills. My mum made me take tablets before. They made me sleepy, dizzy. I forgot stuff, all the time.'

We both heard stern voices and footsteps upstairs. More barrack-room than family sounds. A small plume of dust trickling through the air from the floorboards above. I glimpsed Theo flinching and his thumb poking through a hole into the chair cushion.

'You can come with me if you want,' I said, without thinking. He gave a small smile that collapsed quickly, then looking out the window he stood up.

'The rain has stopped. You should go now.'

'Now?'

'Yes.'

'Will you be all right tonight, Theo?'

'Of course.'

'Will you see me again?'

'Yes. I want to, very much.'

'Then I'll come, the same time tomorrow.'

He nodded, smiling, an arm indicating the stairs from where a shrill voice came.

'Your tea is ready, Theo.'

'Yes Mama.'

At the top of the stairs, Theo walked into a kitchen without a word. I was alone in the corridor, the lounge empty, save for a caged budgerigar edging sideways on a wire perch. When no-one came, I let myself out, lit a cigarette and wondered what had happened. The rain started again.

* * *

In the comfortable back room at the Butchers, Lefty, the barman, had wordlessly set down two pints of Bass without being asked. The first sip, smelling of biscuits baking, and the roaring fire warming my legs, seemed to put the world to rights.

'I feel safe now,' I said.

'What?' said Maddy.

'I didn't mean that. Relaxed.'

This was enough. Just Maddy and me at the end of the day, round a fire. Hard to take my eyes off her. She slipped her scarf off.

'You said you feel *safe* now.'

'I did. I do. It was a bit strange. I'm not sure what's going on there.'

'Is Theo OK?'

'No. I don't think so. But I'm seeing him tomorrow night.'

'Tomorrow? We have a union meeting at the chapel. The new Council want to close the teams down. We *have* to be there.'

'They can't close the teams down.'

'They can. That's the plan. Sell council houses and cut services. You'll still have a job, but you'll share one big office with a hundred and fifty other people. Miles from here.'

She let that sink in and lit a cigarette.

'They're bad for you.'

'I know. Want one?'

'Yes.' My mind was racing again. 'I can't think about the union meeting now. I may have made the wrong decision about Theo.'

I told her everything. What I saw, felt and heard, and finished with my worst fear.

'Maybe you were right,' I said. 'Maybe he should be in hospital. He won't take medication and he had a kind of smile. Could be the sort of smile of someone who has made their mind up. He might do something tonight.'

'Hold on. That's not what he said, was it? I trust Hope too. He may be geriatric but he's smart. Seen a few things. Listen. You think Theo's depressed?'

'Yes.'

'Then who, or what, is depressing him? What's pushing him down?'

'He says it's him.'

'Is it?'

'I don't know. There's something wrong with that house, with those people.'

'Then if he's agreed to see you tomorrow, you should go. I'll stick two hands up for you in the meeting.'

I took my chance.

'Maddy.'

I think she already knew what I was asking.

'Do you fancy going down to the Anchor later? There's a band on.'

I expected all kinds of answers. It was worth a shot. Her gaze was steady.

'Do you want to sleep with me?'

I didn't expect that.

'Because if you do, it's a no from me.'

'Oh. I see. I just wanted to spend some time with you when we're not at work.'

I vainly searched for the right words, to say that I needed to be closer to that simmering energy and intelligence. To feel that warmth again.

'Listen, Jack. You live on your own. I'm with Tim. It would be nice, I think. You make me laugh. But if it got awkward, I have Tim to go back to. He's there for me. Always. You have no one. It's just not fair, on you.'

'So, you're being kind to me, by saying no?'

'I suppose so.'

'It was a crap band anyway.'

Maddy grinned. A big, wide, warm grin. I should have said 'I love you' and be done with it. Sod Tim. Sod everything. I took the glasses to the bar and settled up with Lefty.

When I turned, Maddy had her scarf on, waved, made for the exit, then turned on her heels, her coat whirling out, striding back. She grabbed my lapels, and on tiptoe, kissed me briefly. I felt her pillow-soft lips and closed my eyes.

'It's just a crush, Jack,' she whispered, shaking me gently. 'See you tomorrow.'

***

The next day was colder. Even the railings had a feathering of snow along them. I knocked at Theo's door on my way home and was relieved when he answered it.

'Hello, Theo. How are you?'

He smiled and nodded, standing aside as I clumped into the hall with wet boots.

'Shall I take them off?'

He just shook his head. I hoped he would loosen up.

As I followed him down the corridor, past the empty budgerigar room and down the stairs, I chatted about the weather whilst watching his gait, noticing that he too had such broad shoulders, like his mother.

'Do you swim?'

'I did. I got gold for lifesaving, with honours, and I met David Wilkie. Mama used to take me.'

As he brightened, I saw the chance for us to talk properly and started where we left off yesterday.

'Do you still feel trapped?'

'Always.'

'Then let's just play a game, Theo. I want you to think about being in a deep hole. A dark hole. Completely on your own.'

'Where?'

'In the ground. I'd like you to just peep over the top. Take a look. What do you see?'

'The snow.'

'Good. What else?'
'Mama.'
'Why doesn't she pull you out?'
'She can't. She's talking to my dad's brothers.'
'What is she saying?'
'She's asking them where my dad is.'
'You are so good at this. Can you hear what they are saying, Theo?'
'They don't know. We don't know where he is.'
'I thought your dad had passed away. I'm sorry.'
'Nobody knows what happened. My uncles tell me that he is dead. The court said that he is presumed dead.'
'It sounds terrible for you and your mum, Theo.'

Was it the wrong thing to say? There was a long pause. Where last night the rain had tumbled noisily onto a bin, clumps of snow now slipped silently past the basement steps outside. I waited, even though Theo, slumped to one side in his chair, allowed a strangled sob to escape. His nails pinched the cushion again. He was staring at me. Did he know I was making it up as I went along, using my feelings to guide me? I saw a slight movement. He was rocking gently, a few inches back and forth. Then he stared at me, his eyelashes thick and damp.

'I sometimes think they killed him,' he said, then looked away. Looking at his poster of the young black singer, Sylvester.

'Your uncles killed him?'

'No. I don't mean that. I just think sometimes, they might have done.'

'They might have?'

'He was gay, I think. Like me. He liked men. They hated that. They said my mum made him queer. They said it was better that he was dead.'

'Have you told anyone?'

'No. What can I tell anyone? The police have looked for him. My dad comes from overseas. They checked with the airports, with his family back home in Vittoriosa. Nothing.'

'What do you think?'

'I think he is dead. I think he would talk to me. Send me a message.'

'But there was no funeral. No goodbye?'

'No.'

'I'm so sorry. Theo. Please tell me. What are your uncles doing here?'

'I don't know. They eat the food Mama cooks. Watch the TV.'

'Have they nowhere to live?'

'They live in Epping. They have business in town and then come here. But they know I am gay. They can smell it somehow. They are always watching me.'

'And your mum?'

'She has no idea.'

'Are you sure?'

He nodded, his hands peacefully in his lap, turned them over, examining them.

'I think it's time we got you out of that hole, Theo. Have you thought about leaving home?'

'All the time. It's what I've always wanted but I've got nowhere to go. No job.'

'Then we'll make some plans. I want you to come to my office tomorrow.'

'I can't do that.'

'Who's stopping you? Here's my hand. Let's get you out of that hole.'

At that, he smiled and put his hand in mine for a moment.

'One step at a time, Theo. See you tomorrow. Four o'clock.'

At the top of his stairs, I made for the door when a voice from the kitchen startled me.

'Next time, take your shoes off.'

* * *

Despite London being in the grip of a blizzard, with tales of walkers smothered by avalanches of snow from the towering roof tops, Theo appeared every day at four o'clock for our chat. We went up to a quieter room. From the window, a fresh, white view of London was laid out, the roofs white and stark against a grey, lowering sky.

I put him in touch with London Friend, the organisation that supported lesbian and gay people, and on Friday afternoons we visited the steaming local swimming baths. It was impossible to keep up with him. He would turn, splashing with joy at his own speed and skill. Smiling, and in his element.

'It's like a light has turned on,' said Maddy one afternoon, sitting opposite. 'Do you still think he might harm himself?'

'I hope not. He's doing fine. Councillor Smith has helped sort out a flat for him. Not brilliant, but he's so happy, planning how to move in.'

'Have you told Dr Hope it's working out?'

'Not yet. I still don't know if I'm doing the right thing. At least Theo is seeing someone every week at London Friend.'

'It's working because you're good at putting yourself in other people's shoes, Jack. You've got a talent for this.'

I felt my chest tighten. Rubbed my forehead whilst thinking how to change the subject and in confusion said the first thing that came to mind.

'It's not a crush, Maddy. That thing you said the other night. I don't have a crush on you. I want...'

Maddy held a fist to her mouth, suppressing a laugh. I wanted to curl up.

'Oh Jack,' she chuckled, leaning forward, whispering. 'You're so wrong! It's just a crush I have on *you*. Don't you see? I have a crush on you, but it will pass. You spend too much time inside the thoughts of other people. You forget who *you* are. I'm not the only one, you know.'

'What?'

'With a crush on you. Dr Hope knew what he was doing. That's why he wanted you to see Theo.'

'I'm straight, Maddy.'

'Dr Hope knows that. Theo knows that. There's no harm done, Jack. You helped Theo take those first steps out of the basement.'

* * *

Winter surrendered to spring and the cherry trees in the adventure playground laid their pink carpet of blossom onto the grass. Maddy took her usual holiday in Greece with Tim, and Theo dropped by to say hello. I took on other cases and tried to forget that afternoon in the office when a quiver of hope for something, anything with Maddy, had changed everything for just a few moments.

My last meeting with Theo was to help him arrange his first trip abroad. Near the market, we called into Triangle Travel. They had all the right connections to find a good holiday package and I liked the way Sandra listened to what Theo wanted.

He settled on a hotel with a large swimming pool on the Costa Brava. With luck, some sun, and maybe, new friends. I never saw him so happy as when Sandra pressed a wallet of tickets into his hands and told him to have a great time. He turned to me and grinned. It was the last time I saw him.

* * *

Maddy looked frightened on a Friday afternoon, a few weeks later. Her eyes were darting around and I knew instantly that something was wrong.

'It's Theo,' she said, her voice so different. Shaken. 'He's drowned, Jack. He's dead.'

I sat carefully, both arms on the desk to hold myself up as I struggled with disbelief.

'It was an accident. He was swimming off the beach in Sitges. There is a vicious undertow there. The police say he was waving and shouting because he was in trouble.'

'But he was a brilliant, strong swimmer. He met David Wilkie.'

'The sea can be stronger. Wears you out. Sucks you down. At this time of year, there are no lifeguards. The people on the beach.'

'They thought he was just waving to a friend.'

'Yes. That's what the police said. I'm so sorry, Jack. It's not your fault.'

She walked around and held me from behind, her head down, and a tangle of curls falling over my ears and shoulders. A jumble of thoughts streaming through my mind. His mother and the uncles. It was me who led him to this. To his death.

Maddy just hung onto me as images of Theo swimming swirled about me. He smiled at me again. He was always so free when swimming.

'What are you thinking?' she said, and I looked up to see her eyes were screwed up, unable to stop her tears.

'It's stupid,' I said, picking at things on the desk, realising I was rocking as he had.

'I was thinking, he was swimming out of darkness.'

8
The flicks

Aside from the necropolis at Highgate, and the tomb-yards tucked away in corners of the city, the dead go to the shadow-towns now; the crematoria and cemeteries belonging to boroughs, established at the end of scattered railway lines going north.

We were on our way to show respect for Theo, but I felt dead myself, nursing both a hangover and bruised feelings. How would I get through the day?

Our swaying carriage was olive green on the outside. The paint was peeling but the drabness was overwhelmed by sweet spring air sluicing through the open window. I was so glad Maddy had agreed to come with me to see Theo off. She smiled at me as if nothing had happened yesterday. Last night was heart-breaking.

* * *

We had gone to see a film, *The Deer Hunter*. I expected Maddy to say 'no' and to remind me that she lived with Tim, that feelings needed to be managed like the ropes on a boat, emotions kept tight and tidy. But me? I wanted to let go, and so asked her to come see the film and she said yes. I think Theo's death had brought us closer.

When the lights went down in the Odeon, the throng around us seemed to fade away, and before long we were transported to Clairton, a working-class steel town near Pittsburgh, folded in amongst the snow-capped mountains, and witnessing the last days of young men before they went to war in Vietnam. I was waiting for the scene with Russian roulette and an escape from the Viet Cong, but after a stag was shot and the men became maudlin at the thought of leaving home, I sensed Maddy softly crying. The film had hardly started. I put my hand on hers.

'It's so sad,' she whispered and leant on my shoulder.

'The deer?' I guessed, and hesitated. Her face was in half-light, and then she turned, her eyes gleaming.

'The price paid by so many young men?' I suggested. She was shaking her head, then leaning closer.

'That's Meryl Streep,' she said. 'See how great she is? And that's her fiancé, John Cazales, the guy with the weird hair.'

I had no idea Maddy knew anything about actors. I'd never heard of Meryl Streep.

'Cazales is dying,' she hissed, 'of lung cancer. He was a chain smoker. He died at the end of making this film. Meryl was devastated.'

'I'm not surprised.'

'Jack. They were deeply in love. Don't you see? They had to do what they loved to do, together. Grabbed that moment, acted their hearts out, and then, before the film came out, he died in her arms.'

'Let's not think about that.'

'He was only forty-two. It was a tragedy. It can happen to any of us. At any time.'

'The whole cast must have known.'

A thickset man for whom incipient baldness had not prevented an attempted rock and roll quiff, leant forward between us, and mingling forcefulness with soft tones, suggested we 'shut the fuck up.' He, like half the audience, was smoking a cigarette. You didn't need to light up. A grey cloud hung in the air, shimmering with projected streaks of colour as the drama unfolded.

Afterwards, we headed for the Butcher's Arms. The film had sapped energy from our conversation. I didn't know what to say. I read a review suggesting the director was xenophobic. The towering steel mills were emblematic of America's might. That the scene I waited for was unnecessarily cruel and slighted the Vietnamese. I said all that in my own words but Maddy just sat on the red leather bench staring at her pint.

I got it wrong, of course. I should have stopped there. I went on to tell her about growing up in a factory village. How my sister got out of there as soon as she could, married an American marine who did two tours in 'Nam'. Maddy was looking at me now, listening intently, so I barrelled along with my story.

'I think she hated the base in North Carolina, so she brought the kids to live with us in our village. Every month my sister, my mum and my dad would put together a parcel addressed to the marine base in Da Nang. Chocolate and Senior Service cigarettes. Soon afterwards we had colourful letters from the Viet Cong who had got hold of our details from the parcel's return address. They foraged in the bins. The letters were pretty things, hand lettered, explaining how my sister's husband would die. She would laugh and sob at the same time. The postman used to say, "another letter from the commies".'

'Stop,' said Maddy quickly. 'Don't you see? We must *forget* the past. It's gone. Finished. There's just no point in going over all that stuff. There's just today and tomorrow. You're a Dylan fan, aren't you, Jack? Well, *'Don't Look Back.'*

'I'm not a fan, I just… appreciate…' Stumbling. I had to stop right there. Maddy was glaring at me, or, rather, although it sounds impossible, glaring at herself. About her. Irritated. Impatient even.

'We can't just go on from day to day, as if we'll live forever,' she said, pulling out a packet of Silk Cut and fumbling with a lighter. As it lit, with a soft 'pop' and a sharp smell of petrol, her face was lit briefly by the yellow flame. I thought she looked a bit like Meryl Streep. I saw something new in Maddy every day. It was one of the reasons I wanted to spend all my time with her. Then I made my biggest mistake.

'Do you want to come back to my place, then?'

She just stared at me, a thin smoke column streaking from her cigarette. She stubbed it out only seconds after lighting it. I even made matters worse.

'My flat's just round the corner, Maddy. You know, a coffee or something?'

She pushed her pint to my side of the table and stood up. Swung her coat over her shoulder and looked down at me. I must have looked as shocked as I felt.

'I'm sorry, Jack. You just don't get it, do you?' She waited for an answer, but I kept my mouth firmly shut. She turned to go, then sat on the edge of the bench.

'I'm going to talk to Tim tonight. I need to tell him how I'm feeling.'

'About us?' I caught my breath for an instant.

'No, Jack. Not about us. There *is* no "us". I need to talk to Tim about starting a family. Babies. More than one baby. I need to settle down. I need to *do* something.'

'A cottage with roses round the door?'

With that, she said good night and left. I drank my pint, then her pint. It had her lipstick on, and I ran it against my lips. Then I bought another pint, and after several more, stumbled home. I'd screwed it all up, yet again.

* * *

On the train to the crematorium the next day, Maddy never looked so fresh and carefree, despite her severe black jacket. We talked about how glorious spring is. She didn't seem to mind when we reminisced about mass picketing at the Grunwick strike. It was just another day at work, on our way to say goodbye to Theo.

From the station, the crematorium was less than half an hour's walk, but it was hard to keep up with Maddy who was now in no mood for a chat. As we came up High View Road with the chapel in sight, I said:

'Did you talk it over with Tim last night?'

I needed some certainty. I needed to know. She put a hand on my arm to stop us walking further. Close by the chapel, a black Fiat 500 appeared to be rocking of its own accord like a giant beetle in distress. Then I saw the back seat was occupied by two large, animated men in suits, and in the front, the unmistakable face of Theo's mother, her hair still pulled back with such severity it seemed to stretch her eyes. A fourth person in the front. She saw us and deliberately turned the other way. An argument continued between the family cramped in the shiny little car.

'What's going on?' said Maddy.

'I don't know,' I said, 'but who was the figure in the front seat?'

'I've no idea,' said Maddy, her hand still on my arm. 'But who do you think?'

'It's Theo's dad?' I suggested.

'None of our business, let's go in,' she said, and we walked, quickly, arm in arm up the drive to the chapel. Even then, amidst the tragedy of Theo's short life and the mystery of the third man, I could only think, 'what if this was a church, and Maddy was marrying me.'

I didn't believe in marriage.

* * *

We had made it just in time. It was a beautiful, empty room. A great dome of windows let in the spring sunshine onto rows of upholstered, vacant seats.

'We got the time wrong,' said Maddy. 'Has it happened?'

'We're bang on time. His mother's still outside.'

Then a priest of some kind came through a side door. His face had the look of practised kindliness, but his eyes betrayed him as a bureaucrat and it was clear he wanted to get cracking. Maddy suggested he wait for the family and he nodded, went outside, came back in, went outside again, then pressed a button to start the music.

'How can it be just us?' said Maddy. She was looking about us as if a crowd would suddenly emerge like a surprise birthday party.

Theo's mother had refused to talk to me, to hear my requests for instructions, nor did she answer to any other service dealing with the repatriation of Theo's body and funeral arrangements. In the end, this was a Council funeral, arranged and paid for by my colleagues whose full-time job was to provide a respectful end to lonely lives.

The sound of an insistent heartbeat began to fill the room. It was restrained, steady, controlled but unmistakably disco. We had sat down at the back but I realised my foot was tapping. For once, thoughts about Maddy were overtaken by memories of talking and swimming with Theo.

'What is this?' said Maddy. There was alarm and curiosity in her question.

'It's Sylvester,' I whispered. '"I (Who Have Nothing)". He adored this song. I had to choose something. Why not?' I'd been here a dozen times for the casualties of the city. I couldn't bear another crematorium broadcast of 'Always Look on the Bright Side of Life.'

Then the priest came back, threw out his gown behind him at the lectern, and began the ceremony. Theo's mother and his uncles must still be outside. I got up to fetch them but Maddy gestured for me to sit down.

'We are gathered here today,' intoned the speaker, 'to celebrate the life of Colin.'

'Colin?' said Maddy.

'Who's Colin?' I said. That po-faced little creep had even got Theo's name wrong.

I was about to shout out when the door behind us swept open, and Theo's mother and two uncles marched in, sat at the front, and were then immobile throughout, despite the priest referring to Theo as Colin, his prestigious career in accountancy, and fondness for racehorses. At several points, Maddy restrained me from getting up again. It was over too soon. Curtains opened, the coffin slid out of sight and Theo was gone. Not only forgotten, but wholly misunderstood.

I think it was the harsh emptiness of this end to Theo's life that got to me. Maddy, Theo in the swimming baths. Maddy starting a family with Tim. I just crumpled and bent my head with Maddy's arm around my shoulder, and when I looked up, Theo's family had gone, as if they had never arrived. There was the clattering of an air-cooled Fiat engine in the distance, and the priest walked purposefully up the aisle.

'Did you know Colin well?' he oozed.

There was a kind of volcanic rumble from Maddy. She looked up, pale and sculpted in that white, spring light streaking down from the dome, her lips the only slice of colour, and said: 'His name was Theo, you stupid little man.'

I started laughing. It was a kind of gentle hysteria. A lurching that started in the gut. I clung onto Maddy and she clung onto me. And that's how we left the chapel and headed for the nearest pub. When I looked back, the priest was in the chapel doorway, wringing his hands, looking everywhere about him, except at us.

* * *

Walking back to the station, I blamed myself. I must have addressed Theo's details to the wrong person. I went over it repeatedly with Maddy until she swung me round against park railings, and with one hand on my chest, waved the other around as she spoke.

'Why on earth do you think it's you, Jack? You are *the* fucking bureaucrat. You don't get those sorts of things wrong, Jack.'

I do, I thought. Everyone does. Jesus, she's fierce. But I like that. I like it a lot.

She turned. I couldn't see her face. Then she came back, thumped me in the chest and looked me in the eye.

'To be honest, you're a little bit boring, Jack. You worry all the time. Work is all you think about. That's the only reason you want to be with me, so you can talk about the bloody job. I'm sick of it all.'

She might as well have punched me in the gut. She stood there, hands at her side. One limp red-leather glove at her feet.

'Maddy, you shouldn't have dumped it all on the vicar.'

At this, she smiled through gritted teeth, raised both hands in supplication and brought them down with a growl of despair. When she strode away, I waited, emotionally pinned to the railings. I thought she might be pacing back, to take a run at me, but she just said, 'C'mon,' so I scooped up the glove and followed at a safe distance.

* * *

I slid the window shut on the train. Grey clouds had brought drizzle and our clothes were damp. Maddy said nothing. She was flicking through a diary for no reason I could see. We knew each other so well that silence between us felt comfortable. I was working out what words to use. How to ask about her and Tim. I had settled on a light-hearted 'Hey Maddy, how did it...' when she stood up unexpectedly.

'This is my stop. I'll get off here and out of these wet widow's weeds. I'm sorry, Jack, I shouldn't have shouted at you. I was just...'

She hesitated, pushing down the window to grab the handle.

'...just upset about Theo. Don't forget. It wasn't you,' and then she stepped out as the carriage slowed to a stop. She walked off, hugging herself, her head down against the rain. My eyes seemed sore. I was wondering what the point was in holding on to my hopes when a guard slammed the doors shut. The train lurched forward, and I realised we were catching Maddy up. I raised an arm to wave when she turned, at exactly the right moment to smile, point at her watch, and then mimicked drinking a beer. I nodded.

When I got into the office, I found she had telephoned and left a message with Rose on reception. Eight o'clock in the Butcher's Arms. I was so confused. Was Maddy blowing hot and cold or had I worked myself into a state? Could I change her mind? Had she changed hers? I couldn't wait for eight o'clock.

'I don't know why you go in The Butchers,' Rose had said, holding up the note. 'All sorts go in there.'

'I know,' I said, 'that's why we like it.'

* * *

Before I got to the Butchers, I'd resolved to at least start with a tomato juice, but Lefty had pulled a pint of Bass before I reached the bar.

'That'll put you right,' he said, 'after last night.'

'Last night?'

'Don't you ever have fun? You were miserable as sin last night.'

'Thanks, Lefty. Take for this, and one for Maddy when she comes in.'

'Is it love then, Jack?'

I told him it was none of his business and found a quiet corner. Boring, miserable, and a bureaucrat. I was trying to think of something positive Maddy had said to me. Everything I did seemed to go wrong. Theo would be alive if I hadn't pulled him out of his family. I should get another job. Live somewhere else. And with those plans slowly forming in my mind, I felt a little more certain of myself. Even when Maddy, a beer in one hand, waved cheerfully from the bar and came over to join me, I thought, I can handle this.

'We have to talk,' she said.

'I agree,' I said. 'I've been out of it a bit. Thinking about Theo and wondering what I should do.'

'You could come to some meetings for a start. If we don't start taking some action, the team will be history.'

She pulled out some trade union briefing papers, pointing out the timescale for team closures, redundancy offers and requirements for work in the *Dynamic Service Hub*.

'What's a dynamic service hub?'

'The shop steward explained it all. They're going to redeploy one third of the team clerks to work on a bank of phones. Families will ring in to talk to them and if necessary, we'll go out on visits.'

'Do we get offices?'

'We get a canteen area, and there's a large room full of

filing cabinets. It has a ledge all the way round. We go out, do the visit, come back, write up the notes standing up against the shelves, then go out again.'

'No chairs, no desks?'

'Nope. It seems, if there are chairs, we'll sit on them. So instead, we'll have to go out and do more visits.'

There is a flaw in that plan, Maddy.'

'Of course.'

'Most of our families aren't on the phone.'

'Plus if people want to see us, they'll traipse right across town, and then there's nowhere private to talk to anybody.'

'It sounds awful. But when they think it through, they'll bin the idea. Look, we need to talk about something else. It's been eating me up.' I leaned forward.

'Bins!' she exclaimed. 'I knew there was something I needed to tell you. It's bonkers.'

'About bins? Listen, Maddy—'

'Jack, you'll love this. There won't be any wastepaper bins. No smoking either, for that matter, but they can't stop us smoking. Wastepaper bins. There won't be any. None.'

'I don't follow.'

Maddy fiddled with her pint, twisting it on the beer mat.

'The idea is this. If they have wastepaper bins, we throw rubbish in them, then when they are full, someone has to empty them. So, no bins, nothing to empty, fewer cleaners, saves even more money. '

'What are we supposed to do with the rubbish?'

'Take it home. I suppose they have a point, the amount of chocolate you eat.'

She guffawed and expected me to, but then looked concerned when I just sat there, looking into my pint.

'What is it, Jack? What have I said?'

'Nothing, Maddy. Not now, anyway. It was Lefty. He said I looked miserable, and you said I was boring.'

'I said sorry.'

'I know. I'm sorry too, about the meetings. I'll help. I'll do posters, leafleting, anything. But I need to ask you. Last night you said you were going to talk to Tim. Talk about starting a family. What happened?'

'I suppose I do want a little house with the door in the middle. I'd paint it red. And there would be roses. Me and Tim live in a pokey flat, and we can't even use the garden because the tenant downstairs keeps a fucking Rottweiler in it. It's full of dogshit, and a green mattress, and I just want to grow some vegetables and flowers, Jack. Is it too much to ask?'

'What did Tim say?'

'About what?'

'Moving somewhere of your own. A family.'

'I don't want to talk about it, Jack. It's personal.'

Any other time I would have shut up straight away. Backed off. Changed the subject after saying 'sorry' several times. I didn't. The only way was up.

'Telling me you had a crush on me is personal. Telling me I'm boring is personal. Saying that I only want to be around you so I can talk about work. That's personal. Telling me I'm a bureaucrat is personal. So, listen. I'll tell *you* something. I only want to be around you because I love you.'

I said it. Saying it felt good. There was an awful silence. I'd said rather more than I intended. I hoped she'd be pleased but had the impression she'd heard it before.

'We're good friends, Jack.'

How I hated that.

'But I still have a bit of a crush on you,' I said.

She smiled at that. The first time I'd ever seen a shy, coy smile in Maddy.

'You'll find someone else to love,' she continued. 'I did talk to Tim. He said he'd talk to the tenant downstairs or maybe we could get a little house in Hackney.'

'Who'd want to live there?'

'Yeah. The schools, everything is rubbish. You know Tim's an architect? Not a particularly good one. I mean he's just starting out. But he says we must stay in London. It's where the jobs are. It's where he'll get his break.'

'OK. So you could get a terraced house in Walthamstow or somewhere. Flowers round the back door instead of the front.'

As I said it, I could feel my hopes sinking. Going down like a submarine.

'Did you talk to Tim about children?'

Then it hit me. I had never thought about it before in the same way, but now it seemed natural. I would have children. I would have loads of children. If that was what Maddy wanted, it was what I wanted.

'I did tell Tim how I was feeling.'

'*Was* feeling?'

'He says he'd be left with the baby because I'm married to the job. Love the work too much. Never at home. Drink too much. Smoke too much. So, there it is.'

As she spoke, I realised Maddy was not quite herself.

'Are you pissed?'

'No. Why do you think I am?'

'It's the first time I've seen someone throw a scarf over their shoulder and miss.'

She giggled.

'Me and Sara have enjoyed a bottle or two of nice wine. Thank you.'

'Shall I see you home?'

'I was hoping we could go round to your flat. It's somewhere near isn't it? I thought, maybe, we could go there and...'

The effects of a bottle or two with Sara and a couple of pints seemed to be catching up on Maddy quickly. She repeated herself.

'We could go round to your place and screw.'

'I thought you'd never ask.'

She laughed. I don't think she was joking and it was all I had thought about for weeks.

'I'll get you a taxi, Maddy.'
'But?'
'But we're on duty tomorrow.'
'Shit.'
'Yes, it is. Let's both go home. You'll feel different in the morning.'

We made for the door past Lefty. He nodded and smiled. As we waited for the taxi, I tried to think of something to say. Maddy was having trouble getting her lighter to work. Then the taxi rolled up and she was gone.

9
Intermediate treatment

We called Mike 'the secret policeman' on account of his large, black, gleaming boots and a certain vagueness about his family and other jobs. We assumed the Met. Police had undercover officers in trade unions, peace groups and the local Labour Party. Rumours suggested some had bragged about it when they were drunk, but no-one knew whether to believe them. Maddy put me right about Mike anyway.

'Listen, Jack. He lives with Liza, and she would know straight off. Just don't go round telling people Mike's a secret policeman. It's just a story someone made up.'

* * *

It turned out Mike was a bit forgetful because he liked an occasional spliff. In winter, from our window, I'd see strands of blue and grey smoke drifting from the abandoned outside lavatory in the backyard. I got to like him a lot, and in the summer, when everyone else had gone home, we shut the front door, retreated to the walled yard, and with the help of an impressively long five-skin joint reflected on the doings of the day.

It was just such an evening when young Chas arrived, over the wall. Mike, his feet on a concrete tub of weeds, took a long pull, hid the joint and nodded. His eyes drew my attention to Chas's foot which first appeared over the top of the wall, followed by a leg, then his back towards us as he took in a view. Mike crossed his arms contentedly and launched one of his grand smiles. He was a curious combination. The boots and leather jacket of a back street thug, but the poise of a French aristocrat. He never did anything in a hurry.

Chas, at fourteen, was already an experienced criminal, and his gang had recently been foiled at an attempt on the mailbags at Mount Pleasant sorting office. From week to week he found his cigarette money with the expert use of a spark plug launched with a rubber band against car windows. The catapult punched a neat hole through which he could open a door and empty the car of valuables.

Anyone else would have peeped over the wall, but Chas, convinced the place was deserted at that time of night, heaved his legs over, hung on to the top of the wall, let go and landed safely, facing the wall. I don't know whether he sensed us or smelled the dope. He hesitated. On that still evening I could hear a bee working its way round the yard.

It was the moment we were waiting for. Chas swivelled round and was evidently astonished to find two amused observers relaxing in discarded office chairs.

'Evening, Chas,' said Mike. 'Thanks for dropping in. Just the man I was looking for.'

The skinny, short boy hooked a finger in the belt loop of his baggy jeans and said nothing. Confused but pleased by Mike calling him a man, he leaned against the wall, and scanned the yard for any means of escape. I fetched a plastic chair for him.

'I want to talk to you about a new project Jack and me are starting up,' Mike said and looked across at me. I nodded as if I knew what he was talking about. He was winging it again.

'Fuck off, ponce. You homo,' said Chas.

'We'd like you to get some of your mates together, to meet up with us about a club we're starting.'

'I don't want to go to no fucking youth club.'

'You do. Because this one is just for you and your mates.'

'No way.'

'Listen to me, Chas.' There was a casual, languid authority about Mike's approach. 'You really have no option. That's the "S" from Suzuki on your tee-shirt, isn't it?'

Chas nodded.

'So what?'

'You nearly killed a mum and her kid in a buggy last week, riding that motorbike around the Calder estate.'

'Fuck off, poofter. It weren't me.'

'But it *was,* Chas. I have the photographs. I just got them back from Fennels, the chemists. You were wearing the same tee shirt?'

'No. Weren't me.'

'You might have killed yourself as well. You don't know how to ride that thing.'

'I do so.'

'You can barely lift the bike up. You do realise if your bike racing comes to court, we can have a care order on you straight away. You get to live in a children's home for a few years.'

'No way,' he yelled and made a bolt for the back door. He yanked it open, and we heard other doors crashing shut again as he dashed through the building with a final thud of the front door.

'You didn't have any photographs,' I said.

'No, but the description was surprisingly good, so I knew we had him. He'll be back.'

'I thought you were pretty hard on him, Mike. That stuff about being put into care for a minor offence. It wasn't a public road. It's practically legal.'

'Depends how you word the court report,' he went on. 'If he doesn't kill himself, or someone else with that motorbike, he'll do himself in with glue sniffing.'

'Do people die on glue?'

'Not if you do it carefully. I've tried it. A bit fierce for me, but Chas, he's all over the place. Gets pissed on a bottle of cider, then shoves his face in a crisp bag full of sticky *Evo*. One day he'll just pass out and suffocate himself or go into the canal head-first. He goes mental on it. Never know what he'll do.'

I retrieved the joint from the trough of weeds and lit it again.

'Why does he do it?' I said.

'I dunno for sure. I've got an idea though. All that "ponce" and "poofter" stuff. He might have been assaulted. Plus, he said once he was going to die before he was twenty-five.'

'He said that?'

'More than once. It could be a coincidence, but he seems to believe it. Paedophiles do that, don't they? Tell kids they're doomed. Convince them they're going to die young. "Nothing left to lose. Enjoy yourself while you can." It puts another wedge between children and their parents. Just fucking with their minds really.'

'Shit.' I felt my stomach lurch, realising what we were taking on.

'It's a question,' said Mike, stubbing out the remains of the joint, 'of whether we can offer something better. A bit of honest manipulation of our own.'

* * *

The regular model of *Intermediate Treatment,* to help prevent young people going into care or prison, involved referrals of children on worker's caseloads. There were assessments, forms to fill, and eventually a mixed group of young people, who often did not know each other, were taken ice-skating and later, dinghy sailing on the reservoir. The object was to build self-esteem and illustrate the many, better paths they could take in life. It was also cheaper than looking after them in care, or at a detention centre.

Mike had other ideas. He set them out at a team meeting. Nina, the manager, watched him quizzically over her spectacles.

'The trouble,' he said, 'with IT programmes, is that the boys just go back to their gangs every night. We haven't got a chance of changing their minds about what's right, what's wrong, what's best for themselves. We have to work with the whole gang on the Calder Estate. Use group pressure. Tackle the gang dynamics.'

'Tackle gang dynamics?' said Nina. Half the team looked sceptical, the other nodding, rooting for Mike's controlled enthusiasm.

'It could go very wrong, very quickly,' said Nina, 'and how do you know it will work? Is there any research?'

'Yes,' said Mike. I hoped he wasn't winging it again. 'It's very convincing.'

'Is it?' said Nina. You never knew where she stood on bright ideas. Some she booted out, and others she backed with determination. 'Where? Where is this research?'

'Chicago,' said Mike, reluctantly. He held Nina's gaze. 'It came round with the monthly copies of research.'

'It sounds good,' said Nina. 'Get a team together. Three people, with a fourth as backup. But I want to see that study first.' Liza and Maddy stuck their hands up. Rick and Kate gave a thumbs up.

A fortnight later, Mike waggled the loose gear lever of our ancient Commer minibus, and pulled away from Chas's council flat with a van-load of six young people, and me.

Maddy could not come with us because she was desperately looking for a house with Tim in Enfield. When she told me, I fought hard to control my feelings. Then I saw how leaden her mood was. She was looking around, fiddling with a piece of paper. She wasn't full of joy.

'We had to,' she said, 'I couldn't live in that flat any longer. Not with what happened.'

'What?'

'An argument. Tim saw a stranger having a go at the front door with a machete and then there was a fire. Just a little one. The police said it was deliberate. A fight about drugs. I don't really know. The people downstairs. There's no talking to them. I've just had enough. There's nothing else we can do but move out.'

There is, I thought, and almost said it out loud. You can move in with me. But I just hugged her, and said she'd be fine.

'Good luck,' she shouted above the whine of the engine. Mike pulled onto the main road with a cigarette clamped in his mouth at a jaunty angle. We planned to take the boys camping for a long weekend and check out just how the gang worked. Chas, who had managed to convince most of his friends to join us, behaved as though he was top-dog. We needed to find out if that was true.

10
That thing I said

The minibus swayed and wobbled, the small wheels close together, almost hidden by overhanging bodywork. I had one ear on the boys' chatter behind us, but it was Maddy on my mind. She was invulnerable at work. Strong, decisive and funny, but what was happening at home seemed to unnerve her. I wanted to help. To care for her, but Rick's advice echoed around my brain. *Don't mix work and pleasure.*

Mike loved driving and drove to his own beat. The van had no radio, and Chas's cassette player needed batteries. Mike drummed on the dash then finger-rapped on the door panel. The boys seemed contented, chatting, and already just gazing out of the window.

'Same kind of van the filth use,' said Chas.

'Indeed,' said Mike as the vehicle started to shudder, then spluttered to a halt in Peckham. Mike looked at me, held his hands up in supplication and jumped out to check the engine. With multiple drivers and scrappy maintenance, all the community vans we borrowed were unreliable. I could hear him talking to himself as he pulled at cables and ran his oily fingers along tubes. I wondered, then looked under the driver's seat where the battery was strapped down but exposed. A thick cable hung loose, lifted free of the terminal. Chas, sitting nearest, laughed deliriously. The rest of the boys joined in and pushed each other about with joy. Mike said nothing when I told him. As he reconnected the cable, he smiled at Chas.

The boy was discomforted, having expected a stern response.

Our Commer minibus looked like a poor copy of a Volkswagen Camper Van, with a bullet shape, the speed of a slug and a gearbox stolen from a Hillman Minx. What Mike did next astounded passers-by, our reckless passengers and eventually a police squad car. Our van was supposed to reach sixty miles an hour after a minute, crawling to a distressing seventy miles an hour downhill, with an engine screaming in protest. In crowded streets, forty miles an hour, especially around corners, felt frighteningly fast. Mike put his foot down.

'Stop!' commanded Chas.

'Stop!' screamed the gang as we lurched around a bend and clipped pavement railings.

Behind us, I first heard a siren wail, then saw the revolving blue light flashing in the dull and overcast city streets. Few of the benches had the loose, hopeless seat belts. None of the boys had one buckled up.

'It's the filth,' howled Chas.

'I know,' said Mike and leered at the boys over his shoulder. His eyes. I'd seen them before. They were the eyes of Jack Nicholson. I just gripped the edges of my seat, juddering, when the blue Maxi police car swerved in front of us.

The brakes on the Commer were not practical, or well maintained. A squeal of tyres, Mike pumping the brake pedal and then resorting to jerking up the handbrake. It was an understandable mistake. He had no idea that the handbrake operated on the front wheel drums. The van slewed round and skidded before coming to a rest inches from the duck-blue police car and its alarmed woman driver. She climbed out with slow precision, smoothed her skirt, adjusted her cap, and strode round to Mike, who stepped to the pavement. I was working on my excuses for Nina. Mike was leaning against the wall, his legs crossed casually whilst the police officer kept pointing at the van. To my surprise, she then climbed into the driver's seat, kneeled backwards to address the lads, pushed back her hat, and looked Chas squarely in the eyes.

'Charles,' she began, 'and the rest of you. I am issuing you with a first and final warning. Interfering with the progress of a vehicle in public service is a criminal offence, punishable by a fine up to one hundred pounds or three months imprisonment. Any questions?'

There were none. Chas and his gang looked as puzzled as I felt. We expected an arrest. I expected to drive the van home and tell Nina that Mike was at a police station.

He pulled away with a private smile. I doubt the lads saw. The engine rattled. I hissed, 'Is that even a real offence?'

His look told all. It was a sly grin of satisfaction and later on, at a roadside cafe, he explained.

'Always stay one step ahead. Two, if you can. Much of our work is de-escalation, don't you think? With this lot *we* ramp it up. If we slacken our pace, they will fill the gap with *their* idea of fun.'

'You could have killed us all.'

'It just felt fast. No more than forty miles an hour. I knew what I was doing.'

* * *

The adventure camp was all I feared. Low slung, rusting Nissen huts set in a row in an empty field in Surrey, or Sussex. I still didn't know my way around the south. Chas and his gang ran out onto the scrub land in every direction, and finding only fields and scrappy woodland, ran back together into a huddle. We watched as they spread out again, testing the limits and returning crestfallen. The beating heart of the gang was faltering. Light was falling and they had never, in their lives, been without streetlights. Without shopfronts, without people. An alien place.

Mike searched for firewood whilst I laid out sleeping bags in the boys' hut, cut bread and hid all the valuables.

'Chas,' said Mike. 'The fire's almost ready. Can you sort it, and light it please?'

Chas, a shadow in the twilight, turned to his friends and called out to the only black youth in the gang.

'Frankie. Do the fire, Frankie.'

I don't know what Frankie was doing in the gloom, but Pete, a smaller child with darting eyes and a stoop, shuffled away as soon as Frankie lurched forward. A match was no problem. Everyone but Frankie smoked, so he simply held out his hand and cigarette lighters were thrown at him. He too wore a puffer jacket, like many of the others crowding round now to see him at work.

Frankie gathered a few twigs and bits of dry straw, checked the wind direction, and stuffed them underneath the branches on the windward side. He smiled, a broad and proud grin when the twigs caught and crackled. Faces emerged from the gloaming and more smiles flickered around the fire.

'Sausages anybody?' said Mike. 'Find a thin stick. A green one. Peel off the bark and stick two through your sausage.'

Frankie snorted with laughter.

'With one stick, the sausages will dangle and burn.'

Mike took Chas's attempt and grinned at him. 'Like this, Chas. Not too close to the flames. Here. Rake out embers. Hold your sausage close. Like that. Keep turning it over. Doesn't matter if it gets a bit charred. Tastes better. Next I'll show you how to make eggy bread.'

I watched and copied him, working round the group, laughing when the fatty sausages caught fire. A hand on a shoulder here. Chatting. Everything forgotten except the fire, the spiralling smoke and the stars now laid out above us. Many of the lads fell onto their backs, biting off bits of burnt meat and staring into the glittering dark sky.

I wished Maddy was here, around the campfire. I might have put my hand on hers in the darkness, seen together how these boys who had broken into the Post Office were giggling and bumping shoulders around the fire.

While a large frying pan sizzled with lumps of bread, I watched Pete, holding back from the circle. Cross-legged in the gloom, he nibbled his sausage and looked about him like a frightened dog, protecting his bone. It was too soon to sit alongside him. Time to watch. To try and understand each boy in the group.

And after the bread, stiff with egg, was eaten, Mike appeared with a large plastic bowl, stirring furiously then lobbing into the mix the contents of a plastic bag. From the bowl, he dished out clumps of thick, pink and creamy sauce.

'Angel Delight,' said Chas.

'Right,' said Mike. 'Strawberry and cream, of course. My favourite.'

'Shit,' said Frankie. 'What the fuck is this?'

He held out a lump on his spoon.

'It's a strawberry, Frankie.' Mike held one up. 'I put real berries in it. Try it. Just bite it.'

'S'cool,' said Frankie, and nodded. Around the embers of the fire, the only sound was that of spoons furiously scraping tin bowls.

'Right,' said Mike. 'Let's go to the pub. First, can you piss on the fire for me, lads? Don't want to start a forest fire.'

The group needed no urging. At a distance, we heard the hissing, watched the steam rise, until the boys' voices dropped away when they realised the fire was their only source of light.

***

'I have a torch,' announced Mike. 'But your eyes will adjust. Just follow me.'

At the gate to the lane, he held out an arm and said, 'This way, gentlemen.'

We followed them as they shuffled along until the crescent moon offered enough light to see the verges. Mike nudged me, and I saw, with delight, how Chas, amongst others doing the same, gripped arms and held hands with other lads as they gazed about them, checking out the looming trees, quivering shadows and the dark corners of hedges.

'Our thugs are frit,' whispered Mike as the straggling group clung together for a country mile towards the orange glow of a lamp outside *The Crooked Horseshoe* pub. To one side was a garden. Mike fetched a tray with two beers, bottles of lemonade, a jug of iced water and under his arm, a box of a dozen packets of crisps. The air was still, windless enough to light the remains of a candle on the table. The boys took turns to run their fingers through the flame.

'It's not whether it hurts,' said Frankie solemnly. 'The trick is not minding that it hurts.'

'Lawrence of Arabia,' said Mike. Frankie nodded.

'Tell us a ghost story, Mike.'

'I don't have any. What about you, Jack?'

'Once upon a time,' I whispered, so that the boys leaned in. Magic words.

'My mam told me about the flaming devil of Whistledene. A true story though, and a kind of ghost story.'

'Go on,' breathed Chas.

'Mam was scared,' I went on. 'Shaking a little. Trembling, I mean. She had never told anyone before. Even my dad. My dad's not around any more. He was a railway man. Stepped out of the way of the eight forty to Nottingham into the path of the express from Leicester.'

I let that sink in for a moment, then got into my story.

'My mam, she confessed something to me. How she killed a man.'

Remaining chatter around the table fell away. The candle guttered for a moment, smoking.

'She asked if I remembered when I were a boy and fell on some broken glass. How there was blood all over my clothes and she picked a fresh cobweb from the hedgerow to help stop the bleeding. She learned that from Mother Benson. Not *her* mother, of course. Ma Benson was everybody's mother in the village. Midwife sometimes. She knew all about country medicine. When my mam was a girl and visiting Ma Benson one night, she told her about Old Tom and how he'd been a nuisance around her and her sisters.'

'A nuisance?' asked Mike.

'A nonce?' said Chas.

'Nobody paid old Tom any attention. Everyone knew what he was like, but he tried to make a special friend of auntie Lily. My aunt Lily. She were only thirteen then.'

'So she killed him?' said Chas, incredulous.

'She didn't mean to. Mother Benson said Old Tom were afraid of the little people who live in the woods, the *Green-Man,* and all kinds of beasts of the night. She said my mam should give him a fright, so Mam made up this plan with Lily.'

'Only to frighten him?'

'To scare him to death. That's what they say, isn't it?'

I gathered my confidence. My mother's exact voice in my ear.

'There is now a housing estate, up a hill towards Sedgrave, but once it were a wild place, with a path called Deep Cut because it were a rough old way, dug like a sandy trench through the hillocks. There were trees, bushes, and gorse all up there then, so it were dark, and a lonely place of shadows. Fat Old Tom would hurry up that way to the Plough for a few pints of an evening, so they got ready to set a goat on him on his way home.'

'A goat?' said Pete, his voice barely broken.

'A billy-goat. They got out little candle lanterns, from a box of Christmas trinkets, and tied them to the goat's horns, lit them, then threw an old white net curtain over the goat. As Old Tom came stumbling down that path, they set the goat off towards him and hid behind bushes. It were a proper sight. A ghostly apparition. My mam had to put her hand over Lily's mouth, she were laughing so much. Then an awful thing happened. She said she would never forget it as long as she lived.'

Around the table, the boys were as still as the night air about them. Motionless.

'The flapping curtain began to smoulder and smoke, and just as old Tom came round the corner, the sheet went up in flames and the goat went streaking up the track like a devil from hell. Old Tom took one look, held his chest, and went down dead, right there. She had killed him.

'Mam told me how the fiery curtain blew away, they recovered the lanterns, and ran off to find help for old Tom but he was stone cold dead. Mam just said they found him like that, and none of them, ever, told anybody. She made me promise not to tell anyone.'

'Snitch,' said Chas. Frankie snorted with laughter, swaying from side to side. I had a sudden childhood image of him, rocking in glee on the floor.

'Not a ghost story though, is it?' said Pete from behind someone's shoulder. 'Not like a proper ghost.'

'Ah. But that's not the end,' I said, racking my brain for ideas.

'For whenever the night is still, as it is now, and the moon is small, just like it is now, so the fields and hedgerows are dark and mysterious...'

I made *mysterious* last as long as I could stretch the syllables.

'On these silent nights, there is sometimes the screams of an old man dying, as a fiery, ghostly goat streaks across the horizon.'

'A ghostly goat?' said Mike with a smile. 'Oh dear. No more stories. Can someone pour me some water?'

To my surprise, Chas grabbed a glass, and with effort managed to hoist the big jug with one hand. His look turned from concentration to puzzlement. Only a drip of water fell into the glass. He tilted the jug and I saw an ice cube wedged in the spout. He lifted it further, then the ice tumbled out, the contents sluiced across the table, everybody starting back as the water and skidding ice splashed over our legs and carried with it paper boats of empty crisp packets.

'Nice one,' said Frankie, without humour. Chas was crestfallen. There were no stragglers on the way back and I was uncertain if Chas was still the leader of the pack.

***

It was during the night game that I said it. We planned to thoroughly tire the boys out so we could enjoy a good night's sleep. It was a fantasy. There was never a night of sound sleep. That first night we played a variation of *snatch*. The boys had to remain in the field and avoid Mike and me. If we caught them, we sent each one to their bed as a forfeit.

In excitement they ran about the field calling to each other. The huts were empty. Mike and I were to sleep in one, the boys in another. I lurked between other huts as he wandered the field, bellowing, and herding them in my direction for capture.

I kept still, biding my time, and it paid off. Two figures turned the corner. Two shapes I could see were scuffling and jerking about. I recognised the bent shape of Pete, the thin, wan child from the bottom of Cossington Street. There was Frankie's voice.

'Gimme the box. Give me the fucking money.'

I held back, would have to jump in soon, but needed to see what was happening. Then I saw Frankie's fist holding Pete's arm behind his back, jerking upwards. Pete was clutching something shaped like a toy dog. It was the charity box from the Crooked Horseshoe. Then I saw the box drop, but Frankie didn't stoop to pick it up. It rolled to one side. Frankie still had Pete's arm high behind his back. I heard Pete whimpering. A sob. Then Frankie swung his other arm between Pete's legs. I realised he was gripping him hard, Pete doubling down in pain. I had no choice and leapt forward.

Frankie, at fourteen, was very tall. My height, but thinner. Almost a man. I pulled him round with ease and pushed him hard against the rusting tin of the hut. His face carried a snarl. Pete was crumpled on the floor grasping at his groin, crying out 'You fucker, Frankie. You fucker. I would have shared it with you.'

Frankie tried to pull away. Just seeing Pete's wet, distorted face, I felt like nutting Frankie. For being a bully. A hulk looming in the shadows. For just taking what he wanted. For showing no remorse in his eyes. No fear. He looked at me with contempt. So I said it. It just welled up. It was said before I even knew it, like someone else said it. I had an arm across his chest and my face right in his. I was angry. Furious. I lost it. I hissed, 'You black bastard.'

The moment I said it, I felt cold. Dropped my hands to my side. Frankie just stared at me, spat on the floor, and walked off to the hut. This time it was me leaning back against the iron wall. Pete stared at me and gave me the charity box.

'It was him, sir,' he said quietly. 'It was him what stole it. He hid it and I found it. I was going to give it to you, sir. To take it back. Not right, is it? Charity box for poor kids? Black bastard. That's what he is, sir.'

I told him to go to bed. I would follow on. I couldn't say anything about the way he talked about Frankie. How could I? I was the same. Had sunk lower than any of them. The anger had drained away. I hung my head. What would Mike say? When Maddy found out, she would never talk to me again. I had lost everything in a moment. I lit a cigarette. All I could think of was myself. Only later did I think of Frankie and was appalled all over again. How Frankie must have heard those words, and others, so many times. And now, again, from me. Poor kid.

11
Down and dirty

When at last the fragile moon slipped behind a torrent of cloud and darkness swamped the site, the boys took to their metal bunk beds and curled up beneath blankets.

We listened to their whispering before the snuffling sounds began. We could hear it in our hut where Mike and I sat smoking between nips of navy rum. The strange purring and clicking noise must have been louder next door. We heard Chas accusing one of the boys of joking around. Then the screaming began. Strangled yowls to begin with, then full-throated shrieks of distress.

Mike looked worried. I was still thinking about Frankie. Frankie alone in his bunk, surrounded by white boys and white men. I was piecing together what had happened. Peter had said, 'He took it, I found it, I was going to give it to you sir'. But I'd heard him say to Frankie 'I would have shared it with you.'

'What the hell is that noise?' said Mike.

'Hedgehogs. You'd never believe how loud, how *human* they sound at night.'

He grinned, gulped a glass of Lambs, and cocked his head. 'You sure?'

'Positive. Can go on for hours. Welcome to the sound of hedgehogs screwing.'

'How do you know?'

'I'm a country boy and I did night duty three or four nights a week on top of the day job. Had to. Part of the contract. Then I learned to recognise all the animal calls. Owls as well. I sometimes got called out by townies in their weekend cottages to investigate the sounds of cruelty next door. Foxes calling with hoarse barking.'

Frankie appeared at the door.

'We want to go home. We agreed. All of us. There's animals, and rats and ghosts and everything. We want to go home now.'

I could see Chas and the others hovering behind him. Hunched shapes in the night. Red pinpoints of cigarettes burning bright as the lads sucked on them. Pete, in the circle of light from our hut, wore his blanket like a shawl. I imagined him escaping Colditz.

Mike strode out onto the field, took a lungful of smoke and blew rings into the windless air, held his head back, his chin out, watching for stars. A wood pigeon cooed three times. Three more circles of smoke rippling upwards.

'Rats, eh?'

'You can smell them, sir,' said Chas with uncharacteristic stress on *sir*.

'We seen them,' said Pete.

'Who saw rats?'

Mike's head was still thrown back but his eyes swept down and around the group.

I met Pete's eyes. 'Did you see them, Pete?'

Several seconds passed as he gazed back, then said, 'I did, sir.'

He was lying.

'How big was it?' asked Mike, still watching the sky. Pete held his hands up, suggesting the shape of a large cat.

I scanned the group and realised that not only did Mike think Pete was lying, so did the rest of the gang. Pete was rubbing his hands down his chest as if wiping them. He turned away from me slightly, and looked back. He knew what I was thinking. He had stolen the charity box and Frankie had found out. When Pete said, 'I was going to give it to you, sir,' was he copying Frankie? Was Frankie setting things right? I shook my head.

I needed to think, but I also needed to sleep, and there was something in the air. Something tense and metallic. We all sensed it, for we stood soundless. Mike stamped on his cigarette as an immense explosion of white light flooded the sky, followed in a second by a jolt of rolling thunder. The trees, hedgerows and bushes stood imprinted on our eyes before another sheet of lightening shot down to the horizon. The thunder, crashing and vibrating, came immediately. The storm was a mile away but the rain hit like a wave of bullets, cracking on the roofs of the Nissen huts, a sudden gale snatching at the boys' jackets. They ran for shelter.

'Oh fuck,' said Mike.

'What?'

The boys swarmed out of the shed again.

'Sir,' said Chas. 'The shed, sir. The hut. It's got a metal roof, sir. We'll be cooked alive if the lightning hits.'

Mike looked about him. Looked at me, and the minibus.

'The safest place,' I said to Chas and the group, 'is back in your hut.'

'Is it?' whispered Mike, suddenly silhouetted as a statue in a shattering blaze of lightning cracks.

'The iron roof will take the electricity straight to the ground. Safer than a house.'

'Sir,' said Frankie. 'The bus has rubber tires.'

'I know, it's safer than out here. But the hut is safer still. Get in there. Now.'

Pete alone ran to the van and pulled at the locked handle, looked around him and scrambled to reach the hut before the boys slammed the door.

'The storm's going that way anyway,' I said to Mike, water dripping off his chin as he watched the anvil-shaped clouds gathering momentum across the sky, breaking into clumps, and scurrying south.

Mike brushed water from his eyes. 'You okay?'

'Of course,' I said. But I wasn't. I needed to talk to Maddy. I trusted her. Not so sure about Mike. A friend who was also, in some way, untouchable. When he smiled, his eyes didn't crinkle at the corners like Maddy's did. The nearest phone was at the pub, so calling her was impossible, and I needed to see her face when I told her what I'd done. What I'd said. How I'd begun to feel down. Not just down, but dirty too.

* * *

Shortly after dawn, the adventure men arrived. Hiring the huts came with the bonus of an activity day described as *tough love for teams*.

Mike was stepping into his jeans, so I dragged the door shut.

'I'm Trev,' said one square, sandy-haired man, 'and he's Adam,' nodding at his companion.

'Who've we got?' said Adam.

'Six lads from the Calder Estate in North London,' said Mike.

'It's a gang,' I continued, 'that seems to be run by Chas. He's fourteen. Mike and I think Frankie is a leader too. Some of the boys listen to him. Pete probably robbed the pub charity box last night. I'm taking it back this morning.' I thought, I can phone Maddy.

'Charming,' said Trevor. 'Where are they?'

'Still in their bunks, we were up very late in the storm.'

Adam had already started unpacking a kitbag, pulled the rusty dustbin lid off the remains of yesterday's fire and soon had another blaze crackling, with bread, eggs, bacon and beans in blackened pans.

Pete, blinking, was the first to show his head around his hut door. 'Where's the lav, sir?'

'Just go up by the hedge,' said Mike, 'and mind the nettles.'

'Sir. It's a number two, sir. Where's the shitter?'

'Behind that wooden fence,' shouted Trev. 'Watch your step.'

There was a howl of disgust from the latrine.

Adam chuckled. I stood back and watched them working. The boys clustered round, clutching tin bowls and plates, pushing and shoving to get at breakfast. Adam and Trev grabbed their attention easily. Moving with practised ease around the group, grasping shoulders, then Trev ran a hand through Frankie's curls. Frankie pushed him away with a snarl I recognised from last night.

I guessed they were squaddies. Adam stood back, rolled a cigarette and held it with the lit end inside his fingers, shielding the smouldering glow from sight. Trevor rolled his smokes thin. As slender as prisoners rolled them. All paper and just a few strands of Golden Virginia. Both were neatly dressed. Sharper than Mike and me, but I saw Trev's collar was grubby along the rim. There was a story there. His face was sweaty. My bet was the booze, and I should know. The Lambs rum hung heavy at the back of my head.

Mike agreed we should get the pub money back where it belonged this morning. It was in my duffel bag, and with a wave I set off, looking back to see Frankie's gaze following me.

* * *

Outside The Crooked Horseshoe leaned an 800cc BMW motorcycle with full fairing and blue 'POLICE' lettering. Inside stood the rider, a helmet on the bar and a half of bitter in one hand. A notebook lay unopened.

'That's him,' said the barman, a grin spreading across his face as I pulled the battered plastic collection box out of my bag. It looked like a grinning fox.

'Basil,' he said. 'Welcome home.'

'Basil?' said the policeman.

'Basil Brush,' said the barman, shaking it to check money was still inside. 'We collect for the blind.'

'We're sorry,' I said and explained our project.

'Want a pint?'

'No, thanks. Not for breakfast. I've got to get back. Can I use your phone though?'

'Sure,' he said and pulled a black telephone from under the bar.

They looked at me. I waited.

'Come on, Ralph,' said the barman. 'Let's talk in the lounge.'

I dialled Maddy's number.

'Do you know what time it is?' Her voice had all the stretched-out honey of waking from sleep. I wanted to be next to her. Imagined those curls on the pillow.

'It's ten thirty on Saturday morning and I'm in a pub. There's a policeman with me and he's having a beer.'

'Are you?'

'No. Not after last night.'

'Are you okay, Jack?'

I'm not, I thought. I'm really not all right. I've screwed everything up.

'I'm fine. Tough night though. The boys robbed the charity box from the pub. Basil Brush, whoever that is. For the RNIB. We had a terrible storm. Mike thought we'd go up in smoke with all the lightning.'

'Oh, why are you ringing me?'

'I need to talk when we get back. Can I see you, Sunday night? Down the Butcher's Arms?'

'What is it?'

'I can't say. Not here with the police and everything happening. Not on the phone.'

'Right. See you Sunday then.'

'Thanks, Maddy. Thanks a lot.'

I was going to say something else, about Trevor and Adam, but there was a click, then the purring sound of disconnection.

The copper and the barman were smoking and laughing when I went through to the lounge. I realised everything was red. The bar top, tables, and maroon flocked wallpaper. The floor was a hazardous swirl of reds and pinks stained with years of spilled food. Sticky carpets are the hallmark of neglect.

We exchanged phone numbers. The police would ring Nina to confirm our plans. As I left, the barman called after me.

'It was the *coloured* one wasn't it,' he said. A statement.

I walked back and leaned on the table. Hands flat on the Formica.

'It wasn't,' I said. 'It was one of *us*. A *white* boy.'

The copper looked over his Eric Morecambe glasses at the barman.

'By the way,' I added. 'Careful with those fags. With all that chip and chicken-fat in that thick carpet, this pub could go off like a firework.'

I turned and left, but not before I heard the barman say 'Smart-arse.'

* * *

I took my time walking back, strolling along the lanes, standing in the shade of a chestnut tree as a cloud of butterflies darted frantically about the hedgerow, and I felt my bones warming after the shivers of the night.

When I reached the camp, the boys were on their backs, arms across their eyes. Adam was making tea.

'You're back,' said Trevor. His face was red.

'Up for a game?' said Adam. I nodded.

Mike looked as tired as I felt. 'We've had obstacle courses in the woods and slid down cables between trees.'

'A zip-wire,' said Trevor, pointing with his spoon. 'We zipped from here, to here.'

I didn't like Trevor much. Then the games started.

'Just to warm up,' yelled Trevor. 'We'll play British Bulldog. Have you all heard of it?'

I knew nothing about it. Mike nodded and shot me a glance I didn't understand.

'Two teams,' announced Trev. 'The oldies. That's us four,' he said, pointing at Mike and me. 'And you lot.'

It looked like a game of tag to me. One team were bulldogs and the other team had to reach the end of the field without being tagged by a bulldog. If they were, then they became a bulldog too. Last man standing wins.

'How,' said Mike, 'do we tag someone? Like *tick?* Just touch them on the shoulder? Or are we using a lift? '

'A what?' said Chas.

'Not a lift,' said Trevor. 'We use take-down. Like rugby. You have to take 'em down, lads. Bring 'em down. Used to be called Black Peter or Take Down Black Man. Not you, Frankie. It's not about you, boy. Black Man comes from the plague. It's an ancient game from Germany. The Black Plague. Heard of it? Our bulldog is the Plague-man, running around until you catch it.'

Then he raised his arms, quivering. His face was distorted as he leaned over Pete.

'Huggerawah,' he yelled. 'I am the Plague-man!'

Pete turned his head and walked away to join the other boys.

I looked at Mike. 'I'm not keen on this monster stuff. Not keen on Trevor either.'

He just nodded as we walked to our end of the field. The boys huddled together at the other.

'We are the bulldogs,' cried Trevor, and in an instant the boys rushed towards us, at first in a mob, then darting this way and that. I saw Trevor heading for Pete and handed him off at the last second, then grabbed Pete's shoulder and brought him down in a heap. I checked Pete was okay. He was shaken but jumped up in his new role to catch others not yet taken down.

Trevor's eyes were wide and bloodshot. He stomped off towards Frankie who was too quick for him, whilst Adam tackled Chas. Soon there was only Frankie left in this round. He was cornered and Trevor lunged for him again. Mike barked out, 'Frankie wins this round. Last man standing. Second round.'

Trevor stopped short and lumbered away. We all changed ends for no reason that I could see. Then it was our turn to charge forward and reach the other end. Mike went first and to my astonishment was brought down in an instant at the hands of Pete who did a jig of joy. Mike, now a bulldog, spun round at the thunderous approach of Trevor, who had dodged Frankie. With no one near, I stood for a second, a spectator for a moment, and that was my mistake. Amongst the blur of bodies rushing about, I watched as Mike grabbed Trevor about the neck and shoulders, jerking down so fast, on his knees himself, so that Trevor spun forward, crashing over Mike to land spread-eagled on his back, bellowing like a stuck pig. As everyone watched, I caught sight of Frankie to my left, leaning as if to pick up something, then a flash of his leg, drawn up, kicking with a single piston blow at the side of my knee. I felt it give and bend inwards in quite the opposite direction it should. I crumpled to the floor as Frankie stood over me and said 'Oh, sorry sir,' as I howled in pain.

12

The other side of the road

The back of the minibus had a bench covered in ripped green leatherette. I felt every bump in the field as we trundled towards the gate, and resented the tender care of Pete, leaning over me, shouting.

'Do you want a fag sir? No? We've got some coke if you want.'

Mike shot a glance over his shoulder.

'It's only Pepsi,' said Pete, 'but it tastes the same, I think. It's all we've got.'

Frankie sat behind Mike, impassive, his cheek against the cold window. The rest of the gang were chatting loudly about their adventures and monsters of the night, although Chas appeared to be sleeping. His head slumped sideways on his arms, folded over the seat-back in front of him. I reckoned they were glad to be going home to the city.

Despite Mike's protestations, Trev had wrenched my leg from side to side, and shouting over my wails of pain, declared 'nuffin' wrong with it, mate.'

Adam pulled him off and held him back with a hand on his chest. I screwed up my eyes and felt last night's lightning in my head, crackling between my ears, and shooting down, beyond my knee, in great, throbbing, stabs of pain.

'You need to see someone,' said Adam. 'Something might be broken.'

'We're going home,' Mike announced. 'Get your things, lads.'

One night, I thought. One night was all we managed. All I had managed.

Trev stood at the gate, ready to let us onto the road. Mike slid open his window, an elbow out in his affable way. I propped myself up and saw Trev place a hand on Mike's wrist, then watched as he gripped Mike's elbow and leaned in. Mike's back stiffened, his face impassive. Only Frankie seemed to notice what was happening and shifted around to see as Trevor put his weight on Mike's arm. He was staring into Mike's eyes.

'We'll meet again,' he began in his slow monotone. 'Don't know where, don't know when.' He stared in at the boys. There was something about his gaze. The hair on my neck stiffened. 'But we'll meet again, some sunny day, eh?'

'Sure,' said Mike. 'I'll *enjoy* it,' and pulled his arm out of Trev's grip. Chas had a hand on Frankie's shoulder. I think he would have jumped out and confronted Trev, who, faced with this angry boy, would have flattened him without a second thought.

The gate, sagging away from its hinges, swung open and we sped through onto the road back to London.

* * *

'So it's not broken, then?' said Maddy. It was mid-afternoon in the Butcher's Arms with dust caught drifting by streams of sunlight from cut glass windows I hadn't noticed before. I wished the leg was broken.

'Hurts like hell though.'

'But you're okay?'

'I dunno.'

I was out of sorts. Uncomfortable with myself. I didn't know what to say. She wore a black velvet top that shimmered and glinted with silver threads. That scent of frangipani flowers. I wanted to stroke her back, just to comfort myself, wishing she would stroke mine. Then I had to tell her. Tell her about finding Frankie menacing little Peter in the darkness. Tell her about calling him a bastard, and admitting to myself as well as to Maddy that I'd called him a black bastard. Her hand, gripping a pint, stopped halfway to her mouth. She set it down again and cocked her head.

'Why?'

'I don't know. It even sounded like someone else saying it. And I think it was Peter who took the charity money, and Frankie who was trying to do the right thing. So it's all gone to shit, Maddy. When this gets out I'm finished, aren't I?'

'I doubt it. It happens all the time, and worse. Much worse. But when you're better, I'm going to knock it out of you.'

'What?'

'What do you think? How could you? What a stupid, racist thing to do. He's fourteen, for Christ's sake. You deserve a good slap.'

'I know. I know. I think I was scared. It's all mixed up in my head now. I said it without thinking. I was just so angry at what he was doing. You know. You know, don't you? You know I'm not like that.'

'Like what, Jack? You push a fourteen-year-old boy up against a wall in the dead of night and call him a black bastard? Have you put yourself in his shoes?'

'A hundred times over.'

Then why? For fuck's sake, Jack. I really don't understand. You are one of the most sentient men I've ever met. When Theo was in that deep hole of despair you got right down there with him. You saw him, Jack. You really saw him. And he knew it, and because of that he learned how to be happy. How to live. And I've seen you with Gregory. You are the closest he's ever had to a dad, or,' she paused, thinking, 'maybe an older brother. I can't believe this. I really can't.'

'I know. I don't understand myself anymore.'

There was just the trace of a smile. For once, I wanted to be rescued, but she wasn't the rescuing kind. Not for me, anyway.

'Maddy?'

I realised her eyelashes were fair. That's why her eyes shone so bright.

'What's "sentient" mean?'

I had to duck as she swiped at me, a black web of a shawl slipping from her shoulder.

'C'mon, we're going.'

'Where?'

'To my place. We need to talk and I don't want to do it here.'

* * *

There was no one about. A thin line of newly planted saplings along the pavement. She pulled open the door of her orange VW Beetle.

'Don't you lock it?'

'Why? There's nothing to steal.'

'The car?'

'I wish they would.'

The engine rattled into life and she drove out of town and out of my comfort zone.

'Where are we?'

'Highgate.'

'Posh.'

'Not when we moved in. The rent has doubled. Here we are.'

She pushed open a red front door. I ran a finger over ridges of brush marks. A splatter of crimson on the stone doorstep and the brass lock had a pink smear. Maddy watched me.

'Tim's not much of a DIY guy.' She smiled.

'I thought he's an architect.'

'You don't know anything, do you? He's away, by the way. Just so you know. He's at a conference in Eastbourne. Big new fancy hotel. Trades union event. He's going to talk about the future of council housing.'

'And what's that?'

'He thinks it's well-built low-level houses, with squares and community space for kids to play where families can see they are safe. Fancy a joint?'

Without thinking, I nodded.

'And you? What do you think?'

'About council houses?' she said. 'I reckon they're done for. If Thatcher gets in she'll stop new ones being built and sell off what we've got. Her big mate at the GLC, Horace Cutler, has been doing it for years. The Labour Party talked about it way back when. In the sixties, I think.'

'But it's crazy!'

'Of course it's mad. Stupid. No, it's fucking criminal. You have to see it for what it is. They're extremists. But they don't think,' she said, tapping her head furiously. 'The poor buggers will snap them up. Thousands I expect. But most of them don't earn enough, or work often enough. They'll take out loans, loans they can't afford. Mortgages they can't repay. Or the roof will leak, or the windows will rot, and they can't afford to fix them, so in the end they'll have to sell. Sell up and go into private rented at twice the rent they used to pay. And do you know what? That flat will probably be an ex-council flat owned by some get-rich-git.'

'Oh.'

'Yes. 'Oh' and that's just the start of it. Don't get me going. You're right. Everything is going to shit if we're not careful. If we let them. They're after our jobs. They want to close down the teams.' She lit up a joint. I thought she'd go on about the Tories.

'Why, Jack? Why did you do it? Why did you do that to poor Frankie?'

She passed the joint. It had the sweet mellow smell of crumbled Moroccan hash.

'I told you. I don't know. Can we talk about something else?'

'No. I need to know. You say you were all mixed up. If you ask me, you've been adrift ever since you came here. I don't mean you don't know how to do your job. You're streets ahead of anyone like Nigel. Kate as well. She means well, I know. How shall I put this? You seem to be driven. And sometimes it rubs up the wrong way. Upsets people. People like Nina. You're a bit unpredictable. And here we are,' she said, holding her palms upwards, 'taking it all out on Frankie.'

'I do everything Nina says. I try really hard.'

'Do you think she's stupid? She wants you to say what you think. The last thing she wants is someone with it all bundled up inside, then unloading at the wrong time. It's because you're so bloody nice to her that she's suspicious. She knows what you did up north. We all do.'

Maddy was waving her hands around, including the joint, and I was reaching out, trying to get hold of it for a long, deep, pull.

'You can't go round punching people.'

'I didn't punch Frankie.'

'You punched that manager. That bloke up north who was on the take. Do you want a beer?'

It was getting dark and I was thirsty too. Very thirsty.

'Yes. I do. Thank you.'

Her velvet jacket was across the back of her sofa and her lilac blouse was rolled up at the sleeves. Silk, I think. A faint pattern on it swirled gently.

She stood up quickly, caught her breath at the new altitude, and said 'Woah. Been sitting down too long.'

The fridge was in a large alcove at the back of the room. As she opened the door and bent to get the beers, the light came on, and in that instant I saw the soft dark curve of her body through the thin material. I had to glance away as she rummaged around, squatting down to reach into the back.

Maddy, always so swaddled in jumpers and scarves, and huge tweed coats. Maddy, whose gaze was forever defiant. I had to look again. She was sitting on the floor, still pulling out jam-jars and packets, her hair a halo in the gloom.

'There,' I said, pointing at the top shelf. 'Up there. Cans of Bass?'

She laughed, pulled two out, set one down beside me and said, 'there you go,' and slapped me on the thigh. That leg. The pain was excruciating, and I shrieked with alarm as she jumped back, her hand over her mouth. I screwed my eyes up against the pain.

'I'm so sorry. I really am.'

She knelt in front of me and put her hands on my shoulders as I looked again, to find her smiling face just inches from mine, her fingers pressing into my neck. Her scent and the wisp of Moroccan were intoxicating. Her gaze unrelenting.

I was about to say, I'm too stoned for this, when she said, 'I want to kiss you.'

'You do?' was the best I could think of.

'But I shouldn't. Not for you. Not for Tim. I think I love Tim. But I still want to. I still want to kiss you.'

'You only *think* you love Tim?'

'We've had the best of times, and the worst of times.'

'Is that poetry?'

'Dickens.'

She was still kneading my tight shoulder muscles and looking into my eyes. It wasn't uncomfortable. I felt alive. Her lips parted and I thought she might kiss me anyway. I could only think of one thing. If she fell onto my knees, I could not bear the pain. So I put my hands on her waist to steady her. Lifted them slightly and felt her breasts brush my wrists.

'The first time I saw you,' I said. I don't remember what I was going to say next. She held my head, pulled me forward a little and when her lips collided with mine, I just sank into her arms. I wanted to be held, by anyone. To be hugged by Maddy was everything.

* * *

Maddy persuaded me to talk to Nina about everything that had happened on the adventure trip. She was thoughtful, respected me for telling her but insisted I had to make amends to Frankie somehow and work out why I had lost it. She held up her finger and thumb as if holding an imaginary biscuit.

'You're that close, Jack,' she said. 'I warned you fair and square. Sort yourself out.'

But after that, everything began to unravel as word got out. I was wandering towards the office down Cossington Street when I saw Kate coming the other way, her mackintosh pulled tight across her chest and a scarf over her cloud of curls. I expect she was off on a visit. I know she saw me. I don't know how you can tell, so far away. But she saw me. I raised my hand, waving hello as she turned her head. She crossed the road and examined the contents of her bag, then looked at the houses as she walked past me on the other side. Perhaps I should have shouted. Could she have mistaken me for someone else?

No-one said anything in the office. Rick and Nigel even smiled. Liza just plonked a cup of coffee on my desk as if paid to do it but resenting the work. Mike asked after my injury in a perfunctory way and said I should get a stick out of the aids and adaptions cupboard. For him, it was feeble. I knew he felt let down. That I had abused one of the boys. That I hadn't told him. I didn't have the nerve to ask anyone out after work to the Butchers. Maddy was in court all day with one of her cases, so I went alone.

Lefty the barman pulled me a pint and used a new glass as I was still admiring the foam lacing down the side of the last one. But he wouldn't look at me. Did he know? Did everyone know? Lefty turned away to serve another customer as a shadow fell across the bar. It was Nigel, mental health expert, sometime jazz drummer player and fond of two-tone suits.

'Fancy a game?' he said, nodding towards the pool table.

'I don't play much.'

'You'll learn,' he said, almost kindly. I was willing to take reassurance from anywhere. The balls clacked together in the trough and he began setting them up, leaned his cue against the table, looked up and grinned. There was a tooth missing.

'Nice one,' he said.

I thought he was admiring the neat triangle he'd assembled in seconds.

'Thanks,' he continued. 'Thanks, Jack. We thought you'd come through for us.'

'I'm sorry?'

'Nah. We're proud of you. Sticking up for us, mate.' He ducked his bristly head like a boxer. Still grinning. He peered around. Checked out who was in.

'Standing up for the white man. Takes courage, that does. Especially young man like you. With all those punks, those arty-farty Rock Against Racism lefty types. Those communist thugs in the Anti-Nazi League. Takes guts to do the right thing.'

'Nigel.'

'Don't worry mate. We've got your back. Martin would approve of you.'

'Martin?'

'Webster. You must know Martin Webster. National Activities Organiser for the Front. Bit of a poofter, but he's good. Got some front too. Good one that, eh? Got some front, he has.'

As it slotted together I felt the anger rise like a curdling acid tide inside, and before I knew it, I had him against the wall, my pool cue across his chest, screaming into his face until Lefty pulled me off and Nigel scrambled for the fire exit.

'For fuck's sake, Jack,' Lefty yelled. 'He's an old man. What are you doing?'

'Old man? He's with the Front. He's bloody National Front.'

Lefty held me by the shoulders.

'For Christ's sake. How stupid are you? Half of 'em in here are National fucking Front.'

'Are you?'

'Course not.'

'Then why do you work here?'

'The other half aren't. The other half are left wing punks, trade unionists and the IRA. Some of the precious angels that come in here believe in things you have never heard of, so take my advice. Cool it. I don't want to throw you out but I will if I have to.'

'You haven't said why you work here. With all these people you seem to despise.'

'You don't get it, do you?' he said, shaking his head and heading back to the bar.

I scooped the remaining balls into the holes at one end of the table and realised what Lefty was saying. It was for the money. Of course it was the money. Maybe the craic too. Most pubs were like clubs. They had their loyal people. Regulars who mostly had the same ideas about the world. But the Butchers? It was a strange melting pot of tribes, and the one person who had time for me was a bloody Nazi.

13
Outflanked

I woke up groggy and scared after bells sounded from somewhere. Police-car bells from black and white films. Doorbells that hung in hallways with brass tendrils to rattle them.

It was a phone. My telephone at five-bloody-thirty.

'That you, Jack?'

It was Maddy.

'I'm sorry. I was dreaming. About you, I think.'

'What?'

'Never mind. You rang me?'

'You're on duty, right?'

'At nine o'clock.'

'Nope. Today you need to get down to the Barnsdale Estate.'

'Are you going to tell me why?'

'Stop off at the office. Nina will be there. She didn't have your number.'

'You could have given her my number.'

'I know. Just get up and go, Jack. I'm going back to bed.'

It was half-light. Dawn, and the streets were empty. White, fluorescent light seeping from Cossington Street office windows. I used my own key to get in. Nina's voice was already calling from upstairs.

'Jack. Get up here now.'

She sat at her desk, the phone to her ear, a cigarette in the corner of her mouth, making notes.

'How many? Is that really necessary?'

She put the handset on the cradle.

'Morning, Jack.'

'Why so early, Nina?'

'It's how the police do things. Early call on the Barnsdale. Police are going into number thirty-seven on the third floor, Brixham House.'

She squinted at her watch. 'You need to be there in ten minutes. There's a drugs raid and three children in the flat.'

'Three?'

'There's a policewoman to give you a hand and Maddy is on her way.'

'Not what she said to me.'

'I expect she was kidding. Don't hang about.'

Her voice was more clipped than usual. She held my gaze.

'Anything else?'

'Thirty-seven?'

'Brixham House, Barnsdale. It's next door.'

I dashed down the stairs, thinking fast. I didn't like getting bounced into action. No planning. Anything from the police always turned out to be an emergency.

The cops had a Commer van just like our green minibus, except it was black and without windows. The driver, upright and reading a paper, wound down his window.

'Can I help you, sir?'

'I think you're waiting for me.'

'I'm waiting for the Welfare, sir. '

'Number thirty-seven?'

'I see.'

He turned and shouted into the back of the van.

'They've sent us a fucking hippie.'

There was a murmur from behind him.

'Sorry, sir. Will you go round to the back?'

A door opened. Six or seven officers sat cradling their helmets. A lone policewoman smiled at me. Under the seats an assortment of jemmys, iron bars and wooden bats. A sergeant briefed me.

Drug squad officers were in the courtyard providing surveillance. Uniform would gain entrance and make the flat safe for us to go in.

It started in an instant, the coppers tumbling out of the vehicle, helmets swung onto heads, dragging out a bulging canvas bag.

'New kit,' explained the policewoman with a hint of pride. 'I'm Linda.'

'My name's Jack. Are you assisting me?'

She nodded. Under her cap, a severe fringe of black hair and large brown eyes. A touch of French style about Linda.

'Then please ask me before you do anything about the children. Follow my lead, eh?'

She nodded. Two coppers carried the heavy black bag round the corner as the first shafts of sunlight slipped down into the courtyard.

Barnsdale was an inter-war Greater London Council estate. Maddy had told me it once had fourteen caretakers. Now a GLC van visited most days and Barnsdale had become a shadow of its old self. The tiled stairwell stank and a burnt-out car rusted in the yard. Each floor had a gallery the length of the block. The door to thirty-seven looked ordinary to me. I saw a glint of binoculars in the front seat of a grey Hillman in the yard and thought, I must remember to tell Maddy that I was watching the detectives.

Two of the officers passed their helmets to colleagues in a solemn, rehearsed manner. They bent over the bag, unzipped it, and lifted out a metal, cylindrical contraption with dials and several adjustable steel arms. I watched their faces, for they smiled like a family cooing over a new baby. I turned to Linda.

'Looks like a bloody mortar.'

'Watch,' she said as the two coppers unfolded legs and mandibles until it resembled a gigantic black insect squatting outside the door.

'We borrowed it from a station south of the river,' Linda whispered. 'Druggies have reinforced doors, so we need this pneumatic ram.'

'Doesn't look like a special door.'

'Ah,' she said, tapping her nose, 'that's their trick. Not calling attention to themselves. It's camouflaged. Plate steel if you ask me.'

The arms and legs of the device were braced against the wall on either side of the door and at the back against the wall of the balcony. The officers replaced their helmets and took a handset from the top of the device, attached with a thick curly telephone cord. It had a large look-at-me red button. The sergeant nodded and we all stood along the wall of the flats waiting for the felling of the door. When a copper pressed the button, I expected a cannon thud but instead there was a slow electric whine. The sergeant was perplexed and made hand signals to the officers in charge of the crouching thing.

'Building pressure,' hissed one of the men whilst making winding motions with his hand. There were two rasping beeps, and on the third, a juddering thump followed by an explosive crash as the steel ram, glinting with oil, shot out of the back of the machine, taking six feet of balcony out in a cascade of bricks and a spiralling cloud of dust. I pressed myself against the wall amongst the line of aghast coppers, leaning out to watch the final clumps of masonry tumbling into the yard and onto the unmarked police car. From it leapt the detectives, waving their arms about.

On the third floor, we peered over the remains of the parapet as doors around the estate began to open and tenants in various degrees of undress turned out to enjoy the spectacle of coppers, backs to the wall, wondering, as was I, whether the whole walkway would collapse. The sergeant couldn't contain himself.

'You stupid arseholes,' he hissed. 'How on God's own earth did you manage to set the fucking thing up the wrong way round? You said it was simple.'

'Yes, Sarge,' said the taller, crestfallen operator.

The door to the drugs gang's flat, the very ordinary door to number thirty-seven, opened slowly. Two armed officers drew revolvers.

'Oh my goodness,' said a woman from her hallway, gazing at the gaping hole in the parapet. I'd put her age at mid-eighties, her hair an early morning cloud of feathery white strands. She smoothed her hands on an apron with a pattern of daisies.

'Whatever has been going on?'

'There's been an accident, ma'am,' said the sergeant as pistols were replaced into holsters.

'Well, I should say so,' said the tenant I recognised as Daisy from the ring-around support group.

'Do you mind if we come inside?' the sergeant enquired as I edged along what remained of the walkway and headed for the stairs, pushing past the police in suits coming the other way.

'Don't move,' they yelled. 'We've called the brigade.'

I could hear the sirens already. There was no likelihood at all of children or drugs in Daisy's flat. She was isolated, could hardly manage the stairs and we paid for her telephone so her family in New Zealand could keep in touch. The Barnsdale Estate and Daisy had survived fifty years, only to be hammered by the Metropolitan police.

* * *

I got my story ready for Nina. Something about police intelligence being an oxymoron, but as soon as I got through the door at Cossington Street I knew something was happening. Rose asked me to wait in the kitchen downstairs. Nina was 'in a meeting,' and since none of us had offices, she clearly didn't want anyone upstairs. The door to the yard was open and Maddy was pacing the length of it, a cigarette in one hand, turning as I stepped out.

'You'll never guess what just happened,' I began, but she ignored me.

'What happened last night?'

'Sorry, I mean, I don't know. What?'

'What happened at the Butchers, Jack?'

'With Nigel?'

'Right. What happened with Nigel?'

'You know he's with the National Front, don't you?'

'No, I don't. What I do know is that he's heads down with Nina and it doesn't sound good.'

'I hope he's being sacked. He can't work here and be a Nazi.'

'What did you do, Jack? What did you do last night?'

'It was awful. I had a terrible day. Ever since it came out about Frankie, every right-wing creep has been giving me the thumbs-up and everybody I like has been avoiding me. Everybody. Kate crossed the road to avoid me.'

'What happened last night, Jack?'

'Nigel came all over friendly and said the Front was pleased with me. That they were all behind me.'

'Oh, Jack.'

'So I was a bit cross.'

'A bit cross?'

'I was really upset. I pushed him away, that's all. I wanted him to back off.'

'I was here when he came in. He said you hit him for challenging you about what you said to Frankie.'

'I never.'

'Jack, he's an old man.'

'I didn't.'

'That's not what he's saying and by the looks of it, Nina is furious. She sent Rick out to take over from you on the emergency childcare job just now. How did it go? You're back soon.'

'It was a mess. We'll need to find Daisy Noakes somewhere to stay whilst the GLC make some repairs.'

I was about to tell Maddy everything about last night, about the Barnsdale Estate, about how I couldn't sleep thinking about her all night, but Rose yelled out, 'Jack, you're wanted.'

Maddy put a hand on my shoulder.

'Think before you say anything, and tell the truth.'

'I will.'

I made my best effort at a confident smile and went upstairs.

Nina, in silhouette, sat with her back to the window with Nigel at her side. He looked grubby, unshaven as always, but somehow more crumpled. On his left cheek a purple bruise. He rubbed it theatrically for my benefit. Nina was hunched a little, looking down and writing. She lifted her sad, hooded eyes but not her head.

'Sit down.'

I felt sick. There was something unsettling about how comfortable Nigel looked. He wasn't resigning for being a fascist. Nina and Nigel were the grown-ups, the schoolteachers, and I was feeling small. He looked at her sideways. What had he told her?

Nina went straight to the point.

'I was going to suspend you, Jack. Interview you with someone from the trade union. Kate and Nigel have laid out their concerns about Theo Farrugia.'

'Theo?'

'The boy who took his own life after you sent him on holiday.'

'I didn't send him. Well, I did. I just helped him.'

'You were out of your depth, Jack. He should have been in hospital. He was depressed and you took it upon yourself to do therapy you know nothing about. What training do you have?'

The shock of hearing about Theo brought it all back. I felt cold. Felt the room swirling.

'Every week for two years,' I said, searching for words. 'I did psychiatric and psychodynamic theory, three months in a mental hospital. I've been a warranted mental health officer for three years.'

'You should have known better, then. It's clear from what Nigel and Kate have told me that you were too optimistic. You saw what you wanted to see. You know why Theo seemed so happy? Tell him, Nigel.'

The tension in Nigel was palpable. Despite his calm tone, he could hardly contain his joy. 'Jack, you know, because I said so at the time. I tried to warn you. A suicide risk is at his happiest when he has made up his mind. When he has the certainty of a plan. He was happy because he planned his end. He was going out in style, and I think he wanted to save you the blame, Jack. Very thoughtful of him. A basic mistake on your part, I'm afraid.'

He let it sink in. So did Nina. Maybe they were right. I'd only done what Dr Hope had asked. I remembered visiting Hope just after my first meeting with Theo. Yes. I wanted to be sure. Hope knew Theo well. He was his GP. What was it he'd said? That was it. He'd said it with that wry smile of his, that Albert Einstein smile. He had looked me in the eye and said, 'He will die in hospital, Jack. What Theo needs is a damned good listening-to.'

Nina leaned forward.

'There's a presumption of good faith, Jack. That we all do our best and accept that sometimes we get it wrong. We can't be right all the time.'

'Goodness knows,' said Nigel, smiling with his mouth but not his eyes. 'We've all made innocent mistakes.'

Nina silenced him with a glance. I doubted she had ever put a foot wrong. I wished I had hit Nigel with the thick end of a pool cue.

'But last week,' continued Nina, 'Theo's family came to see me. They have a solicitor and want compensation. I talked to Nigel, and Kate. I think they have a case. It's with the council's legal department.'

I was looking at the floor so I didn't have to see Nigel's face. At the beginning, Nina had said 'I was going to suspend you.' If not that, then what?

'Coming on top of your racist abuse to Frankie Surman, I now have you assaulting Nigel last night.'

'I didn't.'

'Look at him, Jack. Look at what you did,' she said nodding to Nigel, who turned his head again to display the bruise on his prominent cheekbone.

'I didn't touch him, Nina.'

'You pushed him against the wall and you punched him in the face.'

'I didn't.'

'Jack, he has lots of witnesses and I have three written statements here on my desk.'

I tried to breathe steadily but was gasping for air. From feeling a chill, I now felt hot.

'It's lies, Nina. He's a member of the National Front and all his mates in the Butchers are too. I did not hit him. I wish I had. Sorry, Nina. I don't. I didn't hit him.'

I wanted someone with me. I wanted Maddy with me. She could talk for me. She knew I didn't kill Theo. The room was silent for a moment. Just a distant roar as rush hour got under way.

Nigel leaned to one side, his elbow on the armrest. He looked around as if the room was filled with team members.

'I take exception to that, Jack,' he began. 'How could I ever be a member of the National Front? You know very well I'm a jazz drummer. You've seen me play in the Torrington Arms. Jazz comes out of the music of the coloureds, Jack. I may be white outside, but I'm coloured inside. Runs through me like a stick of rock.'

'You said Martin Webster and all of you lot were right behind me. You were proud of what I did. Proud of what I am ashamed of.'

He shook his head slowly, that smile playing on his face.

'No, Jack. You're twisting it. Or you really didn't hear me right. I said to you that if you carried on like that, calling little coloured boys racist names, then you'd find yourself put together with right wing mobs. I was trying to warn you, Jack.'

'I think that's enough,' said Nina. I sensed that even she disliked Nigel's tone.

'I warned you, Jack. You've got form. You hit your boss in your last job and I told you I won't have it here. Well now. I have you responsible for an action against the council for negligence for allowing the death of poor Theo. You admitted to me that you verbally abused a black youth. It's clear there is a pattern. When Nigel tries to give you advice you hit him.' She looked at Nigel. 'Did he butt you? I mean, did he nut you, Nigel?'

'It was a punch, Nina,' said Nigel, barely concealing a smirk. 'With his fist, like this.'

He made a swinging, hopeless attempt at the kind of wild, amateur punch I'd never use.

'So I'm afraid, Jack, that this is gross misconduct. Misconduct of the worst kind. You've got a track record; you've done it again and I have all the proof I need. I'm sorry, Jack, I'm going to have to let you go today.'

'Let me go?' A dark chasm seemed to open. I felt dizzy.

'You are dismissed, Jack, and not before time. With this kind of misconduct, I just can't have you around. You're not fit for this work. Not fit for this team. Give me your mental health warrant.'

I felt for my identification card and gave it to her. She slipped the card out of the plastic wallet, ripped the document into tiny pieces and threw them into her bin.

'And your office keys please.'

'But Nina. I didn't. He's lying.'

I saw she had noticed I was wet around my aching eyes, fighting back my tears. I was embarrassed, tired and all at sea.

'The keys, Jack. You can collect your stuff on the way out. There'll be a letter from the director by the end of the week. You'll be paid until the end of the month.'

I put the keys on her desk and fled. I couldn't take any more. I didn't stop for my things on my desk. I just ran out of the building, afraid of meeting Maddy. Afraid of meeting anyone. It seemed that after the explosion on Barnsdale just an hour ago, everything had come crashing down about me.

14
Market forces

Round the corner, I stood for a moment, thinking too hard to put one foot in front of another. In the window of Bob's Antiques, I saw my reflection. Wild hair and a shapeless jacket hanging off my shoulders. I walked away from that glimpse of a loser. I had everything in my hands. Cossington Team felt like a family, and I might have had Maddy too, but I'd thrown it all away.

When I think of someone, their smell comes to me. I hold my dad's old railway waistcoat and can almost feel him close to me. Turning past the community garden I noticed a trace of tropical flowers in the air and wondered if I'd ever see Maddy again. The day was warming and still, like a lonely Sunday afternoon.

The family at Cossington Street. My friendship with Maddy. I had fooled myself that I was part of that. An illusion, and I saw that now, always pretending until I believed it myself. Dad had said the Welfare wasn't a proper job. He saw it as something you do for a while before you find your feet, and I still hadn't found mine.

Church Market was loud, and furious with colour. Opposite Triangle Travel there were racks of moth-eaten furs outside Cohen's Costumiers. Sandra stood at the door of the travel agents, unbuttoning her neat grey waistcoat, the warmth of that early summer's day on her upturned face. Did she know what happened to Theo? A wave from Sandra. A flutter from the hip to say hello and a cheerful smile while I was thinking of Theo who drowned alone whilst waving. Now, as with every night since his death, I lived again those moments of booking his escape with him. I thought he was taking a break from his family, but maybe Nina and Nigel were right. He was running away from himself.

Triangle Travel reminded me how raw Theo's excitement was at the thought of his adventure. His hopes of meeting other young men. Was it possible that all along he had planned his suicide? Planned it when we were swimming together up and down Sally Street Baths? In the Dolomites Cafe we had laughed aloud at what he should pack. I said condoms and a straw hat and he said, 'You know I'm saving myself for you,' and giggled so much I began to laugh. It was enthralling. Not his sentiments, but his confidence in mocking me. I remembered how I believed that with our help he had become free and could say what he felt at last. In those last moments I ever saw him, I had chided him.

'Don't say that, Theo, you know I'm straight.'

'I get that, Jack. I seen your face when Maddy's around. You light up. Those shoulders of yours go back, like this,' and he wrenched his own back comically, sticking his chest out.

There's an instant when the people you work with let you know they are moving on. Theo, who had needed my friendship and support to climb out of his private darkness, was able to poke fun at me. I loved it even more now, for I was certain he had no intention of drowning himself. He was waving. The Spanish Police said so. He was calling for help. He wanted to live. Theo had a place of his own that he loved, had found friends, and saw that holiday as the first of many. He told me he wanted to fly on Freddie Laker's Sky-Train to the States and see Sylvester live. Nigel was wrong. Theo had not killed himself.

I threaded my way through the throng, every person on their own trajectory between fruit, veg, kitchen utensils and fashion jackets. I needed breakfast at the Dolomites Cafe and when I got there was surprised to see the vagabond prince behind the counter. Gregory nodded and beamed at me.

'Hello man,' he said, deftly working a monstrous Gaggia machine. 'Take a seat. Ilaria will catch you soon.'

I sat tucked away in my usual corner where months ago I'd fallen for Gregory's ten-quid vase swindle. His threadbare baggy trousers had gone, and I took it all in. A crisp shirt, a shave and a haircut suited to his lofty attitude.

'Two weeks,' said Ilaria when she brought my fried breakfast. 'Best worker we ever have.'

'What?'

'*Si, e bravo*,' said loud enough for Gregory to hear. He caught my eye for a moment, and forgive me, I thought, how strange that Gregory had a job, and I didn't. I was almost broke and one salary cheque from eviction. I ate breakfast quickly.

'You did good,' I said on my way out.

'She done it,' he said, indicating with his eyes an older woman in another quiet corner, quietly stirring her Marocchino.

'Oh, brilliant, Gregory.'

'No problem, Jack. Put your money away, man. This one's on me, all right?'

'No, no, Gregory. I can't let you.'

'You can. I owes you. Remember? I knows you often pay me out of your own pocket. I'm getting this, okay?'

'Yes. Thanks, Gregory.'

'Call me Greg.'

'I will, thanks,' I said and had to leave, the brass bell tinkling as I pulled the door shut and stood by the grey brick wall, tears welling and dripping down my cheeks.

'You all right, love?' said an old woman half my size. She held a pair of garden canes from which dangled a bright array of knitted doll's clothes.

'Yes, I'm fine,' I said, looking down at her upturned face. 'I had some fantastic news.'

'What about, darling?'

'Someone I know. He's got a job and I think he's very happy.'

'That's nice, ducks,' she said. 'You take care now,' and wandered off up Church Market, holding her fashion rails above her head.

'Lovely stuff for your dollies!' she cried and disappeared behind the stalls.

* * *

I needed to sit down and threaded my way through the stalls to Marco's for a coffee, squeezed round a metal pole that held the ceiling up, and found a seat by the window. The doll's clothes seller had startled me. Her fragile appearance had an ethereal quality. I wouldn't have been surprised to be told she had died decades before. She was *of* the market, rather than in it.

A newspaper lay forgotten on the table. A half page advert proclaimed *Labour Isn't Working*. The Pope, elected a month earlier, had died and a Bulgarian defector had been killed with a poisoned umbrella tip on Waterloo Bridge. I picked it up to read how the first test-tube baby was getting on, when a hand gripped my shoulder. Before I turned, I recognised Linda's voice. She was out of police uniform and finishing a bowl of De Marco's ice-cream. Grabbing her bag, she slipped round to sit with me.

'What a mess this morning.'

'It was hilarious. Not at the time. Afterwards, I mean.'

'Awful. I feel so sorry for the lady.'

'Daisy. Her name is Daisy. We know her. I think she'll be all right. She's probably seen worse.'

'Do you mind if I get a coffee, and we could talk a bit?'

'Sure.'

I had nothing else to do. Her eyes were even larger, darting about, with too much blue makeup between her lashes and eyebrows.

'Are you okay? Shouldn't you be working?' I said.

'Oh no. I've been on all night. That was my last job. We were at Barnsdale at four thirty this morning, waiting for you.'

'Yeh?'

She looked at my hands and smiled a gaping grin of a smile. And pulled down the zip of a thin-leather jacket. Beneath it, a brightly embroidered waistcoat.

'I got a hell of a fright last night in the mortuary. Do you know it? Down by the gasometers.'

'I do. I've been a couple of times.'

'At midnight?'

'Never.'

'Those bastards down the nick. Kings Cross. Been there as well?'

'Lots, for work that is.'

'They said I had to get used to dead bodies. We see them all the time. Breaking doors down, climbing through windows and there they are, sitting in an armchair or on the toilet. Dead.'

'So why a trip to the mortuary?'

'Well, I haven't seen one yet. A body, that is. So, they said, it's all part of induction. You go and see a few and they talk you through it. The sorts of things you might expect to see.'

'Okay. Makes sense,' I said, thinking, nothing ever prepares you for the visits where they've been sitting there for weeks.

'They took me in. There were three of us policewomen, and a young copper. The funny thing was, all I could think of was that I was expecting a marble slab. Something elegant and proper, but it was only a huge, tiled tray, and a sinkhole between some feet sticking out from under the sheet. I couldn't take my eyes off them feet for a minute. I saw this man in a white coat on the other side. He must have had the shroud pulled up a bit because he was doing some sewing. I asked him. I said, "What are you doing there?" and he looked right at me and said nothing for a while. My sergeant said, "You'd better tell them, Frank," and this Frank, he leaned over and said, "I has to put all the bits back in after we've had a butchers. No pun intended. I sews 'em back up neatly. I'm sorry love, is it upsetting you?"'

I watched Linda's eyes. They were still moving, sweeping round the room. Was she still on duty or still in some sort of shock? Anxious perhaps.

'What a night you've had, Linda.'

'Oh. You remembered my name? You're all right. What was yours?'

'Jack.'

'Oh yes. Jack. The others on the team, they called you "that hippie." No offence.'

'None taken.'

'I quite like hippies myself. Do you like my waistcoat?' She held her jacket open, the geometric patterns mixed with shimmering silver and gold threads.

'I do.'

'I made it myself. Anyhow. Do you want to know how it ended, at the mortuary?'

I had already guessed but nodded. She wrinkled her nose.

'It smelt in there. Chemicals and something else. I thought, is that it? So I said to him "Are you going to show us then?" He made a rude joke, and he leaned over the body and started to lift the sheet back.'

I almost felt it. I could have been there.

'Whoosh, this naked bloke that was lying on the slab, he sits up sharpish, pulls off the rest of the cover and says, "Hello darling, want some of this?"'

She looked at me for a reaction. I didn't know what to say. I'd heard it was a prank played on new recruits but pretended to be shocked. The words came out funny, 'Oh my gosh,' but she didn't notice.

'I know. I nearly jumped out of my skin. The young copper. He fainted and hit his head. There was blood and everything, so I went back out to the van and had a fag. Here, do you want one?'

She took out a packet of Rothmans. I shook my head.

'To cap it all. The man on the tiles. He's one of the inspectors. What a nerve. Listen, what sort of music do you like?'

'Depends on my mood. I usually like a bit of country rock or Neil Young, but right now I'm up for the Clash or the Stranglers.'

'I've got plenty of LPs you'd like, and I got the Clash on cassette. I copied it from a mate's record. White Riot. I live round the corner. Golden Lion Street. Do you fancy coming round? I don't have any dope or anything, but I've got some rum. We could have a bit of a dance.'

'It's only eleven o'clock.'

'Right. But I've been up all night and I bet you haven't had much sleep either. I can't go to bed yet. Not after last night. But I could do with some fun.'

I was fumbling for what to say. She saw that and said, 'For a laugh, like. We can mess about, and I like talking to you, but to tell the truth you come across a bit vacant.'

'I lost my job today.'

'What? Not because of the job on Barnsdale? That was all down to us.'

'I know,' I said, and I wanted to tell her about everything. A chance to talk to someone, anybody, but she grabbed my wrist and tugged me out the door, back into the throng of the market, me blinking, with streams of people shifting like shoals of fish in the bright sunlight and the barking calls of stallholders all around us.

* * *

'Come on,' she said and dragged me round a corner where all the discarded cardboard lay. There were no shops here, only shuttered windows and doorways. She stopped and said, 'Here we are,' pulled my shoulders down so she could reach, and kissed me. A short, perfunctory kiss. Almost tenderly, she wiped her lipstick off my mouth with her forefinger and with three keys, set about unlocking a brown door.

'Can't be too careful round here,' she said. 'Some dodgy people round the market. They want me to live in police accommodation, you know. To keep an eye on us, I think, but I don't want that. I can take care of myself. Come on up.'

As I went up the stairs, my legs felt heavy, and I realised I was tired. I needed to sleep and anyway, what about Maddy? She once said we could be 'pillow friends'. She told me her future was with Tim. All her family and friends expected that. They would buy a house, and despite what Tim said now, I guessed they would have children.

Maddy had explained that pillow friends were proper friends. That we could secretly sleep together and be honest and free with each other. Tell each other the things we couldn't say to our partners. That was when I said, 'Maddy, I don't have a partner. I've got no-one to cheat on,' and she got mad at me and said, 'well you'd better find someone, because it's got to be equal. Anyway, I'm not saying we can't sleep together. I'm saying we can never be, well, *together*.'

Linda was pouring rum into two tumblers. I could smell it from across the room.

'Christ, it's strong,' I said, taking my first sip.

'It is,' she said. 'The sergeant gives out bottles sometimes. It's over-proof. He says it knocks you up to dance and knocks you down to sleep.'

'Where does he get it?'

'Notting Hill, I think. I dunno exactly, but I like it. Better with Coke, or bitter lemon, but I haven't got any.' She appeared serious for a moment. Her jacket hung behind the door and now she opened her waistcoat and stood with her back against the wall. Beside her was a sash window overlooking the quiet, dull street, and beyond it, the distant bustle of Church Market. I wondered if Maddy would be having lunch in the Dolomites Cafe round the corner. Would she remember Gregory?

'Do you like them?' asked Linda, pulling her waistcoat behind her and pushing out her chest. She was wearing a black shirt with white polka dots.

'I'm sorry?'

'I mean. Do you think they're all right?' she said, looking down at her breasts.

'They're fine.'

'Are you sure? Do they seem normal to you?'

I swallowed another searing mouthful of rum.

'Perfectly, absolutely normal. Um. Can I have some more of this?'

'Help yourself.'

I did.

'You see, I can't be sure.' With a hand on one hip, she put the other inside her shirt, as if looking for something. 'Do you think they're the same size? Because, sometimes, when I check in the mirror, they don't look right to me. They don't feel right.'

'I wouldn't bother if I were you. I wouldn't. I'm sure it doesn't matter anyway.'

'It does to me. I don't want to be a freak.'

'You're not. You're great.' Wondering what else to say.

'Come here,' she said, and reached out to pull me to her. I tried to put the tumbler down and spilt the contents over the table. It was a delicate table, with candy-twist legs, the fumes of rum spreading across the table, filling the air.

'I'm sorry. Let me wipe it up. It'll ruin the wood.'

'Don't bother. I don't like it. Anyway, it's not mine.'

'All the same.'

'Here,' she said, pushing my hand to her breast. 'Are you sure? Do they feel okay to you?'

I felt both, attempting to behave like a disinterested doctor. A firm stroke there, and a little squeeze here. She had a point. Linda was young, and I expected softness. Her breasts were hard, like taut muscle. I was wondering what, or if, to say anything when she kissed me again, but her arms weren't around me. She was pulling off her shirt and waistcoat, and without a bra, as she stood against the wall again, I saw a fierce and unsettling gaze.

'Tell me the truth. Tell me you like me.'

'You're wonderful, Linda, but it's a bit soon, isn't it? I'm not sure I'm ready. What do you want?'

'I want you,' she said. 'Watch me.'

So I did. All she wore now were black, baggy trousers. They were thin, almost translucent and fluttered a little from the breeze from the open window.

'My eyes,' she continued, pointing at her face. 'Don't look away.'

I daren't. I didn't want to anyway. Everything today had been different to anything I was used to. I didn't care anymore. Now, I wanted Linda. I wanted to fold her in my arms, to lay down with her on her rumpled bed and sleep. Tiredness washed over me, until I realised she had a hand down the front of her trousers. Her eyes were fixed on mine.

I focused on those huge, blue rimmed, staring eyes. Liza Minelli in *Cabaret*. She had one hand flat against the wall, and the other working between her legs. For a second, I thought she was in a kind of trance.

'Will you help me? I want you to help me.'

I hesitated.

'For fuck's sake, come here. You can kiss me again if you like, but I want you to do this for me now,' she said, looking down at herself. Her short hair was wet and tangled, a single bead of sweat running down the centre of her chest. One hand was still spread against the wall behind her, but now she bent forward, cat-like, as if to pounce, still staring at me.

This has nothing to do with me, I thought. It's not sensual. It's lust. I walked closer, and she took my hand again, guiding it.

'Here,' she said, as I felt her knickers strain against the back of my hand.

'Like this,' she added, and pushed herself against the wall while I did as I was told. My senses were brighter; everything pin sharp. The aroma of Wray and Nephew rum mixed with that of hot-dogs from the air outside. And her smell. For a moment I thought it was an earthy perfume, but it was her own, intoxicating sweat. The wall was papered with a small green floral design. The same Laura Ashley pattern as on the walls of the Cossington team office. On the wall behind Maddy's desk. Behind my desk.

I don't know how long we stood there, her eyes locked with mine and her breathing turning to panting, gulping for air. I was alarmed when she began to shake, quivering so much I thought she might be having a fit. Her legs gave way and she sat down heavily, breathing hard. Her face was wet, her lipstick smudged and an expression of triumph on her face.

'That was fucking brilliant.'

'Yes, brilliant,' was all I could manage, although, as far as I was concerned, there wasn't a great deal of fucking.

'Are you all right?' she said. 'Here?' her hand between my legs. 'You can go in there,' she added, nodding towards her bathroom. 'You can go in there and sort yourself out.' It took a few seconds to realise what she meant.

'I thought we might, like, go to bed now. I'm tired and we could have a cuddle,' I said.

'You mean, sleep together?'

'Yes, just sleep if you like. We're both knackered, aren't we?'

'I can't,' she said, 'I'm back on duty in an hour or two.'

'I see. Okay. We didn't talk much. I thought you wanted to talk.'

'I wanted you, Jack. That's all I wanted. Don't tell me you didn't want me.'

'I don't know what I thought. A bit of a laugh and listen to some music maybe?'

'You're dafter than you look, aren't you? You don't even know what you want. If you did, you'd take it.'

The way she looked. The impish confidence and those proud, sweaty breasts. I did want her. Should I do something about it?

Before I could decide, she went to her bathroom, turned, and said 'Jack, make sure you pull the downstairs door hard, properly closed. I'll see you again sometime, all right?' and shut the door. I could hear the bath running, poured myself another rum, gulped it down, took a Rothmans, and left, making sure the door was firmly shut behind me.

15
Winklers and wood panelling

My scruffy black 2CV was still outside Cossington Street Office from early this morning when the parapet on Barnsdale fell away in a cloud of dust and I still had a job. Come to think of it, everything in this city was dirty. The cars, the windowsills. Even leaves on the trees were dipped in dust.

I was rolling back the roof, wondering if I should drive home after a couple of rums, when I saw Rick coming out of Ahmed's newsagents.

'Don't go,' he said, a great thick arm across the door, leaning on the car. 'I need a hand tonight. After tea.'

'You haven't heard?'

'That you've been sacked? Well I never. Didn't see that coming.'

He grinned and went on. 'It's off the books. You don't get away from us that easy.'

'Rick. I've been up since five thirty, I'm knackered, and I've lost my job. '

'All the same. You smell like the Butcher's Arms after a hard night. You shouldn't be driving. What have you been up to?'

'I met someone down Church Market and had a few rums.'

'I hope she was worth it. Kate was in Marco's Café and saw you dragged over the road.'

I didn't know what to say, so I did what you do when there's nothing left to say, and just stared at him. Doing what we do, we're both experts at staring, eye to eye, and letting that hole between us get bigger. Refusing to jump in. Screw the small talk.

'I need you, Jack,' he said. 'Mike's up to his neck with the naughty boys...'

'Don't call them naughty boys.'

'What do you call them? Let me think. Does it begin with B?'

'We call it the intermediate treatment group.'

'Mike's busy and I need someone to give me a hand with some winklers.'

'What?' I said, without the slightest idea about Rick's 'winklers'.

I was sitting on the wheel-arch. It was hot from the sun all day but I felt a faint chill. 'I'm exhausted. I can't help you with anything. Ask Maddy or one of the others.'

'There's nobody else that's willing to do it. '

'Nigel?'

'I don't work with him. Don't trust him. Maddy suggested you were right for this one.'

'What's the job? Can't it wait until tomorrow?'

'No. They're coming round to Olive's around seven tonight.'

'Who are?'

'The winklers. Surely, you've heard about them? They winkle secure tenants out. Some of the squares round here, the Georgian four-story houses are worth twenty to twenty-five grand.'

'Surely not that much?'

'The prices are shooting up for good properties, but you can't sell one that has a tenant in the basement because they probably have a cast iron claim to stay. No one wants to buy a house with somebody else's grannie in the cellar. So those houses go for ten grand at most. Some developers buy them up cheap and pile the pressure on for the tenant to leave. They'll offer them five hundred quid, stuff dogshit through the door.'

'Why don't they call the police?'

Rick looked up at the clouds.

'For a start they'll just send someone like your Linda round.'

'She's not my Linda.'

'And she will just have a cup of tea and tell them to ring the station, and if they do get a call, they'll make sure they're too late to do anything about it.'

'Because the developers...'

'Exactly. Fifty quid here, fifty quid there. Then it's sorted. The tenants take what's offered and put it down on a new rental or move in with their family. Immediately, the house is worth twenty-five grand and by the time they've done it up with a cheap and flashy conversion, they can sell four posh flats for ten or twelve thousand quid each.'

'And Olive?'

'She's had the offer. Three hundred to get out. She said no, so she's had a door window put in, fireworks through the letterbox and a bin full of rotten food waste tipped down her stairs. She's getting another visit tonight and they'll make a final offer. You and me are going to be Olive's grandsons.'

'How old is she?'

'Eighty-five, but she's right as ninepence and won't be scared out easily. She just needs a bit of family backup. Might be a bit rough though.'

'I don't mind that. In fact, I'd quite like some of that.'

'I'll see you here at six thirty then. Go and sober up. Get a coffee or something.'

Rick crossed the road into the Cossington Street office and I went back to my corner in the Dolomites Café around five o'clock, ordered a large black coffee and fell asleep before it arrived, because it was cold when I woke up with Rick's meaty hand on my shoulder.

Ilaria set down another cup for me.

'I thought you'd be here. It's okay and still half an hour to go,' Rick said.

The shadows outside were long down the empty market street. The coffee tasted sublime and at last I had something to do.

'Did Nina ask you to do this?' I said.

'She prefers not to be told about some things. Maddy knows. Kate told her, but that's it. They're coming up afterwards and driving us to a party.'

'I'm not sure I'm ready for that.'

'You will be. Come on, let's go.'

* * *

'They said they'd be here at seven on the dot,' said Olive, answering the door in her basement flat just off Richards Road. The tarmac on the road was thin in places and I saw some cobblestones poking through. They reminded me of Eric on the corner, staring out of his window for sixty years.

'Where do you want us?' said Rick, looking around. 'Nice place you've got here.'

'I've lived here for fifty years,' she said, 'and I don't plan to go anywhere else just yet.'

We stood in her front room with windows having light from above and her front-door opening directly into the room.

'This is my parlour,' said Olive, 'and those buggers will be coming in that door so I'd like you in the kitchen out the back and when I shout "Roger," you can come in.'

'Roger?' I said.

'That's the signal,' said Olive. 'Are you new at this, love?'

'He is,' said Rick, 'but he's handy and you got to start somewhere.'

We obediently filed into the kitchen.

'I'll leave the door open so's you boys can hear what's said.'

Rick nodded and took out a silver-coloured Dictaphone, checked the mini-cassette was the right way round and looking at Olive's baffled expression said, 'With a bit of luck we'll get them on tape.'

'I don't care about that,' said Olive. 'I want you to show them what's what. A ruddy good hiding.'

'It's the Rent Act,' said Rick. 'Last year. It's made harassment like this illegal, and if we can prove it, the new landlord's in real trouble.'

Olive looked unconvinced. 'It may be criminal, but the filth ain't going to do anything about it, are they?'

Rick might have agreed, but there was a loud rattle at the front door, and Olive went to open it. We listened.

Aside from Olive, there were two voices making respectful greetings and saying, 'How are you, love?'

'I am not yours or anyone else's "love",' said Olive loudly, as if she were deaf.

'There's no need,' said one man with the clipped tones of an officer or a gentleman. The other sounded like a schoolteacher with adenoids. Rick and I looked at each other. They weren't the typical East End thugs I'd imagined. If they were ex-army, it might be altogether different, except looking at Rick, a mountain of a man, we probably had the odds on our side. I was thinking Trevor, the boozy one at the camp, was the first wrong bloke I'd met out of the army, so I doubted these two were squaddies. Unless one was a major.

And then the conversation became louder, with Olive saying, 'I don't want your filthy money,' and the nasal one droned on about how four hundred quid was very fair.

'Very fair indeed.' I thought for a moment that there were three men in Olive's parlour because the bloke with the posh voice had lost his graceful vowels and was becoming insistent on Olive hearing him out.

'Listen to me, Mrs Chapman. Listen to what I have to say to you. This is what is going to happen.'

Rick was holding the Dictaphone up to the crack in the doorway, hoping to capture an incriminating threat but then Olive cried out 'Roger,' and to my surprise yelled 'Clive, get in here now.'

'Come on then, Clive,' said Rick and yanked the door open.

Olive was staring up at a tall man, whippet thin, standing over her.

'These,' she said proudly, 'are my grandsons. I'd like you to go now and leave me alone.'

An awkward silence followed. Long enough for me to take in Olive's parlour, the wood panelling with its peeling green paint, the spectacular cut-glass lamp and Olive, sparking up a Park Drive cigarette.

I like to know where the heavy, pointy things are, and apart from the lamp there was nothing except whatever these men carried in their pockets.

'What did you say is going to happen?' said Rick to the beanpole looming over Olive. I had one eye on the other shorter and square man. He had a boxer's broken nose. Funny how voices can be deceiving for there was nothing of a teacher about him. He wore a large gold earring so clearly hadn't bargained for trouble and ripping it off might be an option if I needed to add an incentive.

Apart from surprise, I couldn't work out what else they were thinking. I expected they got payment by results and short-arse's handmade suit was worth at least fifty quid.

'I would like Mrs Chapman to accept our very generous offer of five hundred pounds sterling to vacate the property,' said the tall bloke. It was the *sterling* that irritated me, as if it made the offer more valuable. I glanced at Olive's face. She wasn't afraid, and she clearly loathed what they stood for.

'Go on, sod off,' she yelled, pointing at the door and using her other arm to get out of her chair.

The thin man made the mistake of moving to push her down again, his hand outstretched.

I thought Rick would drop him right there. Years as a miner had left him heavy with muscle but he just took the man's wrist in a firm grip, twisting gently.

'I think it's time to leave for good,' he said as the man bent towards him. The other man didn't move but was staring at Rick. I glanced at the crystal lamp with its beautiful Corinthian column of glass and a silver volute at the top. Fixed above it, a lamp-oil bowl and a slender blown-glass chimney. It was gorgeous but I knew broken nose wouldn't hesitate to lay about him with it. It was the perfect weapon, so when he made his move, I got there first. Olive, who we both assumed would leave us to it and phone for the police from her kitchen, sat calmly smoking her fag.

'We're not here for any trouble,' said the thug. Rick had wrenched the taller man into a chair and was controlling him simply through his grip on the slender arm.

'But you're making trouble,' I said. 'Grandma told you to leave her alone.'

'Olive,' said Rick, 'It's time you called the police. We can wait until they get here.'

'Sorry, ducks,' said Olive. 'No phone. Never needed one.'

The thin man looked at broken nose. I saw he was hovering over the chair cushion as Rick turned up the pressure, his victim neither sitting nor standing and distinctly uncomfortable, but valiantly said, 'No fucking phone, Leo. These ain't family. How come they don't know there's no phone?'

Leo, for it was he who had the stillness and nose of a fighter, was now having to decide his next move: take care of me or go to his mate's aid and take on Rick. He made the same decision I would and came for me. That way, Rick might come to my aid, and let go of the creature in his grip.

His walk was reassuring. Not full on and not barrelling forward. He came at me sideways as if uncertain of his first move.

Whatever he was thinking, he'd had fair warning and those expensive lapels were irresistible. A foot taller than him, I just grabbed him and butted his head on the sweet spot. He was too late to thrust my arms apart. Too late to counter the blow. My brother told me to strike as if to drive your head through the other man's forehead. It stops the instinct to hold off at the last instant. So he went down heavily, stunned but not unconscious. He lay propped on one elbow. His wallet poked out of his trouser pocket, so I took it, found a private club membership card in the name of Leo Trowler and stuffed it all back in his pocket.

Rick let his man go. The thin man looked shaken and went over to Leo and said lamely, 'Are you all right, Leo?'

I saw a look of tenderness. He looked back at me.

'What have you done to my brother?'

'I'm sorry, what's your name?'

'Edward.'

'He asked for it, Edward. It might have got very nasty,' I said. I thought about the lamp. 'So it had to stop.'

'You could have killed him.'

'He might have killed me. Listen, if you come into an old lady's house and menace her, you deserve what you get. What you do is...'

I couldn't think of the right word but Olive completed my assessment.

'You're scum, now get out.'

'It was our first job,' said Edward, lifting Leo to his feet and backing towards the door as if we'd rush them. The door opened and Maddy came in with Kate behind her.

'All right?' she said to me.

'Sure.'

'It's just that, there's blood on your head, here,' she said, pointing vaguely to her forehead.

'Oh, it's not mine,' I said. 'Trowler here has a split head. Nothing really.'

'I see,' she said, glancing at Trowler, who was feeling for the injury himself.

'I could get you a tea-towel or something. Some cold water?' She headed for the kitchen, but by the time she got back, Leo and Edward had shuffled out, their career as winklers off to a bad start.

* * *

In the back of Rick's cheap car, sleep was overtaking me again. Rick was explaining how Nina had planned to fix it so the housing department would buy Olive's building and modernise it for rental back to Olive and the tenants upstairs who were on short term leases and facing eviction. Maddy sat in the front, so all I could see was her hair as she chatted with Rick about work. Kate was in the back with me but quiet and staring out of the window. She looked like Julie Christie in a Marks and Spencer mackintosh.

'Where's the party?' I said and Kate, still gazing at the last rays of sun, said, 'It's outside London, Jack. Somewhere in Essex, I think. It'll take an hour or so to get there.'

And with that I lay back and didn't wake until it was dark and we were surrounded by the twitching silhouettes of trees bending in the wind. A full moon lit black scudding clouds, ripping along above and behind the trees.

'Christ, the wind's got up,' I said.

'Welcome back,' said Rick. 'We were worried for a while you were concussed but you're okay, aren't you?'

'Yep. Not even a headache.'

'We're nearly there.'

Maddy turned round and said, 'There's lots of people going. You deserve a good party.'

'Do I?'

The car was bouncing along a lane, in a landscape full of shadows and movement in the scattered moonlight. I saw what looked like a circle of giant machinery; a wagon train of bulldozers and cranes. Another building site of little boxes, I supposed.

'Here we are,' said Rick, pulling into a large yard with a score of cars parked up on the gravel. Outbuildings on either side protected the house from the gale so some windows were open, and I could hear Debbie Harry singing 'Heart of Glass', her backing track to the rhythmic soughing of the trees around what looked like a manor house.

Inside, despite flashing lights and a throng of dancers, I could see the room was entirely panelled in oak, but unlike Olive's dull paint, these walls were waxed and glinting. Near the fire, some had a reeded pattern like the glass in my front door. The fireplace of arched stone had the embers of a log fire. Above, a vast plasterwork ceiling with galleons tossed on rolling waves towards pale shadows of palm trees and mythical beasts. At the back of the large room, children were running and sliding on the polished floorboards, miming into imaginary microphones.

Maddy and Kate were dancing together so I left in search of the kitchen and found it off a nearby gallery. There were no pictures on the walls, but it was too glorious to call a corridor. I had fallen in love with the house, feeling it had sat here in the midst of a wood for centuries, and the kitchen was enormous too, crowded and loud with chatter.

A barrel of beer was racked up to one side and I pulled a pint for myself. A slim, disconsolate looking man stood nearby staring across the room. He had large, dark, kind eyes surrounded by black curls, a rough beard and a corduroy jacket.

I caught his distracted look and said, 'Such a lovely house. Arts and Crafts, isn't it?'

'Much older,' he said, laughing gently. 'Much, much older. Did you see those oriel windows and the wonderful panelling in the reception room?'

'I did. Is it your house?'

'God, no.'

I liked him already for his soft voice and his manner. He was clearly sad about something, so I thought I'd chat to him when an odd sort of man worked his way through the room, said 'I'm sorry I have to leave,' and went quickly, followed by two awkward men in suits. He had thick black wavy hair, a rough scrub of a beard and wore an oversized Barbour jacket with a farmer's flat cap.

'Who was that?' I asked.

'You don't know? You really didn't recognise him?'

'Should I?'

'Everybody knows Prince Charles.'

It took a moment to register.

'What's he doing here?'

'Stopped off on his way to Northamptonshire. His girlfriend's up there. Sarah Spencer, I think.'

'But why would he stop here?'

'Haven't you noticed? No pictures, no rugs and nothing but glasses in the kitchen? Tomorrow this gorgeous house is coming down. Demolished. First the scavengers come in and take the joinery, the oak panelling, doors and even the stone lintels. All the tiles will be taken down and carted away. Then they'll bring in the wrecking ball.'

'They can't, surely not. It's just stunning, this house. How old is it?'

'Elizabethan. Nobody's sure. It has a mix of styles.'

I thought of the encampment of bulldozers. Tomorrow it would march on this house.

'So Charles was here...'

'He was part of the protest. The campaign to save Summerwood House. That's what this place is called. Most of us are historians, or local activists. I'm an architect.'

'I still don't understand why. Why take down this beautiful, beautiful house?'

'Compulsory purchase,' he said, 'and by next year the construction of a huge orbital motorway will be carving its way through this hill, this wood and what's left of this house.'

'Shit. That's terrible. I just can't believe it. Another motorway?'

'The M25. It will encircle London.'

'I'm sorry. That's awful,' I said, unsure what to say.

He looked me up and down.

'You're with the Welfare, aren't you?'

'Yes.'

'I'm Tim. You probably came up tonight with my partner, Maddy.'

16

The red dress

Finding Tim was a shock, more so as I liked him before I discovered he was Maddy's Tim. That Tim. The boring, career-obsessed Tim who Maddy loved out of loyalty and remained with for safety. Against what? From the start, I thought Maddy could take on the world. That's why I liked her. She always knew what to do. How to handle people.

'Oh. So, you're Tim,' I said, with a cement mixer churning into action in my gut. 'I'm Jack. Maddy has told me so much about you.'

'Like what?' he said, standing back a little. I could see him counting the ways I fell short. I needed a bath, clean clothes. My face felt like a clammy, shapeless thing.

'Your ideas about proper housing for people. Communal spaces and room for children to play.'

'Just back from a conference,' he said, 'about building housing for the community with safe spaces for kids surrounded by houses, like an old-fashioned Georgian square where everyone can keep an eye on what's going on.'

And I was round your house then, I thought, so happy to be with Maddy, and you couldn't keep an eye on us. But nothing happened. Nothing will, now.

'She talks a lot about you,' said Tim.

'Who, Maddy?'

'Who else?'

'Of course. I'm sorry, Tim, I'm tired. Been up all day. A lot's been happening.'

'She says you're talented, got a gift for the work. I think she really admires you.'

What was he doing? Where was he going with this?

'Sometimes, when I'm worried about work, I wonder if she might leave me.'

'For who?' I said, with a laugh too loud to be convincing.

'She goes on about you all the time. She's a bit of a free spirit. I've always known that. It's why I like her, I suppose. But it has its downside.'

'I guess so.'

'Are you…' He looked around for a moment. '…with anyone now?'

'Me, oh no. Not at all. I dunno,' I said, grasping for a way out. 'Sometimes,' I said, 'I'm not sure what I want. I think I might be gay.

'Yes,' I continued, to my own despair. 'I mean, we're all a little bit this, a little bit that, aren't we? I like to let my feminine side out now and again. Not that I've, you know, enjoyed what it is, what gay guys do.'

I looked at Tim's impassive face and carried on regardless.

'There was a difficult moment when someone I was working with liked me that way. I mean, it happens with women too. But you deal with it professionally. Put a kind of wall around it, if you know what I mean. With each other too, in the team, sort of. A kind of invisible barrier because we're not allowed to, you know, get close, because it's bad for the team. And anyway, it would get really complicated…'

'So you fancy Maddy then.'

'Not my sort.'

'No?'

'Not at all. No, she's too…'

'Unpredictable?'

'Exactly.'

'Because things are a bit shit at the moment, between us I mean. And now things are bad at work. Did Maddy tell you?'

'About?'

'About my job.'

'You're an architect?'

'For the council. We design new housing, swimming pools. Everything from offices to public lavatories.'

'Sounds brilliant,' I said, relieved that the heat was off a little.

'And now it's all for nothing. The Tories are set to win the next set of elections and their plans are ready. Our architect team is to be closed and they'll bring in contractors. All our experience and everything we've learned will be thrown to the winds. It's happening everywhere, so we'll all be hunting the same jobs. I never imagined I'd be on the dole. I might have to rely on the money Maddy brings in to pay the rent, keep a roof over our heads.'

'Surely, for a while, the benefits will cover the rent?'

'It's a figure of speech, Jack,' he said with a trace of irritation. He took a sip of his beer and looked over my shoulder.

'Ah, there she is. My Maddy.' A smile transformed his miserable face.

'I just met Jack,' he said to Maddy, who was glowing from the joy of the dance.

'Oh, hello again,' she said to me. 'You've woken up,' and turning to Tim she said, 'He slept all the way up here.'

'Even with Rick driving that old heap?'

'Don't be so awful,' she said, poking him with one finger. 'Rick's a great driver.'

'It's that old car I was worried about. Did you come up with Kate too?'

'Yes. She didn't get a word out of Jack here.'

'She and Rick are an item, aren't they?'

'Oh yes, lust at first sight,' said Maddy.

No, don't say that I thought. I tried to signal.

'Jack here,' he said, nodding at me.

'Jack says that you have a sort of invisible wall around you at work. You're not allowed to get off with each other. "Bad for the team," he said.'

'Hah,' said Maddy, swigging from a bottle of wine before pouring a glass, her eyes alive with excitement. 'Is that what he said?'

Oh no, I thought. For the love of God *don't*.

'He doesn't know the half of it. You don't, Jack. You seem to see everything except what's under your nose. Kate with Rick. Mike and Liza.'

'I thought so,' said Tim. 'It's like one big incestuous family.'

'And it's different elsewhere?' said Maddy. 'Anyway, in case you're jealous, I haven't slept with anyone in Cossington Street.'

Thank you, I thought, thank you, Maddy.

'Not yet anyway.'

Tim burst out laughing, spluttering into his pint.

'Anyone in mind?'

Please Maddy. I beg you.

'I only have eyes for you,' she said to Tim with a sense of warmth I both resented and was grateful for. She stroked his cheek. 'Come on, sweetheart,' she said and took his bony hand, pulling him away. 'Let's dance. Dance to celebrate the house. It's the weekend,' I heard her say, just before she caught my eye over Tim's shoulder. And then I was alone in a kitchen full of strangers, gulping the last of my beer and wondering what else Maddy had said. What else was there to say? A kiss? Some bloke at work with a crush on her?

'Can I get you another beer?' said a young man in a leather jacket. He wore steel-rimmed round glasses and had a joint in the corner of his mouth.

'I'm Matt. This is my parents' house. I'm just here to see the old girl off. This house I mean. I don't think Pa can bear it, but I've got used to the idea now. Thanks for coming. It means a lot to us that we go out with a bang.'

'I think it's glorious,' I said, no longer worried what I said. 'I'm heartbroken it's being taken down. I love it all. The setting in these woods on a hill, the stone walls and great oak timbers.'

'All kept together with slabs of mortice and tenon joints, oak pegs. Hardly a nail in sight,' he said. 'It's always been a happy house. This hill is called Mount Pleasant, and we like to think that was about the light. It streams through the trees of a summer's evening and catches the house with a wonderful golden glow. Not so happy for the priests, of course, back in the day when priest hunters were on the prowl for their prey.'

'Are there hiding holes?' I said.

'Two,' he went on, with just a little pride. 'Maybe more. There's a false fireplace upstairs where a priest died of suffocation and another in the corridor near here. An amazing place. Do you want to see it? There's an old story there's another secret room somewhere.'

'Of course,' I said. The crowd was getting larger, louder, and all of it contained within the friendly grip of this great old house.

I followed Matt out of the kitchen and further down the panelled corridor, away from the party. 'Sympathy for the Devil' kicked off in the hall and I thought of that Jagger film, *Performance*, made with James Fox. I'd watched it a few years ago and it stuck with me. The old house, flashing lights and a sense that anything might happen.

Towards the end of the long gallery, it became much darker, and the floor was cluttered with brushes, bits of twine and leftover cardboard from the packing up of the house. Matt handed me the joint.

'Here, hang on to this. Go on, take a draw. It's Lebanese.' So I did, while he fumbled for a light switch, cursed and lit a match instead.

'Here,' he said, twisting hard at a small, carved corner of the panelling.

'See?' he said as the panelling swung in to reveal a space larger than I expected. On a long oak plank of a seat lay a rusting, green cylinder Electrolux vacuum cleaner, a collection of Victorian bottles and a crumpled box of Tide washing powder under the bench. Then the match went out and he lit another. As he did, I ducked down, tracing my fingers across the bench until I felt Matt's hand softly stroking my backside and turned round to find myself in his embrace, his face upturned, and his other hand gripping my groin.

'All is lost,' he said. 'What have we got to lose?'

He had a point. It felt like I had very little to lose. That's what someone said to me once.

'You'll never make thirty,' said my old English master, pressing me against the wall in his garage. 'You drink, you smoke, you ride motorbikes like a maniac. You've got nothing to lose, and you know how I feel about you. Cost you nothing, make me a happy man and you will enjoy it, I know you will.' It was the look of him, not his hands, that frightened me.

The oily stage manager in the town theatre, stroking my cheek, telling me that a simple favour to him would set me free. He had that frantic gaze too. It upset me. Unnerved me. I saw it later in the eyes of a young teenager behind the wheel of a stolen car. From my window at Cossington Street I sometimes saw it among the glum betting men idling outside the bookies over the road. Most were downcast but a few had that wild, wide-eyed stare. It wasn't even desire. It was the prospect of possession. I loathed it.

Matt kissed me. His lips full and soft, and his beard smelling of beer and cigarettes. One hand cupped my arse and the other gripped my shoulder, pulling me closer to him. Then, standing back a little, he said, 'Do you?'

'No, I don't,' I said quickly. Unsure what he meant. 'In fact, I've never done that.'

'Your first time then? That's okay. We can be gentle. As gentle as you like.'

'But I'm not. I don't think that is what I want.'

'I heard you talking to Tim,' he said. 'There's only one way to find out.' Just before he closed the door, I caught another glimpse of his excited face. Then we were in total darkness except for a sliver of light from under the secret door.

'We'll have to be quiet,' he whispered, 'unless you want to be found out.'

'I don't,' I said, 'and I don't want this, either. I'm love with someone else, Matt.' I flailed about for a handle to open the door.

'What's love got to do with it?' he said without irony. 'You are what I want, and I can give you what you need. Right now.'

His hand caught mine and brought it down to his reptilian prick. I recoiled, stupidly wondering how he'd got that thing out so quickly. Instincts kicked in. I wanted to punch him. More than that, I wanted to nut him, but even then, I thought how butting people was becoming a habit and decided to treat Matt professionally.

'What I need,' I said, 'is for you to put that away and listen to me.' I found a brass doorknob with my right hand and instantly felt safer. 'I don't want to have sex with you, and I don't like the way you tricked me into here.'

I pulled the door open and he stood there blinking from the dim moonlight in the gallery outside, his cock quickly secure in his trousers again. Behind his glasses, I saw a single tear in the corner of his eye. That intense stare he shared with some other men had dissolved.

'I'm sorry,' I said, 'about you losing the house. I don't think this would have helped, though.'

'I made it up,' he said. 'The house is not mine. It belongs to Bruce, a family friend.'

We were walking back towards the main hall.

'Don't you have a partner?'

'It's over. It's been over for weeks.'

'Maybe you should talk to him. Just talk. After all. What have you got to lose?'

He didn't notice my small joke and when we reached the hall just said, 'Thank you,' and walked over to the fireplace.

* * *

I was going to fetch another beer when a hand caught my arm and when I turned, there was Maddy, beaming and holding out her scarlet dress. 'Do you like it? I changed upstairs.'

'I do. I like it. Where's Tim?'
'He's gone.'
'Gone? Why?'
'He saw me with my arms around another man,' she said. 'In fact, the man who owns this place. Well, he did, until they took it off him.'

She pointed to a tall, older man by the fire.

'I don't think he's got what you want, Maddy.'

'And do *you* know what I want?'

'No, and I don't think you do either.'

She was quiet for a moment. I thought how different she looked. At work, almost the tomboy, clambering over railings and dashing towards explosions, but here, tonight and in that dress, she looked as if transported into a thirties house party. The room was lit by the fire and scores of candles.

'No one cares if the house burns down,' she said. 'By the end of the week it'll be rubble anyway.'

An insistent beat throbbed through the room.

'I know that song somehow,' said Maddy.

'It's Sylvester,' I said. 'Theo's favourite.' I wanted to change the subject.

'Why did you have your arms around that man?' I said.

'It was just an idea I had,' she said, and I realised she was a little tipsy. 'He's good looking, don't you think? A kind face and a sense of humour will get you a long way.'

It didn't sound like her.

'I did it because it was the only way to get rid of Tim.'

My heart leapt but it was wrong. 'You're playing with fire, Maddy.'

'I don't care. I wouldn't mind if Tim pulled me away. If he took me home. Took me upstairs. But it's always the same. He just walks away. I knew he would, and I knew that if he did, then I'd have you to myself.'

'So, do you know what you want, then?'

'I want you,' she said with a broad smile. 'At least for tonight. We don't have to screw, but we must talk. We never talk properly, and I want to hear more about you.'

'You don't want to sleep with me?'

'I can say no, just as easily as I can say yes. Remember when I said we could be pillow friends? That we could just meet to sleep together? I was thinking about that. About how I don't just want you to touch me. I need to talk with you about the things we never say. About the things that really matter.'

'So, you don't fancy me.'

'For goodness' sake,' she said. A touch of impatience in her animated face. Her eyes bigger, bluer than I remembered from that first day I met her. When she stumbled, and I fell for her.

'Yes,' she said. 'I do have feelings for you, but to be honest, Jack, I can find men like that any day of the week if I look hard enough. There's something different about you. Something right from the start.'

'Me too.'

'And I don't know what it is. I haven't figured you out yet, Jack, and I need to do that. Let's grab a bottle of wine. Do you know anywhere we can be alone? I can hardly hear you in here.' She put her hands to her ears, a wineglass dangling from her little finger.

'I think I know somewhere nice and quiet,' I said.

'Not outside.'

'No, ' I said. 'There's a place somewhere in the heart of the house. I'll show you.'

17
Inside out

I grasped Maddy's hand, grabbed a bottle from wooden crates by the door and left the room, excited to feel her fingers pressing into my palm.

'I hope you like white wine,' I said, holding up what felt like a very heavy bottle.

'That's champagne,' she said. 'I do like champagne. Bruce just emptied the cellar.'

'Bruce?'

'He inherited the house just before it was condemned. He is an old friend of mine.'

Behind her, two open windows gave out onto a silvered lawn. The breeze had passed, leaving stillness in the air, and moonlight caught spikes of wet grass at the edge of the trees. Maddy followed my gaze and gripped my arm.

'Look. The spirits are leaving.'

I plainly saw three grey, hooded figures drifting slowly towards the trees.

'Shit,' I said.

Maddy stifled a laugh.

'You need a drink,' she said, holding out her empty glass, 'and so do I.'

'What did we just see?'

'Wraiths.'

She leaned towards the window, that same moonlight gleaming on the red dress.

'It's a thing,' she said. 'Bruce told me about it, but I've never seen it before.'

'I don't believe in ghosts,' I said, 'but I just saw three.'

'I never imagined,' she said, and when I looked at her, she wasn't following the last wisps of phantoms but looking at me. Her expression caught me unawares. I really don't know, even now, whether it was the starlight, the champagne, or that red dress.

She too faltered.

'I never imagined that I would,' she said, and emptied her glass, one hand on the stone windowsill. 'That I would see them. It's because of the marshy ground down there. It's the warm, wet air. It rises from the soil and condenses into columns of foggy air in the cool of the evening. It's just the conditions. They make magic. You see them by ruined abbeys at twilight on a summer's evening.'

As she explained the spectral scene, her gaze never left my eyes and she set her glass down without looking. It was at the edge, poised to fall. I didn't care. I wanted that moment to continue for a little while longer. I prayed that it would, with my centre of gravity lurching this way and that.

'They kept fish in ponds near the abbeys,' she went on. 'To eat of course, but the same conditions. Warm, moist air rising.'

She stopped as if breathless, one hand smoothing her dress along her thigh.

'Will you kiss me? Not like the time I kissed you at my flat. I wanted to see what you tasted like, and I was drunk.'

'You're a little tipsy now.'

'Are you going to kiss me or not? It is your turn.'

She put both hands behind her on the ledge. The glass fell into tinkling shards on the floor. I tried a half-hearted peck on her lips, my hands on her hips, but she put one arm over my shoulder, pulling my head down, the other round me, drawing me closer, her mouth softer than I remembered. A trace of tropical perfume brought back the moment we first met.

At the other end of the corridor, people were coming and going between the kitchen and dancing in the lounge. Sooner, or later, they would begin to wander, exploring the house.

'I promised to show you a secret place,' I said.

'You must believe I'm awful. I treated Tim badly,' she said. 'You don't know the half of it. I let him think I'm on the prowl, throwing myself at Bruce and teasing him about you. It's true. I am...'

'A bit mixed up?'

'Yes. A bit mixed up. Kiss me again.'

This time, our embrace was looser. Her hands were by her side as I held her, and I realised she was on tiptoe.

'Be careful, Maddy. There's broken glass everywhere.'

'You too,' she said. 'Be careful around me. I don't want to hurt you, Jack. Not ever. Not once. I won't mean to, but maybe I can't help myself.'

'Down here,' I said, leading her to the end of the corridor. In a corner of the oak panelling, I found the finely carved vine leaf, twisted it carefully and with a nudge of my shoulder, the panel swung into the priest's hole. Maddy gasped and stepped inside as I fished for my Zippo. She closed the door.

'This is exciting,' she said as our eyes adjusted to the small room. 'What are you looking for?'

'I'm not sure,' I said, scrabbling about at the back of the low, wooden bench.

'You've been here before?'

'About half an hour ago. Matt showed me this place, and he said there's a larger room somewhere. I think this first bit is a sort of decoy.'

'But you didn't find it.'

'Something happened, so we left,' I said.

'You must tell me.'

I turned round, and saw her face lit up by her own lighter's flame.

'What happened, Jack?'

'He tried it on with me, that's all. It was nothing.'

'With you?' she said, a hand stifling a guffaw.

'Why not? Is there something wrong with me?'

'For a start, you're not gay. Are you?'

'No, but I pretended I was. Just for a moment when I was talking to Tim. I think Matt overheard.'

She sat down on the bench.

'Why did you tell Tim you're gay?'

'I don't know. It was stupid. I thought he believed we were having an affair.'

'We're not. Are we?' she said.

I stopped searching for some lever or ancient button and wondered how to answer Maddy. If kissing and hiding in a secret room wasn't having an affair, what was?

'Oh Jesus. You didn't hit him?' she said.

'No. I didn't. But I did say I was in love with someone. To make him stop.'

'Was that the truth?'

'Yes, I've told you before... after Theo's funeral,' I said.

'Did you?'

'I was trying to tell you how I felt.'

'I'm sorry,' she said. 'I've been, what did you say? Mixed up.'

'I expect men say it to you all the time. That they love you.'

'Only to get into my knickers. They don't mean it. I ask them "why do you love me?" And they don't have a clue.'

'I do.'

'Yep. I suppose you could make something up.'

I glanced up at Maddy, about to say how cynical she was, how I didn't need to make up stories about why I loved her, and I saw she had lit an old candle in a jam-jar, holding it in her lap with both hands, staring into it, tears dripping down her cheeks.

She put the jar aside to wipe her cheeks with the heels of her hands.

'Don't say anything,' she said, putting a hand on my leg, then she leaned into me, her head on my chest.

'I had half a mind to seduce you,' she continued. 'Stupid idea. I wanted to get you out of my system. Get it over with and get on with my life. Tim's thinking about children, now. He seems keen.'

'And the cottage with roses and stone walls around it?'

'Why stone walls?'

'To keep your children from running onto the road.'

She spluttered a little, wiping tears away, then grinned.

'You're doing a home visit already, to see what an awful mum I am.'

'You'll be grand.'

'Everything should be good, but it's all wrong somehow and I don't know why.'

I needed to change the subject, upset by the thought of Maddy and Tim beneath the eiderdown whilst kids ran loose downstairs.

'Let's find that hidden door.'

'Above this beam,' she said, 'if you tap it, then it's obviously plaster on brick. See how dense it is?'

I nodded. That energy I loved was bubbling through her unhappiness.

'I think this whole section above the bench pivots from the centre. Which means that at this end,' she said, shuffling down the long bench, 'you only need a piece of wooden frame in this corner to stop it turning.'

I took the candle to the oak frame bordering the corner.

'See,' she said, 'there's two knots in the wood?'

I saw what she meant, got out a half-penny piece and found it slotted into the rough surface of one of the blackened knots. It turned, allowing a three-foot length of the frame to come away.

'So, you'd have to be locked inside here,' she said. 'Unless there's another way out.'

'Be my guest,' she said, indicating the way to push open the door.

Maddy was right, one end swung inwards, the other swinging out behind us. The grin on her face was infectious.

'Hand me the light,' she said. 'Wow, it's incredible. Come, have a look.'

I rolled over the ledge and a smoky warmth hit me. It was the heart of the house and bigger than I expected. About five yards by six and set into one wall, a closet or recess bed of the type I'd last seen in a Glasgow tenement, but centuries older. Stout curtains remained, to allow privacy between those huddled there in more hostile times.

'Look at this table,' said Maddy, sweeping her candlelight over it. 'It looks almost new.'

'Because it's always so dark in here,' I said.

There were cuts on the surface of the table where once someone had sawed meat or bread and three high-backed dining chairs along one of the walls.

Maddy scrambled back out of the room and returned with the champagne.

'This is so special,' she said. 'We need to toast.'

'To us?'

'To this amazing place. You can almost smell the history in here.'

'Rats,' I said. 'Maybe that's what you can smell.'

We took turns to sip from our only glass. Maddy swung the door shut then looked around the room, finding more candles in an old cupboard. These she placed on the table and lit each until the room was ablaze with light and quivering shadows.

'We'll suffocate,' I said, as the candles spluttered and burned. 'A priest died upstairs in a smaller hidey-hole next to a chimney.'

'But we have our own,' said Maddy pointing. She was right. A small fireplace and grate sat in the corner. I went over, and from it felt a faint gust of night air. Maddy called me back to the table. We shared a single glass of champagne, quiet at last with only the faint and distant bass thump of dance music.

She looked about her.

'No droppings,' she said. 'So, no rats. Or mice.'

'Maybe they have a special place to shit.'

'They don't,' she said, suppressing a giggle. 'They can't help themselves. Rats and mice don't have rectums. That's why they leave a tell-tale trail.'

'Do you know absolutely everything?'

'I know about rats. I had two when I was little.'

'It's been the strangest of days,' I said as we faced one another. 'From your call early this morning to go down to the drugs bust, the parapet falling away. I thought I was done for. Sacked by Nina. Then Rick gets me to help chase away the winklers, and here I am with you in a priest's chamber in the middle of the night.'

'I think you left out the bit about Matt. He groped you?'

'A bit.'

'He has a habit of doing that. It's a sort of sport.'

'Maybe. I think he was upset about something else. It's all right, though. I can deal with it. But it brings back memories of another sort. When I was a boy, and it winds me up sometimes. Men who like boys. They all pretend it's normal. That it's something special, when it's only special to them.'

'Matt's not like that,' she snapped. 'He's not into boys.'

'I know that. But still. How would you like to be cooped up, just out there, and some stranger feeling your bum and exposing himself?'

'It depends on who it was, I suppose.'

'You're not serious,' I said. 'Does anyone want sex with someone they really don't know?'

'It's not my fantasy. But it might be yours.'

I looked at her and remembered lunchtime with Linda.

'Rick told us on the way up. You were asleep in the back with Kate. How you met our famous Linda, the popular copper,' she said.

'Oh God.'

'How could you leave that bit of your day out?'

'Pushed it out of my mind. I wanted to forget it. Wasn't much fun anyway,' I said.

'I know. Rick told us all about it. The whole story.'

'I didn't tell him anything. Not a word.'

'You didn't have to,' she said. 'Rick says the same thing happens to everyone she takes a fancy to.'

'Oh.'

'Yes. Rick sees and hears everything.'

Maddy went quiet, then caught my eyes as I looked about me.

'Was it good sex then, with Linda?'

'It wasn't really sex. I didn't have sex. I suppose she did.'

'Sounds awful. So, your best sex then? Ever?' she said.

'I don't think I have. Not great sex. I've had different sex. Not with men. But I got tricked into going back with two older women once. I thought that'd be exciting. But it was soon clear that one of them was just going along with it, and when I went to the bathroom, there were all the kids' toothbrushes and rubber ducks.'

'Oh, Jack,' said Maddy, covering her mouth. 'How terrible.'

'And you?'

'Nice girls don't tell.'

'But you're not that nice, are you.'

'There's only been Tim, ever since college.'

'No.'

'It's true. At the time it was all so exciting. We were going to build a new world after the revolution. Socialism was inevitable. Tim was going to build houses for the community.'

'The sex must have been all right, though,' I said.

'I thought it was. I didn't know any better. I still don't. But you know, he has this great big drawing-board at home, with fantastic diagrams of houses with courtyards and gardens, then he swears and there's a splodge of ink running down the board. He gets all upset so I hug him and say, "can't we cover the stain with white paint or something?" and he starts shouting, saying it's ruined, and can't I see that. He can be passionate about his diagrams and pictures, but the sex? There has to be something other than a hug, a fumble and tossing about.'

'So that's it. Just you and Tim?'

'Well, almost. My first time was with a teacher. Mr Griffin. I was sixteen and I had to have an abortion.'

'I'm sorry.'

'Don't be. But it's never left me. I think about walking on the beach on the Gower Peninsular. Would it be in joy with a strapping son at my side, or in desperation and depression at my life lost? No money. No career. And now? A cottage with Tim shouting upstairs and children playing out on the lawn. God knows.' She looked miserable.

'I'll tell you what,' I said. 'Since we're having so much fun, and it's only midnight, I'll go and get another bottle of bubbly,' and I clambered through the low, wide door, pulled it shut, and slipped out into the corridor. The only light came from the kitchen doorway at the other end of the corridor, so bright I had to squint. There was a silhouette of a man in the corridor waving his hands around. The unmistakable shape of Tim, and by the way he swivelled round, he must have seen me.

'Jack,' he yelled and rushed up to me.

'You're back,' I said. 'Someone said you'd gone home.'

'You mean Maddy. *She* said I'd gone home.'

'Oh yes. She might have told me.'

'I know all about you. Where is she?'

'What do you mean? Why would I know?'

'Because you are fucking my wife.'

'Your wife? You're married?'

I looked at his screwed-up face and thought how interesting he was. How angry he seemed to be, but I see a lot of angry men and with Tim it didn't feel right.

'We will be,' he said. 'Just as soon as I get my redundancy money.'

I wasn't afraid of Tim. Aside from being shorter than me, he was too handsome to start a fight. Too careful of his looks. I decided to tell him the truth.

'Maddy and me have not been screwing.'

'Oh, fuck off,' he shouted. More real in his anger this time, but still, something about his manner had me wondering.

'Matt knew straight away you were just putting it on. Could tell you were pretending. How you were in love with someone else. You're in love with Maddy. The way you look at her. The way she talks about you.'

The way she talks about me? Then I had to risk it. Just step off a cliff and say it.

'I am in love with Maddy,' I said. 'We haven't slept together because she loves you.'

I glimpsed the faintest of smiles on his lips. Here we go. I said it.

'But there's something wrong, isn't there?'

'What?' and fiercely, 'What do you mean?'

He knew I had guessed right. I could tell. I had to be quick before Maddy came looking for me.

'You're not in love with her. You never have been.'

'We've been together for years.'

I knew then, I was right. Who says 'together for years'?

'That's all it is, Tim. You and Maddy are just partners. An arrangement that suits you, but it must have been difficult when Matt was the man you loved. Perhaps you still love him. The man who loves you. Getting married was the last straw, I expect. Did he finish it, or did you ditch him? Does Maddy know it's all fake? '

'I don't know what you're talking about.'

But he did. I could see it. Feel it. Lies and secrets.

'I could tell Matt was in a bad way, but I didn't know what it was. It was you, wasn't it? You, who told him it had to end, and then marrying Maddy. What for? For her money?'

'Money? What do you know? Is she in that hidden place? That fucking room?'

'I doubt it,' I lied. 'It's full of rats, I'm sure.'

He was obviously repulsed and swallowed quickly, looking around.

'I'm right, aren't I?' I said.

He pushed me in the chest, shoving me aside. I didn't have to hit him. He was already broken.

'Stay out of my fucking life,' he screamed over his shoulder.

Fat chance, I thought. I'm just getting started.

18

Leviathans

Tim charged past our hidden door with his arms flailing, down the dark corridor. In the distance, a sudden rectangle of orange light, then his thin frame bent forward as he stepped down into the cellar. It must be huge, I thought, with coal holes, boot-rooms and a pantry. I hesitated. What to say to Maddy? Play it by ear.

Slipping back into the warmth of our refuge, I found her asleep, an empty glass and her feet together on the table, her crimson dress drifting above her knees, her head open-mouthed and lolling over the chair. A deep, rasping snore shook the air in the room.

Even now, as her hand shuddered, navigating her dreams, she looked strong and invulnerable. I knew better now. Understood how at work, however uncertain the challenge, she felt a calm sense of a way forward. At home, with Tim, a hollow sense of loss? Did she wonder, perhaps, why going home at the end of the day felt awkward, as if the job was never complete? Wrote office reports until the streetlights flickered on. Reluctantly driving home, did she glimpse that shadow of lovelessness? Did she not feel alone with him?

Maddy gave a little sigh, tried to stretch, and instead turned awkwardly to one side, her hair across her face and her neck exposed to the candlelight. I needed to kiss her neck softly and as lightly as I could.

Her snoring became steady sleeping sighs and as I reached her shoulders, I could taste her scent of jasmine and vanilla-orchid in the air, bent closer, the softest brush of her downy hair on my lips and half an inward breath to sense the warmth of her.

It had always been more than friendship and affection. More than my admiration for her skills and kindness to others.

Desire, so often momentary and casual, had taken hold of me; was shaking me until I had to admit to myself what I had sometimes pretended. I had told Tim the truth, that I loved Maddy, and now that I understood him, I allowed myself to imagine a future with her. I sat near to her, wondering how we might feel as the decades went by. Might we celebrate the turn of a century together?

The distant beat of the music faltered and quietened. Then echoes of shouting and somewhere nearer, a desperate cry of 'Maddy!' She flinched, and rubbing her neck, sat up and seeing me, I hoped for, then saw, a growing smile.

'What was that?'

'They're calling your name.'

'Who?'

'I think it's Tim. He's back and he's looking for you.'

'Oh, no.'

'Do you want to see him?'

'No, not now. How do you know it's him?'

'I met him,' I said, wondering how much to tell her. 'He knows how I feel about you. He said as much.'

'What did you say?'

'I told him we hadn't slept together.'

'Christ,' she said, in a low voice, looking around her, as the voices came closer.

I slipped a wooden peg into a crevice at the end of the wall panel.

'Maddy?' Then a scraping sound. Somebody had found the antechamber. Kicked the zinc mop bucket. A match lit. Two voices. Tim and Matt. A yell.

'Maddy!'

Then to each other.

'He said there were rats in here.'

'Never,' said Matt. 'Never seen any. But there's another space somewhere behind this wall, I think. Bruce told me.'

A flurry of tapping, knocking, and whispering followed. Maddy sat impassive at the table, a slight smile on her face.

'Maddy?' shouted Tim. 'Everyone's going. We're going home. Are you in there?'

Maddy held my gaze.

'Maddy?'

A long moment. They must be listening. Everything quiet.

'She's gone. I knew it. Gone with that bastard.' Footsteps and the slam of the outer door. We sat looking at each other, afraid it was a stunt to lure us out. Maddy's eyes glinting in the guttering light of the candles.

Minutes passed. From elsewhere, a slower, softer beat of party music resumed. I put a finger to my lips, felt a slight, anxious, metallic taste in my mouth before I leaned forward and kissed her, my heart beating fast, senses sharper, and her dress soft and warm to touch. Her hand on my neck, my cheeks hot. Unable to take my lips away and pulling my jacket off before putting my arms around her to keep her close, I felt a tremor as I traced my hand down her spine.

'I'm sorry,' I said. 'Shall I stop?'

'Why?'

'You sort of jumped a little.'

'Don't stop,' was all she said, put her chin on my shoulder, held me tight, then pushing me back, cupped one ear with a hand, listening with mock alarm on her face. Nothing stirred. We were alone. She stood and eased herself up to sit on the table, legs dangling, smiling, and felt with one hand for her collar, opened three buttons, her chest flushed and damp, pulled at her dress to fan cooler air onto her body, slipped a hand to her breast and said, 'It's so hot. Why is it so hot in here?'

'I think the chimneys are clustered around the middle of the house,' I said. 'Around us, the stones are warming up.'

She grinned. I pulled off my shirt. It was wet with sweat.

'I'm sorry. I must smell like a horse. I haven't changed for a day or two.'

'Come here. You smell good. I want to hold you,' she said. And she did. Caressed me as I always wanted to be touched.

Kissed furiously this time as some of the candle flames shivered and died, then fell to exploring each other while asking ever more silly questions.

'Do you like ice-cream?'

'Raspberry.'

'Pistachio.'

'Motorbikes?'

'No,' until it became hard to think and we lost ourselves in the pleasures of making love.

* * *

We woke naked, sprawled on the table, the air cooler and the music long gone. As I opened my eyes, Maddy was propped on one elbow, watching me by the glimmer of a single remaining candle.

'We should go to bed,' she said, looking over her shoulder at the curtained chamber set in the wall. Inside was sacking filled with straw, a wooden box full of tapers and an oil lamp. Maddy lit the lamp and set it out on the table, pulled on her dress and clambered into the recess. Coarse woollen blankets and the scratchy sacking made sleep impossible until I pulled on my jeans and shirt again. I put an arm around Maddy and held her breast as she pushed her backside towards me. I still couldn't sleep, thinking all night about Maddy, losing my job, about Nigel and the National Front, but mostly about Frankie and the things I'd said. Maddy had told me I needed to put it right, and she was right, but I had no idea how to go about it. Sleeping with Maddy had somehow stripped away my fog of uncertainty. Of running away from dilemmas. I was restless, got up and checked my watch by the lamplight. Early morning. Everyone must be asleep or left for home. Then distant shouts in the corridor outside. Tim and Matt again? Had they come back? Louder voices.

'Clear.'

The clack of boots along the corridor.

'Check.'

'Clear.'

'Check.'

'Shit,' I thought, as the call and response faded, followed by a low diesel grumbling.

'Maddy!' I yelled, reaching to grab her arm.

'What?'

'They're clearing the house. They're pulling it down!'

'No, they're not. They must salvage it first. Soft strip it. Everything in this house is worth money.'

'I really don't think so. Get your shoes on, Maddy.' Aware that I was screaming, waving my arms about.

'Calm down,' she said, just before an explosive, cracking sound filled the air, with the floorboards vibrating, glasses falling, and a plume of dust and broken mortar cascading from the fireplace, the smell of earth and chalk in my mouth. A wall seemed to sag. To settle.

Maddy wrenched at the panel giving access to the outer chamber as another thunderous crash seemed closer than the last. The false panel, our way out, wouldn't budge. I yanked out the peg keeping it shut but still the door wouldn't move an inch. Maddy hitched up her dress, bent to one side and gave one end a powerful kick. It moved. She kicked again and it flew open. We scrambled out into the darkness of the broom cupboard. I felt desperately for the doorknob to let us out, a rush of dust under the door, then I had it open, blinking in the glare of sunlight. Shielding our eyes, saw out of the cloud of smoky dust, the yellow arm of a gigantic digger launching its predatory lunge at the outside wall of the corridor, half of it gone already.

This time it swooped to one of the beautiful, shallow bay windows, and with the roar and rattle of its massive engine and hissing pneumatic arm, the jaws gripped the top of the stone and wood. It jerked upwards, glass panes and slates tumbling and splintering. Long, grey net curtains twisted, shivering in the freshening wind, clinging onto the metal rail of the window, hauled up into the sky; the fluttering wraiths, tortured and banished from their centuries-old home.

* * *

Was it a moment of deafness or real silence? Standing in what remained of the oak panelled gallery in a swirl of powdered masonry, watching tumbling brick and stone, slates sliding on other slates, all coming to a crashing halt amongst the pitter-patter of grit and stones. The yellow leviathans around us seemed surprised, retreated a few feet, then with a hiss of complaint seemed to relax on their haunches like a pack of giant dogs. Then the shouting began.

Amongst the scurrying men, one huge figure ambled towards us. Rick looked the part with a helmet and leather jerkin. I turned to Maddy. She was covered in ash-grey dust apart from her blue, startled eyes and wet lips. I stretched out my arms and saw they too were powdered with grime.

'I knew,' said Rick, 'you stupid bastards would be around here somewhere. Imagined you in the woods like two little doves. Searched everywhere. And here you are. Proper Hammer Horror. You OK?'

I looked at Maddy, who nodded. As we walked uncertainly away from the ruins of the house, a small man in an even smaller suit dashed towards us but stopped at Rick's warning hand.

'Are there others?' he yelled. 'Any more?'

We both shook our heads. Unable to talk. Shattered by the fear of death and the lunatic landscape. In the silence, a tumbling cast-iron length of guttering fell to the ground, clanging like a chapel bell. It began to rain, great splodges of deep red spreading over Maddy's dress.

A fence had been erected overnight, and beyond it, more demolition equipment, vans marked 'Leverton' and a small white Renault Four. Inside, Kate was asleep. When she woke and realised who these monstrous creatures were, she couldn't stop laughing, clambered out and stared at us both from head to toe.

'What happened?' she said, as if any explanation were necessary.

Maddy, dragging one hand through her stiff and sticky hair, looked around her, then turning back to Kate, smiled, and said, 'Best sex ever.'

* * *

Rick rummaged in the car boot and came out with an old wallpaper brush and swept much of the filth off us before allowing us into the backseat and setting off.

'Kate and me looked everywhere,' he went on.

'I thought you'd be in the cellar,' said Kate. 'Do you know, they had a room for the crockery, and a room for silverware too.'

'Better still,' said Rick. 'We've turned up some interesting stuff about Nigel.'

'What?' said Maddy.

'Your friend Bruce, the man who owned that pile. He had a box of magazines called Searchlight.'

'Sounds like fascist propaganda,' I said.

'The opposite. It keeps an eye on the likes of the National Front and we went through them last night. Searchlight has spies inside right-wing movements and last year there was a photo of an NF reception. Hilarious. Some of them wearing proper uniforms, but in the corner, a jazz band. Look at the drummer at the back.'

He handed me the magazine from a box in the footwell.

'That's Nigel.'

'I think it is, and judging by the smile on his face, I don't think it's an ordinary booking.'

I peered at the half page photograph captioned 'Dance of Hate at the Fascists' Ball'. Behind Nigel's band was a banner on the wall. 'Keep Britain White.'

'I told you. I said he was in the Front.'

'I think there's more to it than that. Let's get you home first. You need a wash and I need some sleep.'

From behind us, a dull thump then a roar like a huge waterfall. I looked at Maddy, but she was already asleep.

'Dynamite,' said Rick. 'They're in a hurry.'

* * *

Rick took us all back to the flat he shared with Kate, and they went straight to their bed. Maddy and I had a bath and wrapped towels around ourselves afterwards. I crawled under the blankets in Kate's spare bedroom while Maddy brushed her hair in front of a wardrobe mirror. The towel slipped and her hip jutted out, a black and pink bruise near her waist.

'You're hurt,' I said.

She turned round to see where I was looking. 'Oh,' she said, covering it with the towel. 'It doesn't hurt. Why are you smiling at me?'

'I like looking at you.'

'I feel the same. And it's funny. I like you looking at me. It feels all right, if you know what I mean. Comfortable. I'm comfortable around you.'

She shifted her towel to her shoulder, letting it drape down one side of her body, still damp and pink from our bath. 'Somehow, when Tim looks at me, it's like he looks at me, but he doesn't see me.'

'You've been together a long time.'

'I love him. I still love him. He tries so hard. It's just that it feels sometimes like he needs me, but he doesn't want me.'

There it was. The chance to tell Maddy what I was certain of. That Tim and Matt were an item. Matt loved Tim. That was for sure. I wasn't certain Tim had finished it, and if he did, then why would he want to marry Maddy? Money? I didn't really believe that. Not the way he looked when I accused him of it. He was facing the dole, but Tim could get a job for sure.

'What are you thinking?' said Maddy.

'Whether Tim will find out about us. How I don't want it to stop.'

'I don't want it to stop either, and Tim's going to find out for sure.'

'How do you know?'

'Kate,' she said. 'Now she knows, it'll be on the local news.' Maddy held up one hand, fingers flapping like a glove puppet.

'Why did you say it? I was wondering about that.'

'I don't care,' said Maddy, 'I really don't. It was true anyway. Best sex ever.'

I didn't know what expression to put on my face. Tried out a few. Maddy laughed.

'I mean. I don't mean. Oh, it's not like you're athletic or anything. It's not gymnastics, is it. It just felt good to me.'

'Good?'

She threw her wet towel over my face and held it down tightly. Giggling. Pulled it off.

'Right,' she said. 'It felt right, it felt close, it was fun and I loved it.'

I saw for the first time the sandy freckles on her shoulders.

'We'd better have another go, then.'

19
C'mon Inn

We slept all day on Saturday but had to eat and came down to Kate and Rick's kitchen in a house where every wall was white and abstract blue paintings were stranded around the rooms.

'What can I get you?' said Rick, hovering by the fridge as we sat like children at the table. Maddy still squinted in the afternoon sunshine, half asleep and thoughtful.

'Breakfast?' I suggested, and Rick smiled without complaint.

'I must go out soon. I'm going to the No-one's Inn. Want to come?'

'He means the C'mon Inn,' said Kate from her armchair without glancing up from her forensic task, painting her toenails silver. 'We used to call it the *No-one's Inn* because nobody used that pub, so some church group took the lease and it's still a pub, but without alcohol. It's a youth club now, so it's called *C'mon Inn*.'

'Are you running it, Rick?' said Maddy.

'Me? No, I cook there once a week. A lot of our kids use the place and it's a way to meet up and show them how to make a few of my famous dishes.'

Kate snorted, but I was impressed.

'You can skip breakfast,' said Rick, waving a frying pan, 'and we can eat in an hour. I'm making pork chops in mushroom sauce with new potatoes and peas. If the boys aren't in "care" yet, many of them soon will be, so cooking's a good thing to learn.'

'Kids don't eat mushrooms,' said Kate.

'We'll come,' said Maddy, and so we did, but first Rick drove around Green Lanes, stopping off at a butchers and emerging with a bulging bag of chops, packs of spuds and mushrooms from a greengrocer and frozen peas from another local shop.

'Are you paying for those?' said Maddy, but Rick just winked and said, 'Favours.'

'Nina said we shouldn't do, or take, favours,' I pointed out.

'There's favours,' said Rick, 'and there's *favours*,' and pointed at the peas. They were out of date.

'I'm just taking them off their hands,' he said, and parked up round the corner from the freshly painted C'mon Inn.

Rick, Kate and Maddy went in first, hauling bags of provisions and a duffel bag stuffed with sharp knives. I was looking up and down Cossington Street, thinking how it had been my manor for such a brief time. A few months in the job and it seemed like home and the team, my family. The street was a place of work, settled now for the evening, warmth rising from the pavement flags and a single, parchment leaf drifting down to the gutter.

'Jack,' Maddy said.

She hung off the door frame, waving. Something about her I found hard to place. Same old Maddy, but what? Happier? I put the thought that I had made her feel different out of my mind. We were back at work. That's what she liked.

I followed her into the bar and stepped into *Bugsy Malone*. Children as young as twelve sat around tables playing cards and board games. An older boy stood by, chalking scores as youngsters threw darts at a board hung on a nail. It rattled as the arrows thudded home. In the background, softly, I could hear the Commodore's wretched single, 'Three Times A Lady'.

Behind the bar, I recognised Sandy from the Bridge youth club. Helping her was Chas, a tea-towel over his arm and looking every inch the barman. He was dwarfed by the majestic mahogany bar-furniture and mirrors.

'What can I get you, Jack?' he said.

'Later,' I said, checking with Maddy, who nodded. 'I think I'm doing some kitchen portering.'

'No problem,' said Chas as I walked round the bar. 'Just make sure you wash your hands.'

'Sure,' I said. 'Chas. What's in that other bar over there?'

'That?' he said, turning his head towards what had been a snug bar. 'That's our *Smoking Room*,' he said proudly. 'Just for older kids like me.'

* * *

I followed Maddy through double swing-doors with glass panels etched and cut with fine swirls and plumes. Once a luncheon or function room, decked in its day for weddings and funerals, the large space now echoed to the snap of pool balls rattling around two tables, and beyond those, three table-tennis games were in play. Above, a vaulted and ornate skylight failed to evacuate the musky smell of armpits splashed with Brut and Jovan.

A score of girls, all in high-waisted baggy jeans and trousers, lined the walls on benches and at small tables. It seemed like every young person in the neighbourhood was there. At the far end stood a small stage and beside it a table with record decks, boxes and a pair of large speakers from which the familiar voice of Olivia Newton-John sang 'You're The One That I Want'.

I heard a small intake of breath from Maddy and followed her gaze. Behind the disco table a door stood ajar and in the shadows beyond I saw the familiar ducking and diving movement of a figure in a grey and blue two-toned suit.

'What's Nigel doing here?' she said. She looked at me for a moment then said softly, 'You'd better get out of here, Jack.'

I wheeled round to the right and went through a door next to a serving hatch. In the kitchen, Rick was dusting a pile of chops with flour and dried herbs.

'Nigel's out there,' I said. 'I think he's putting on the tracks.'

'Oh,' said Rick, apparently unconcerned. 'I've seen him here before. Everyone in the team takes a turn to help out now and again.'

'But Nigel?'

'There's something else I've only just realised,' said Rick. 'Out there, I was wondering for a while but I'm sure now.'

'Sure of what?'

Maddy came in. 'It was here. It was bloody well here, Rick. Think of that photo in *Searchlight*.'

Rick nodded.

She was right. Nigel and his band had played for the Front here. On the wall at the end had been the banner Keep Britain White. It was the same room.

'I told you what he said to me in the Butcher's Arms,' I said to Rick. 'He's a fascist bastard and shouldn't be anywhere near these kids.'

'Interesting you should say that,' said Rick, lighting up an enormous enamelled stove.

'I think you should get out of my kitchen,' he added. 'It's getting crowded in here.'

'I thought you needed some help?' I said.

'I did. But I don't need you now. I have all the help I want,' he said with a wry smile just as Frankie came out from the pantry with a selection of bowls and jugs. It all came rushing back. That night when I said that thing to Frankie, when in my tiredness and fear of a boy no more than fourteen years old, I was stupid and racist. Someone, or something, inside of me was no better than Nigel and his vicious friends.

Frankie stared at me, pulled his shoulders back and said, 'Hello, sir.'

'You don't have to call me *sir*,' I said quickly. The air in the room seemed still for a second. The clattering of pans had stopped.

'I do, sir,' he said. 'I must.'

'Oh no. Call me Jack.'

'I will call you sir,' he said with a cool stare. 'My mum says I must call you sir.'

Each time he said 'sir' it felt like a precise punch in my gut. I remembered what Maddy had said. Something I had needed to do.

'Then I'll come and see your mum,' I said.

His eyes resolute. Not a flicker.

'Yes, sir,' he said, setting the crockery down on a stainless-steel counter. He walked back to the pantry.

'You haven't been yet?' said Maddy.

'No, but I will. I think I'll go to the Butcher's Arms now. See you later?'

I could see she was thinking it over and Rick just nodded.

'No problem. I want us to talk about what we do tomorrow in Tottenham.'

'It's a Sunday,' I said with thoughts of crisp white sheets, coffee, colour supplements, and Maddy.

'Yes, and the National Front are on the march again. You might meet up with your old pal Nigel.'

That was Rick. Generous, loyal, but pitch-perfect when sticking the verbal knives in the back.

20

Trouble in Tottenham

The tube to Tottenham was crammed with an assortment of protesters. Maddy had found a seat and I swung from a roof strap next to a group of men wearing dungarees, check shirts and yellow construction hats. Rick, Kate and others from the team were elsewhere on the train, already separated from us by the crush to get on the platform and the train.

At Wood Road, three organisers of the counter-demonstration directed us outside whilst a furtive man, too old for his leather bomber jacket, searched the crowd, pointing some to another exit.

We met Rick and Kate on Gatehouse Road by Barclays Bank to carry out the first part of the plan. The National Front had had the gall to set up an information stall stacked with newspapers and booklets, protected by a ring of young men.

Kate and Rick approached the two men shuffling and propping up their propaganda. Rick seemed friendly, chatting and waving his hands around. Kate was nodding, leafing through some of the material. Maddy nudged me as Rick's voice became louder. When he slapped a hand on the table, it drew the attention of their minders gathering behind him. That was our signal. I lunged forward as Maddy pulled a mail-sack from her bag and snapped it open. With just two wide sweeps I emptied the table into the sack, and we pelted down Dove Road.

I looked over my shoulder. Two of the youths had scrambled towards us, only to be grabbed by Rick, yanked backwards to the floor by their collars. Rick backed away with Kate, mingling into the increasing swell of anti-fascist protesters.

'What shall we do with them?' said Maddy. We hadn't thought about that. Behind the shops were scattered bulging plastic sacks and giant steel containers.

'Paladins,' said Maggie in triumph, heaving the sack as high as she could, up, over, and into the bin, leaflets fluttering down into the mud. She grabbed most of them and threw handfuls over the edge of the bin. I looked at the titles and stuffed some in my bag. Maddy gave me a hard stare.

'Know your enemy,' I said.

* * *

Circling round to the High Street, the chanting became louder.

The National Front is a Racist Front. Stop the National Front.

It was like emerging from the tunnels into a stadium. There were angry roars and calls, for in the distance, a cluster of wavering flagpoles with union flags turned into the road, advancing slowly towards us. Against the damp concrete walls of buildings and the dull grey sky, sagging like a soiled sheet over us, the flags' colours and movement drew our gaze. Each side of the marching Front was a single line of police officers wearing gaberdine mackintoshes. The protest shouts fell away to individual calls but from the marchers we heard their own refrain.

British Jobs for British Workers, Keep Britain White.

This was the moment we had waited for. They shall not pass, I thought. We were ready. Over the road, by the bank where the Front's stall had been, yellow construction helmets flowered above the heads of a wider, surging crowd, ready to take back the street. More police emerged from behind us, linked arms in front of us and attempted to push us back. There were too few, and we were too many, jostling and pushing. I saw the ragged band of white supremacists moving towards us, a hundred yards away, surrounded by anti-fascists throwing police helmets, placards and eggs.

'We must stop them,' I said but Maddy looked doubtful.

'I don't want anyone hurt,' she said, with a determined look. 'Not even them.'

'They're scum,' I said. 'Vermin.' Even I sensed I was being carried along by the throng, the yells of 'Stop the fascist front.' We could not let them pass. *I* could not let them pass. So, I stepped out into the street, turned on my heel and took a good look at the men advancing up the road with their flags, their leather jackets and placards.

I called to both sides of the road. Waved to my comrades.

'They shall not pass,' I cried. I heard Maddy shout something. I yelled 'Stop the Fascist Front! Stop them here!' and looked back at her. I could not hear her but reading the words she mouthed at me was easy. 'Come back, you stupid, stupid man.'

But I couldn't. How could I? I'd stepped off a cliff. It wasn't a dilemma. Any walk back to the sides was a walk of shame. Of defeat. The marchers were a few yards away. I could not stand down but already, without anyone joining me, I began to feel afraid. I looked around me again. The yellow helmets were there, but remained on the pavement. What for? A group of punks looked up for a fight but were held back by coppers with grim faces. Just one push and we could smother the road with hundreds of anti-fascists. There were few policemen on Maddy's side. A couple of snorting police horses were behind her, their riders chatting as if unconcerned by the riotous assembly. A red marine-flare went off, soaring over the march in a red plume of smoke.

At the front of the march, before the union flag wavers, was a ragged bunch of young men. Youths, looking from side to side. Walking with fear like Chas and his gang down that dark country lane.

I shouted 'Stop!' and they did. Looking at my upraised hand instead of the ground, they halted for a moment, their column crowding up behind them, then moved forward again. Leading by example had been a complete failure, so I had only one option left. I hit one of them, a swinging punch round his head.

'Aww. That fucking hurt, you bloody hippie,' he said, holding his ear. I was ready for the next one, for my fears dissolved as I saw them as they were. Thin and frightened. Poor kids caught up in fantasies of a Britain where they had jobs. Where they meant something. Where their dads could be proud of them.

'Stop!' I repeated in my own vain fantasy that alone I could prevent this march. They shall not pass, I repeated to myself just before a uniformed, hurtling figure charged into me from the side, an arm round my neck, his other hand grabbing a chunk of my hair. As he wrestled me to the pavement, I glimpsed the National Front moving past, then a blur of someone leaping on my copper's back. I strained to look, finding Maddy with an arm round his neck, pulling back and yelling, 'Run!'

I took the chance, wrenched away the arm that was gripping me and dashed down the street with Maddy not far behind and catching up.

'I told you not to. How could you be so stupid?' she yelled.

We reached a park near the tube station and stopped for a moment.

'You're right. It was the stupidest thing I've ever done,' I said.

'I wouldn't say that, but you are a liability.'

'Am I?'

'You and Mike on your stupid expedition. The way you treated Frankie. Punching Nigel.'

'I didn't punch Nigel. I just put him up against the wall.'

'You and Linda.'

'That wasn't me. That was her.'

'I don't know why I love you.'

'What?'

'Never mind. I've had enough. Let's go back to Kate's flat. She said Tim is on my trail and it's time I faced up to him.'

I nodded and we walked in silence back to Wood Road station. She loves me, I thought. Absent without leave from the demonstration, we found ourselves in a half-empty carriage heading back into town. I felt in my bag for the last of the Front's leaflets. Under a bold union flag the Front *Statement of Policy* proved boring and predictably unreadable. *The Economy* (five pence) contradicted itself in several places, so I opened *The Case For Economic Nationalism* by John Tyndall (ten pence).

'They want to get out of the Common Market,' I said to Maddy who just put her head on one side and sighed.

'I voted to leave the Common Market in seventy-five too,' I continued, holding up Tyndall's booklet that advocated the same policy. Maddy looked mortified. A slew of National Front brochures slipped from my lap to the floor.

'Scum,' said a bloke with ripped jeans, eye-shadow and spiked hair, jerking his arm up with two fingers stabbing the air. 'Up yours, you fucking racist.'

I stood up. You have to. You're just a punch-bag if you sit down but the ageing punk started shouting, 'Fascist,' and that caught the attention of other travellers from the demonstration who began to gather around.

It was Maddy who defused things. 'We robbed the NF stall,' she said. 'We nearly got arrested and had to leg it.' She started to rip up our stash of propaganda, stuffing it into the litter bin.

Left to ourselves again, she put a hand on my knee and having got my attention, just said, 'That's the second time today, Jack. I don't want to have to keep rescuing you.'

She had a point.

21
Home visit

When she came to the door, the first thing I heard was Frankie shouting, 'Not him, oh no!' and the sound of a door crashing shut. I was surprised, for Frankie's mum was not as I imagined. Small and graceful, she had the poise of a ballerina. Unsmiling and half the size of Frankie in every way.

'I'm cooking,' she said.

'I put a note through the door to say I was calling.'

'I know that. What you want?'

'I'd like to talk with you.'

'I think you done enough talking already, don't you think?'

'I've come to apologise,' I said.

She had the look of someone who'd heard that and more besides. 'To me, or to him?'

'To you both.'

'If you want to say sorry, then you say sorry to him first.'

Frankie's voice, muffled, came from up the stairs.

'No Mam, no. I don't want to see that man. Tell him to go.'

'Get down here.'

The way she said it, I would have jumped down the stairs, no argument, and Frankie did too. He stood with his hands by his sides and his head down.

'And you,' she said, with a tilt of the chin at me. 'What you say now?'

I looked at Frankie, his fingers working at his trouser seams.

'Frankie,' I began but he just turned his head to one side with the faintest chuck of sucking his teeth. His mum allowed it, her eyes flitting between us.

'I just cannot forget that night, and what I said to you,' I said. 'I keep going over it again and again and I don't know...'

'Frankie not a bastard,' she said. Frankie looking for the floor to swallow him whole. 'But he is black, like me, and there's no doubt about that.'

'Frankie's dad has gone home,' she continued. 'Gone back to Grenada.'

'I don't know Grenada.'

'You might call it the Spice Island. Grenada. Belonged to you British until a few years ago. It is in the Caribbean, south of Barbados. You have heard of Barbados?'

I nodded. Frankie sat on the arm of his mother's sofa.

'My husband has gone home to work with the trade unions there. Working for justice.'

'It must be hard for you, with just you and Frankie.'

'You will never know. I work cleaning the floors at the Tate Gallery in the day and government offices at night. Frankie has a weekend job.'

'He's fifteen, right?'

'Him just fourteen.'

Fourteen, and I was afraid of him that night. He seemed big to me. Powerful. Here, in his mum's sitting room, he looked fourteen. He looked sorry for me. For me.

'Frankie is like his dad,' she went on. 'You call him names because you think that because he's black he took that money. Frankie always want to do the right thing. Just like my husband. He was trying to take that money back from the boy. The thief.'

'I know. I realised that. I took it back to where it belonged.'

'He's not a thief, and he's not sub-normal.'

'What?'

'Frankie goes to a "special school", they call it.'

'What?'

'The ILEA. The education people at County Hall. They saw Frankie and told us he needed extra help. They said he needed a school that would be good for him. Frankie has a good head on him. He very good at maths, at design, at making things, and taking all my things apart. My husband said they will look after him properly. That the school here holding him back. So, we let him go, on the bus every day to his special school. Then I found out. They say it is a school for sub-normal children. I tell you. It full of black children. Seems we are all sub-normal.'

'No. Of course not.'

'It not what you *say to us*. Who are you? Mr Jack? It what you do. What all of you do.'

'Frankie is not... he's not sub-normal.'

'You think I don't know that? Frankie could be an engineer. Work on aeroplanes. And you know what he do at special school? He's watching videos. Playing games. The teachers, some of them, like you. They call Frankie names. They don't care.'

'Not me. I am not like that,' I said, but in that instant, I realised I was like that. I had been, that night on camp, and I had not before thought what boys like Frankie faced. What his mum faced every day. Not even tried to stand in their shoes.

'I don't quite know what it's like for Frankie,' I said, struggling to find the words, 'but I am beginning to understand.'

'You think?'

'Understand a bit about people like me. About people who do what I did. I saw some of them in Tottenham. I know some of them. I lost my job because of what I did to Frankie.'

'You did? Then I am surprised.'

'It was part of it. That and what happened to one of my cases. A young man. He died.'

'One of your white boys died. And you think you got sacked because you call my son a black bastard?'

I saw Frankie flinch. His mum had her hands on her hips.

'What you said to my son, it happen every day. If not to him, then to me. Sometime loud. Sometime like a whisper in my ear. But that family, they lose their son? They're going to sue you. Sue the Welfare.'

192

'They can't. That's the thing. There's a presumption in law that I did my best. That I tried my best. And anyway. What happened. I don't believe it was my fault. '

'You don't?'

'No. But what I said about you,' I said, turning to Frankie, 'I am deeply sorry for. Every day I see how wrong it was. Most days, many of my friends will not talk to me because of what I said. Worse than that, some people I thought were my friends, they have told me that they are proud of me for standing up for white people.'

'So you are proud too?' she said.

'I am ashamed. Completely ashamed.'

'So you go to Tottenham and march with your friends?'

'Not to march. To stop the National Front marching.'

'And did you stop them, Mr Jack?'

'No.'

'And you think it's just the National Front that hate black people? Hate me? Hate Frankie?'

'No. I know it is not. Now I know how deep this is. I've seen what the police do too. Now you have told me about Frankie's special school, I will try to do something about that if I can.'

'You will?'

'Have you any papers?' I tried to smile. 'I'm good with papers.'

Frankie's mum turned. She had a sheaf of folders ready on the table and began to pass them to me, but held on tight, staring at my face. I tugged gently at the folders but she had them gripped in her small hands.

'Why you say that to my son?'

'I was tired.'

'Because you was tired?'

'I hadn't slept. I thought Frankie was hurting another boy. I thought he had stolen some money.'

'And for that you call him those names?'

'I didn't mean to.'

She held the folders tight.

'I was a bit frightened.'

'Of him?'

Frankie looked away again, hiding his face with his hand. I realised his arms were slender and bony.

'I don't know. I don't know why. I just did. I can't tell you.'

'I don't need to know, Mr Jack. Happen all the time so's I stop wondering. But you. You need to know. You had better find out why that thing came into your head. Came in through your ears and came out through your mouth. You understand me?'

'I do.'

'Because you cannot do your best if you do not know where them words came from.'

'Yes. Look, I'd better be going.'

'No sir,' said Frankie. 'One minute.'

His mother seemed surprised too.

'I'm sorry,' said Frankie. 'For kicking your leg, sir. For karate. When we played British Bulldog. You are still limping. I saw that yesterday.'

'It's going to be okay, Frankie. I don't blame you.'

He slipped upstairs before the door shut behind me, and from the street I heard his mum scream, 'Frankie!'

* * *

I headed back to Rick and Kate's flat, but I really wanted to go home. To sleep, to think and work out what to do next. I was shaken by meeting Frankie and his mum, but it was not as rough as I expected. I wanted to catch up with Maddy, for she had set off to see Tim and to collect some of her things. We planned to meet at Rick's and go from there to my flat and start looking for a place of our own.

There was a door to the garden in the wall of a side road and once among the sunflowers and beanpoles of Kate's garden I paused for a moment, giddy with the still warmth of a walled garden, and sat at a little café table.

Kate must have seen me for she came out with a mug of coffee, sat down, and pushed a packet of Dunhills towards me.

'Help yourself,' she said. 'You missed Maddy. She came back and went out again.'

I lit one of her cigarettes. 'Is she okay?'

'Not really, Jack. To be honest, I don't think it's been great for her to get mixed up with you.'

'Thanks Kate, but I think that's Maddy's call.'

'Maybe. I thought Rick warned you off, didn't he?'

'He told me about Tim, yes. When did Maddy leave?'

'Just now.'

'What's going on, Kate?'

'I can't say. I think she's left you a note. A letter. It's in the room upstairs. She told me to tell you.'

'About the letter?' I said. I stubbed the cigarette out, my heart beating.

Kate looked down as if searching for something on the ground. Checking her toenails.

'She said "sorry". She said to tell you she was sorry, and a bunch of other stuff that I can't remember.'

'What other stuff?'

'I don't know. She was in a hurry.'

'Rushing out as I arrived.'

'Something like that. Listen, Jack,' she said, levelling her eyes with mine and pointing with her cigarette hand at me. She meant to be forceful but wasn't carrying it off. Her voice faltered.

'She had to put a stop to all this. It's making her unhappy, Jack, and deep down you know that.'

'I don't. It's not true. What have you said to her?'

'She said she made a mistake. She was drunk. The whole thing with the party and that old house. Jesus, Jack, you nearly got her killed. She loves Tim, don't you know that?'

I didn't want to hear any more or look into Kate's face for a moment longer and dashed into the house, past Rick in the kitchen and upstairs. The windows were open and traffic sounds invaded our bedroom with broken exhausts growling.

On the bed was a flimsy blue envelope of sorts. A folded aerogramme with its red and blue bars around the edge. It fell open when I picked it up.

> Dear Jack,
> What a coward I am. I will, I promise, meet you soon but I can't right now. I could not bear to see your face when I tell you that I have to go back to Tim. I went to see him, to tell him it was over and that I wanted to be with you, but I couldn't do it. The moment I saw him, saw how hurt he was, I knew I'd done a terrible thing.
> It's not you, Jack. It's never been you. It is all my fault. I was having trouble with Tim and I think, looking back, I used you. And now I know I've ruined everything. He's been so understanding. Anyone else would throw me out for behaving like that but he wants me back and I have to stop seeing you.
> Tim and I have been together years. His parents, my parents, all the holidays. He needs me and I think I need him. In a way, I love you, Jack. I have loved you, but it's not enough just to want to sleep together. I have responsibilities. It was always wrong because of the work we do. We both need someone else. Someone who doesn't do the mad things we have to do, day in and day out. I'm sorry, Jack. I really am. When I've sorted all this out, when I've settled things, we should meet again just to talk. I never, never wanted to hurt you and look what a mess I've made of everything. I've got to go.
> Love
> Maddy xxx

I sat down on the bed, began to sob, and keeled over with the weight of it all. I thought I had everything, and it had slipped through my fingers. All I could do, staring at her letter, was focus on that lonely word left on its own in a sea of light blue, tissue-thin paper. Love.

22

Shadows

I grabbed what few things I had and headed for the front door, hoping Kate was still in the garden. The house smelt of baking bread. Rick saw me, came out of the kitchen and caught my arm.

'Where are you going?'

'Back to my flat. I haven't been there in days. Not since the drugs job on Barnsdale.'

'Jack. Have something to eat?'

I ignored him and carried on. 'Not since I got sacked, since you took me on that job with the, what is it?'

'The winklers.' Rick smiled.

'Not since the party and spending the night with Maddy. I need to go home.'

'Stay.'

'I can't. I'll see you later.' I almost ran and fumbled with the door, giving time for Rick to put his great arm, smothered in flour, across me. Again.

'Will you stop doing that?' I said.

'What?'

'You did it when I was getting into my car. I'm not a kid. You're not my dad. You can't stop me leaving.'

Sometimes you hear yourself say things, and shame grips you.

'I won't stop you. Just talk for a moment, please,' he said.

My eyes were stinging. I'd had enough.

'You know what work's like,' Rick said. 'We do it all the time. Hold people.'

'What?'

'Here,' he said softly.

Before I could say no, he put those dusty white arms round me, and losing what was left of my pride, I dug my head into his chest. He smelt of Brut. I hate Brut.

'It's over,' I said. I knew it was lame. 'I'll never meet anyone like her again.'

'You won't,' he said. 'You can be sure of that, but you'll meet someone else that's different, completely different. Not like Maddy at all.'

'I don't want anybody different.'

'No. I know. Look. You're covered in self-raising. Let's just wipe you down.'

'I don't care,' I said, pulled open the door and left.

When I looked back, wiping my eyes with my knuckles and feeling globs of flour on my lashes, Rick was standing on the pavement, smoothing his hands on his apron.

'I'll see you at the Butchers,' he called. 'Eight o'clock.'

* * *

My place was a mess. I'd got up days before in the middle of the night to do that sodding duty call on Barnsdale. Mike called it the dogwatch on account of it being dogs like us with no family or kids to worry about who turn out on the call. It was Maddy who'd rung me. Almost yesterday it seemed, and I had high hopes, but now, I knew it was just a fantasy. Always had been. Kate was right. We were lucky to survive the bulldozers. I had memories of nights with Maddy, and that would have to do.

Outside, on the giant brick wall, Woody Allen and Diane Keaton still stood by a great city river discussing their nervous relationship. Only the top of the weathered poster remained, their heads in black and white, faded to grey, and a pink declaration to one side:

Funniest Movie of the Decade...
Woody Allen's Breakthrough

I shook my jacket out the window, took off the rest of my clothes and ran a bath. It was almost cold, so I stood ankle deep, soaping myself, splashed myself down, and wrapping a towel round me, collapsed on the bed. I was almost asleep when the phone rang. It was Rick.

'Be there at eight,' he said and put the phone down.

It rang again. I knew who it was.

'Jack?'

'You know it's me. Why are you calling me? You said you had to sort things out.'

Just her voice had been a jolt.

'I wanted to ask you something. It won't take a moment. I saw Rick. He brought round a cake, and I have no idea why. But he said something.'

'What?'

'He said that when I see you, and I don't know when I'll see you, he said I was to ask you about Tim.'

'Ask me?'

'He said I needed to talk to you about Tim. Why did he say that?'

I guessed why he'd said that. I knew Tim was gay and in a relationship with a lover that Maddy believed was just a friend. Perhaps he was bisexual. It was none of my business.

'Jack?'

'Still here.'

'What is it, Jack?'

'I don't know what he's talking about. Goodnight, Maddy.'

'Jack! Don't go. You do. I can tell. You know something. Tell me.'

'It's nothing, Maddy. Nothing.'

I pressed the phone cradle to cut off the call and dropped the phone on the floor. The dialling tone purred for a while and then fell silent. No-one could call me again.

* * *

A fusillade of banging on my door woke me. From the shouts, I gathered it was Mike, let him in and fetched a dressing gown.

'It's time we went to the Butchers,' he said.

'Not you as well.'

'Rick sent me,' he said, pulling the makings for a joint from his pocket.

'Not me,' I said. 'I don't want anything.'

'You need a drink. Will you get dressed now? Mostly you just have excuses for a beer, but I think you have reasons enough tonight.'

'Does everyone around here know my business?'

'You mean Maddy?'

I went to my bedroom, searching for a clean pair of jeans, a shirt, another jacket and put Fleetwood Mac on the record player. The LP was skipping the odd track, but I found myself swinging along with the beat.

'Maddy?' Mike shouted. 'Nothing to do with her. There's something we need to talk about.'

I wondered if he was going to tell me what it was. Something he and Rick had cooked up just to get me out of the house. It was a ruse I'd use.

'Come on,' he cried.

I was looking for some Y-fronts. No clean ones to be had, so I pulled my jeans on without any. Who cares? I needed to know what was going on with Mike. It felt like there was something that I knew nothing about. I wasn't sure if it was a secret, or something unsaid. For all his energy, ideas and skill, sometimes, and only sometimes, when he was there in front of me, he wasn't really there.

'Are you done yet?' he said, leaning into my bedroom, smiling, 'because I can't stand listening to *Rumours* anymore.'

I grabbed my bag and we left.

* * *

Mike took me along passages, between and behind shops. I loved them. All those different names in all the towns I had lived; the alleyways, jittys and ginnels.

Above the darkening chasm between the stores, low-slung grey clouds swam, but beyond, at the very end of all we could see, there was the makings of a fiery sunset over Bones Brothers department store. I was gawping at it outside the Butcher's Arms, thinking how, like the blanket of snow at New Year, this orange spectacle was becoming bigger than the whole of London.

Mike dragged me inside by an arm. I saw Rick at a table and pulled back a chair. It clanged against the pressed-tin imitation-oak panelling.

'There you go,' said Rick, pushing a pint of Bass across the table. I stared at the famous red triangle on the side of the glass.

'First ever trademark, that,' said Mike, smiling.

It was good not to feel so alone.

'I'm sorry, Rick,' I said after a long silence. 'I didn't mean to shout at you.'

'You won't be the first,' said Rick.

'And you won't be the last,' added Mike.

'If you're here to warn me off Maddy, I don't need to be told.'

'Rick told me about Tim,' said Mike. 'The love that dare not speak its name.'

'You did know then,' I said to Rick.

'Not interested,' he said. 'We need to talk about you instead. Mike, tell him.'

Mike sat back, checked the tables around us, and leaned forward. There was a background hum of conversation and brown, whirring fans struggling to drag out the rising cigarette smoke.

'We've been digging around,' said Mike.

'We?'

'Kate, Rick and me,' he went on. 'Nina knows. She smelt something about Nigel's complaint. He knew things he shouldn't have known.'

'Kate,' I said, 'will barely talk to me after what I said to Frankie.'

Mike looked away.

'Kate thinks you're an arsehole,' said Rick, 'but you're *our* arsehole. We all make mistakes. Maddy said you went to see Frankie.'

'I did. And his mum. I wanted to ask you about ILEA special schools.'

'Sure, but later. Kate knows all about them. How did it go?'

'Good, it was good, until I got back. Until Maddy left me.'

I realised it was in this same corner Maddy and I had often sat. How she smiled when she was tipsy.

'Let's talk about Nigel,' said Mike. 'Turns out he knows the family of Theo.'

'My Theo, who drowned in Spain?'

Rick nodded. This was getting interesting. I knew Theo didn't kill himself. He couldn't do that in water, deliberately. He loved water, all of it. I just knew he wouldn't want it to end that way. He was waving for help.

Rick carried on, swatting away smoke from Mike's cigarette held languorously away from his own nose.

'Nigel knows Theo's uncles. They run businesses of a sort overseas but also in London. They have some kind of leverage on Theo's dad. We don't know why.'

'Theo thought he was dead,' I said.

'He's very much alive, but they are putting the squeeze on him, and his wife, to sue the council for the death of Theo. Theo's mum wants nothing to do with it, which is how we found out about it.'

It was here in the Butchers that I'd had Nigel against the wall, a pool cue across his scrawny ribs. Maybe I should have taken him outside.

'They can't sue, anyway,' said Mike. 'You have Crown immunity so long as you're acting in good faith. Doing the best you can.'

'Nina said I was unprofessional. Isn't that the same thing?'

'She doesn't think that now. Maddy knows mental health work. She talked Nina through what you did. She read all your notes and talked to Theo's mum. His mum said you worked miracles with Theo.'

'She never said so at the time.'

They both stopped, took a sip of bitter. Mike took out a notebook. Rick and I looked at him. It gave me time to think.

'There's more, isn't there,' I said. 'You said, "*You* have Crown immunity," but you didn't mean me, did you? You were looking at Rick and me. Like you're a lawyer or something. Why didn't you say, "*we* have Crown immunity"?'

They were both silent. Mike stared at Rick.

Rick looked into his beer, at Mike, then said, 'because he isn't one of us. You must not breathe a word. Not yet anyway. He's a cop.'

'Not the fucking Special Branch.'

I stared at Mike. For the first time ever, he looked at me like a real friend. He seemed relieved and had lost that actor's grace.

'I'm part of the SDS. It's a section of Special Branch but even they don't know what we do. I *was* undercover, for years. I'm resigning next week.'

He stubbed out his fag. The aluminium ashtray skidded across the table. The precise Mike had become clumsy.

'What the fuck is the SDS?'

'It's the Special Demonstration Squad, set up in the sixties,' he continued.

'So, you've been spying on us all along. Why us? We're just the bloody Welfare. That's all we are.'

'It's complicated.'

'You have to explain,' said Rick.

'I joined it because it sounded exciting,' Mike went on. 'The eyes and ears of the Met. No regulations, no uniform. No shifts. It seemed kind of glamorous in a seedy-spy kind of way.'

Oh no, I thought.

'And what about Liza? What does she know? You've been living with her for years.'

'Nothing. I've got to tell her soon. Next week. I'm dreading it.'

'But why? Why Cossington Street?'

'It was wrong. But see it from their point of view. We're the Demonstrations Squad. Think about Grunwicks. Massive demos. Every man jack of you.' He grinned. 'Sorry, Jack. All of you. Even Nina. Every morning at six a.m. Down to stop the scabs crossing the picket line, then back to work at nine, and most of you back down there after work. That's commitment. You're all lefties.'

Was that an insult? I wasn't sure. It was all coming out now.

'We don't go round infiltrating the right. Too dangerous. You lot wouldn't ask us to go and knife someone just to prove yourself. They would. Most of them are criminals in one way or another. We don't need to infiltrate the NF. Most of them are so bent we can twist their arm. Turn them into informants.'

'I can't believe this. You can't say we're all lefties.'

'Liza. Take Liza. All right, I regret everything I did. All of it. But I wouldn't have met her otherwise and I love her. You know that, don't you? It didn't take long. She's as lefty as they come. She organised a school-pupils strike, for God's sake. There's a whole group of people round here arguing for so-called children's rights. The right to bunk off school, that's the latest.'

'School students,' said Rick.

Despite his admissions and regret, I could see Mike was still defensive.

'Kate? What about Kate? You couldn't call her a radical,' I said.

Rick shook his head. Mike tapped a finger on the table.

'She was eighteen when she and the other women's libbers bombed the Miss World contest.'

'Not proper bombs,' said Rick.

Mike swung round to him. 'Look it up.'

'Rick here?' I said, lifting my pint in Rick's direction.

'The Battle of Saltley Gate,' said Mike.

I didn't understand. Never heard of it.

'Years ago, in the '72 miners' strike,' said Rick. 'We'd shut every mine and the only fuel getting out was from Saltley coke depot, so a few dozen Staffordshire miners set up a picket there. Stopped a few lorries. Birmingham police sent hundreds of officers. Tons of fuel trucks going in, day in, day out. That's when we called for help, from South Yorkshire, South Wales, trades unionists from Birmingham. I was there when they arrived.'

Rick, that tower of affable brute strength, sat there and raised his hand to his face. I couldn't believe it. He wiped away a tear.

'It were the greatest show of solidarity I ever saw. I'd come the day before, and in one moment there were so many police. Had us backed up against the fence. Lorries freely going in and out. The next, we heard this roar. The tramping. The songs. And over the hill, marching, came thousands, thousands of miners, trade unionists from West Midlands and then it were all over. It were our Agincourt. The police folded and closed the plant. We'd won.'

He sat back as if exhausted. Mike just looked at me.

'Nina?' I said.

He nodded.

'What about me?'

'I had you down as an anarchist. An unguided missile.'

'How could you, Mike?'

'It was my job, stupid. Just like you have your job.'

'But you were good at *our* job. Did you get two pay cheques? What happened? Why are you resigning?'

Rick got up to get more pints. Beyond him, on the other end of the bar, I saw Doctor Hope, complete with hat, lifting a shining glass with evident pleasure. Mike followed my gaze with a smile. It was the golden hour. That's what they said, but it was only a matter of minutes. Something about the road, the way at this time of year the sun fell. Everyone knew about it. As the sun dropped, an orange glow streamed through the room, threw letters and patterns from the cut-glass windows across the floor. Streaks of red and gold slipping across the walls.

'I just couldn't do it anymore,' said Mike.

I wanted to believe him, but right then, I was still angry.

'I think it started in Lambeth,' he went on. 'I went there to get intel on the Anti-Nazi League demo against the NF who were parading up and down, provoking the community.'

Rick brought a set of pints back.

'It was peaceful. A lot of pushing and shoving, then the SPG piled in.'

'The Special Patrol Group,' added Rick.

I nodded, pretending I knew all about the SPG. I was thinking of the van outside Barnsdale. Were they the SPG?

'The SPG are a law to themselves,' continued Mike. 'They seem to operate on their own.'

'Like you,' I said.

Mike paused, sipped his beer and went on, and on. After all these years, he was off the leash.

'They're thugs. Tooled up with lead coshes and crowbars. All the coppers in the Met want to get into the SPG. It's like a toytown SAS. They drove into Lambeth and van after van of cops arrived. They provoked anti-fascists by writing "NF" in the condensation on the windows. The police cornered fifty demonstrators against the churchyard walls. Several demonstrators were dragged screaming and crying to the police station. Every one of them had blood over them. I know the SPG did it. They bragged about it.'

Mike was holding his pint on the table between his palms, twisting it around ever faster. His story was just tumbling out of him.

I said I was going to the gents but instead I went outside. I needed air. The street was full of vans and cars hurtling along. The sun had gone down. I felt dizzy. Rick joined me and put an arm across my shoulder.

'You need to hear him out, Jack. There's more you need to know and we need him, Jack. Let's go back in.'

Mike was leafing through his notebook and looked up when we came back. He carried on as if we had never left.

'My governor asked me to take a few soundings. A job, just before we took the boys away on camp.'

'Soundings?' said Rick.

'He wanted me to check out an SPG constable called Douglas. Douglas told me he collected weapons like some people collect stamps. In his home he showed me a leather-bound, lead-weighted stick, Nazi regalia, bayonets, German medals, daggers, whips, and swords. Two days after I reported on his collection, Douglas was transferred out of the SPG to Brixton police station.'

I thought about the botched operation on the estate. The hardware in the back of the van and the enamelled NF badges inside the coats of the filth. Linda and her Jamaican rum. Brixton police had been at war with the community down there for years, raiding restaurants and clubs. That's where the rum came from, of course.

'There's more,' said Rick, 'and it might involve Nigel.'

More? How could there be more? Mike carried on.

'This is where the right and the left come full circle,' he said. 'Among some of you on the radical left, libertarians, there are men trying to justify sex with children. They argue that the laws against child-sex are wrong, and they have a lot of sympathisers. On the right, some in the NF and those loyal to them, have a more *commercial* interest.'

I must have looked puzzled. He went on, tracing lines on the table with his finger.

'They are using boys, and some girls, to rake in money. Exploiting vulnerable kids. They know where to find the most charming kids and they have connections everywhere. The awkward youngsters, they have delivering drugs.'

I thought of Mike, rolling joints with one hand. What a hypocritical liar he'd been. Was he telling the truth now?

'We suspect Nigel is in on that,' said Rick, 'but we don't know where the kids come from. Children's homes?'

In the mirror behind Rick and Mike I saw a woman come in. Smart jacket and a briefcase. Saw her put a hand on Dr Hope's arm, order a drink and sweep the room with her dark eyes. She settled on us. It was Nina. I heard her footsteps as she approached, then the shock of a flat, leather-gloved slap around my ear.

'Jesus, Nina,' said Mike. 'You can't do that to your staff.'

'That was for Maddy,' she said. 'He's not on *my* team, and in the Butchers I can do what I like.'

23

Grand Union

Mike fetched me another beer. I watched his gait, for he'd regained that subdued swagger, his chin aloft and head slowly turning as he took in the bar-room and the Butchers customers. Now I knew that, for all these years at Cossington Street, for all that time with Liza tending him after he broke his leg skiing, he was a bastard undercover cop.

They grew beards, left their ironed shirts at home with their wives and swapped slacks for grubby jeans.

Except Mike. There he was, clean shaven, a hand pushing back through his thinning hair, leaning at the bar, reading the room. And aside from a neat black leather jacket, his sooty cord trousers had the shadow of a pressed crease, ending at polished copper's boots, worn by a copper. Always a copper.

Nina's swipe, cuffing my ear, had not hurt. All I felt was embarrassment.

'Why'd you do that?' I said, holding my ear as if I was in pain.

She just looked at me. An unflinching gaze, as if sizing me up for another whack.

'I told you,' she said at last. 'For what you did to Maddy.'

Her words were whispered across the table, only the plume of a neglected cigarette between us.

'You are trouble,' she went on. 'You are a problem because you are all over the place.'

She was right about that. Was that all down to me, though? I couldn't help my feelings for Maddy.

'I am bloody angry with you,' Nina hissed, looking around, leaning towards me so that I moved back in case she took another swipe. What she said next took me by surprise.

'You were right about Nigel,' she said. 'The day after I sacked you for punching him, his purple bruising just disappeared. It was fake, like all the lies he told me.'

'Have you sacked Nigel?' asked Rick.

'No, not yet,' she said, nodding towards the bar. 'He doesn't know what I've found out. I talked to Larry. Asked him if he'd barred Jack.' She glanced at me. Larry, who'd pulled me off Nigel. Larry, whose pub stitched together all walks of life. Nina turned to me.

'He said Nigel was goading you. That you put him against the wall.'

'I did.'

'But you didn't hit him.'

'No,' I said, my excitement rising. 'I didn't and Theo didn't die because of me.'

'I know that, too. But not because of you, Jack,' she said. 'Because of Kate and Maddy doing your homework for me.'

'I told you,' I said. 'I really did. I told you, Nina.'

Nina took a sip of her beer, lifting her glass with her smallest finger extended in my direction.

'You did no such thing. Nothing you said made much sense. You offered no evidence. Bawled like a ten-year-old. You didn't come back to me when you'd calmed down. How can you stand for your families if you can't advocate for yourself?'

I put my hands flat on the table, then turned them up in supplication.

'I told you about Nigel and the NF. I told you I didn't hit him.'

'You *would* say that,' she carried on, 'but what am I to think? You dropped your last manager to the floor. Never mind the reasons. Did it not occur to you that it could have ended your career? That if you'd handled it properly, *he* would have been sacked instead?'

I was going to talk about being stressed and not being myself, but Nina just went on.

'You did the same thing to one of those winklers.'

'It was self-defence.'

'It was over the top,' she said. I looked at Rick. He just had his usual faint smile.

'I thought you didn't know about that, Nina.'

She leaned back, crossed her legs, and just stared at me. I felt she was reading everything about me.

'I love her,' I said. It was all I could think of. That's why Nina slapped me round the head. That's what she said. That was what this was all about, wasn't it?

Nina swayed a little, like a cobra choosing an angle to strike.

'You racially abused a fourteen-year-old boy.'

'I know. Nina, I know. I don't know why. I don't know where it came from.'

She lit another cigarette from the smouldering end of her last one.

'That is why I have trouble with you,' she said, shaking her head slowly. 'You know everything, but you don't even know yourself.'

'I never wanted to hurt Maddy,' I said. 'I would never hurt her. I love her, Nina. Anyway, it's all over.'

'I doubt that. How can I have you both in my team? Just think about this, Jack. Do you love Maddy? Or do you want her to rescue you? Because that's what worries me. It will wear her out, and in the end, when you come to your senses, you'll resent it all. It will end badly.'

I was going to protest. Tell her I didn't need rescuing. I'd do anything for Maddy. I'd apologised to Frankie. I would make it all up to them. But Nina just got up, gathered several empty glasses, and turned to us before she left.

'Jack. I'm having you back if you'll come back. Meanwhile, I want a plan about…' she looked around, '…the other thing, and keep him,' she said about me, 'away from Nigel.'

She swept over to the bar, gave Larry the empties and left without a backwards glance. On the table was a manila envelope covered in scored-out office addresses and labels.

The latest was simply my name. Nina had used the most recycled envelope in the office to give me my papers, and I was back in service.

I stuck the package in my shoulder bag. We all had them, full of files, reports, guidance-books, and tuppenny coins for phone boxes. Maddy used old halfpennies because they worked too. I gripped it on my knees like a terrified patient awaiting root canal treatment. When Mike asked me if I wanted another pint, I shook my head.

'Let's go,' said Rick. I didn't ask where. I just followed him out of the Butchers and into the dark night.

* * *

The gongoozlers had all gone home. Those crowds of sightseers and drunks loafing around the locks and bridges of the Grand Union canal, gazing at the boats, hoping for collisions and unscheduled plunges into the filthy water. Not that you needed to swim. In places you can stand up to avoid drowning. People said bodies were often found in its cold embrace. Dredging for one body, you're quite likely to find another.

Although the street above was flooded with the acid orange light from tall sodium lamps, down on the towpath it took a while for my eyes to adjust. Overhanging trees and roadside hoardings left the canal in shadows. Lights opposite and the blue-black sky above were reflected in the rippling water, the arch of a bridge completed into a circle by the dark, mirrored waters below.

'Let's grab a seat,' said Rick when we reached a bench opposite a half-sunk and derelict houseboat. From his bag, Rick drew out a couple of cans.

'It's all I could find tonight,' he said with a look of embarrassment, holding out a can of Tennent's lager. He turned it in his fist to reveal a pin-up photograph of *Marie* on the back of the steel can, her blouse open to the waist.

'That's truly awful,' I said, taking it.

'I know,' said Rick, lifting *Erica* and ripping off the pull-ring with a pop and gassy sigh.

'Wait until you see mine. The beer's terrible, too. I blame the Scots.'

Now it was cooler, somehow a cigarette felt comforting, from that first phosphorescent spurt of lighting it to the taste of resinous wood and warmth. We sat in silence, watching the ripples from unseen animals foraging on the bank.

'Where you from?' he said, scratching his bristly neck and waiting.

At last, I told him how growing up in a Midlands village was a little less ordinary than I first thought. I had assumed all villages had brickyards, breweries, hosiery and bootmakers, farms, ten pubs and a fine Norman church.

'My dad, a railwayman, buckled on a leather harness with chains at midnight to clear the express line of dead bullocks. My mum counted the number of coils in the filaments of light bulbs.'

'Every bulb?' said Rick, incredulously.

'A sample,' I said. 'Quality control for eight hours a day glued to a microscope.'

I wanted to tell him how my dad read me stories every night and brought me a small toy if a grateful passenger tipped him. I was loved, and never beaten like the kids I worked with. I didn't tell Rick that. It felt wrong, so I chose instead to talk about my older brother leaving home for the Royal Navy at fifteen. A boy polishing steel dustbins at Ganges training centre at Shotley.

My brother Daniel, terrified at climbing a 142-foot mast every few weeks and glad to leave the regime, then hospitalised in Mombasa when two ships collided.

'Most of all, I remember him teaching me Morse Code on a little machine. He had his finger on top of mine and said, "You've got lovely eyes." I think he surprised himself when he said it.'

Rick said nothing, letting me go on, miming with my hands the incident of the destroyer, *Hogue*, rammed by the cruiser *Mysore*, crushing my brother's best friend in front of him at dead of night on the foam and star-streaked ocean. I loved my brother then.

'Until he went on those subs. Submarines,' I added. 'Waiting for weeks under the northern icecap with their nuclear engines,' and again, Rick listened and watched as I described my brother gazing up, imagining through the ocean the lonely polar cap above. Rick shivered.

'They call it the silent service,' I said, 'in more ways than one,' and drew a hand across my mouth, zipping up my lips.

There was a minute of silence as we both watched little silhouettes of rats scurrying on the hulk on the other bank. They ran in lines, a flowing stream of rodents, outlining the shapes of the cabin roof until, in a breathtaking moment, from what was left of the cockpit, a shape emerged; grey, thin, and elegant, with a yellow beak, poised to strike.

'Fuck me,' said Rick. 'It's a heron.' In that instant the bird plunged its head down, snatched a rat and launched itself into the evening breeze, flapping slowly down the canal with her prey still wriggling in her mouth.

When the bird had gone, I threw my cigarette into the canal.

'I thought they caught fish.'

Rick laughed.

'I'm not sure there's any fish left. Though I've never heard of herons taking rats.'

I thought about my story.

'Are you sure you want to hear this?' I said. Rick looked relaxed.

'I've got all night,' he said. 'Anyway, Nina said I could take a day off tomorrow.'

'So you'll report back to her on me.'

'Nope,' he said with kindness in his voice. 'She just wants you to be heard. Thinks you're dwelling on stuff. Stressed out.

What we do under stress, I sometimes think, is that we revert to childhood behaviour. We are angry, and we cry. For what? And if not careful, we start blaming people, becoming victims ourselves. You must have done PVR at college.'

'I don't remember,' I said. I really didn't.

'Perpetrator, victim and rescuer,' chuckled Rick. 'A bit simple, I know, but there's some truth in it. That we cycle through those roles unless we are careful.'

'I don't do therapy.'

'We're just talking,' said Rick. 'I'm telling no one about you.'

I looked at him carefully. I trusted him. Or at least, I wanted to trust him.

'My brother was never the same,' I said. 'It might have been the claustrophobia in those submarines. They humiliated him too.

'He bought me my first proper bike at the shop on Barrow Road. A Coventry Falcon. I loved it. The next day he started pelting me with apples in the garden. Hard ones, then stones and rocks, and I just lay on the ground curled up as he called me a "bastard".'

'A bastard?' said Rick.

'A bastard. A little shit. He said my dad wasn't my real dad. But I did nothing, nothing to him, you see? Nothing!'

I stopped, ashamed of myself for blurting it out, took a pull at my can of lager and felt the cold fizzing down my throat and spreading out across my chest.

'My mum stopped him. She sent him down the pub and told me never to talk about it. I didn't. You're the first I ever told. My dad thought I fell off the bike. I was bruised and cut all over.'

My eyes were damp, but I stopped myself from crying. Used my palms to wipe away stray tears.

'Did he do other things?'

I nodded, but didn't talk about the arm wrenching, the broken wrist or when I thought I would suffocate. I was glad when shore-leave ended. Glad when my brother went back under the sea. Half of me hoped he would drown.

'I threw the bike in the canal,' I told Rick. 'I said it was stolen.'

He nodded, looking up and down the towpath. 'Not this one.'

'As it happens, yes. The Grand Union. It goes all the way from here, up North to the Midlands and beyond.'

'Is this why you joined the Welfare?'

'No.'

'To rescue others?'

He let that sink in. I felt forced to think about it, but was then distracted by figures stumbling out of the blackness under the bridge. A man and a woman, swaying to and fro, their voices becoming louder.

'I don't want your fucking ring,' she said, pulling at her hand with the other until her arm flew into the air and there was a tinkling sound before a moment of silence.

'Oh shit,' breathed Rick. 'I think we're about to have a domestic.'

The woman, a slip of a girl, stood back and stared at the water.

'Oh my god,' she said. 'Oh my god,' again, with a hand to her mouth now, looking back at the man, a shapeless shadow in a billowing puffer jacket.

'It's none of our business,' I said.

Rick leaned forward, elbows on his knees.

'Depends,' he said.

The couple were less than ten yards away, the man with his hands on his hips, staring at her.

'Do you know how much that cost?' he yelled, and without waiting for an answer he lurched forward. Surely, he must have seen us, motionless on our iron bench, sipping at new cans of Tennent's.

The man swung a punch at the woman but missed, swung round, and grabbed her.

'You stupid fucking cow,' he screamed. 'I'll fucking kill you, you filthy bitch.'

He was shaking her wildly. She tottered on heels, waving an arm, then slapped him. A good whack across his face. She might have drawn blood, for he wiped his nose with his cuff. Rick looked at me. It could only get worse.

'Always a mistake, I think,' I said in a low voice, 'to get involved in a domestic.'

'But it's the mistake we are compelled to make,' said Rick, standing up and stretching his arms.

'Let's call the police,' I said, clutching my bag.

'And how do you plan to do that?' whispered Rick. 'The nearest callbox is half a mile away'.

The man's jacket was slipping off his shoulders as he pressed the woman against the wall behind the path. His hands were at her neck when Rick sauntered over.

'Can I have a word?' he said.

The man spun around. 'And what the fuck has this to do with you?'

'Not a lot,' said Rick. 'But I don't want anybody to get hurt.'

'Hurt?' said the man. 'I'll fucking kill her.'

'No, you won't,' said Rick evenly. I was ready, to one side, behind him. I just wished I wasn't there. That this wasn't happening.

The boyfriend had one hand on her neck and the other jabbing a finger at Rick.

'Just fuck off,' he yelled.

She was pleading. Waving her hands about. Sobbing. Reaching around her.

From the corner of my eye, I saw two swans gliding through the glassy surface of the canal, glancing at us as they slipped by.

'I'm sorry,' said Rick 'but you can't do that...' and stared suddenly at the man's hand. He had let go of the woman and had a kitchen knife in his fist. I don't know where he had it. I didn't see him draw it. It was just there in his hand. Maybe it was intended for her, but now he waved it at Rick.

'If you don't fuck off right now, I'll stick you with this,' he shouted.

There was something about him. The sniffing, sour look, and hatred. A bloody cokehead. I thought. Always the worst. Drunk too.

Rick started. 'Let's talk about this, eh?' but the man ran at Rick, who had his hands outstretched. Standing by the edge of the canal.

'Kevin!' yelled the woman as Rick easily grabbed the man's wrist and used his leg to sweep the bloke off his feet. He landed heavily and groaned. Rick picked up the knife and threw it into the water then bent over Kevin to lift him to his feet. That was when I saw the girlfriend lurching towards Rick, a hefty piece of fencing held over her head.

'Leave him alone!' she screamed at Rick, who looked up, holding an arm over his face as she lunged at him.

I did the only thing I could think of and used my shoulder to nudge her firmly. The fence pole fell to the floor as she tottered, swayed, screamed, and fell face forward into the canal.

Somebody must have heard the commotion, for that's when the cars and sirens arrived.

'I didn't hit her,' I called to Rick. 'I didn't. It were an accident.'

'Brenda,' yelled Kevin, struggling with Rick's knee on his chest.

Brenda was at the bank, shoulder deep in the water, her hair full of weed, making feeble efforts to clamber out.

A police officer and a policewoman rushed down the embankment, grabbing hold of bushes to keep steady. The female cop got to us first, scanning the scene. It was Linda.

'Hello, Jack,' she said. 'We can't keep meeting like this.'

Rick, his knee still firmly on Kevin's chest, started heaving with laughter. It really wasn't funny.

24

The wrong horse

'Let's go,' said Rick, pulling me along the towpath. 'I'm hungry and I expect you are.'

'I want to go home,' I said, but Rick insisted, hooking his arm into mine and heading off under the bridge. Beyond that, a towering lock-gate, water gushing from splintered timbers, over green slime.

'I'm not sure I want to see Kate right now,' I said. 'I mean, I will. I know she's helped me with Nina and everything but...'

'I thought we'd go to my other place,' he said.

'Your other place?'

'Friends. They're friends of mine.'

* * *

It was a huge Georgian house. A woman answered the door.

'Come in,' she said, without asking my name, or saying hello. 'I am Birgit.'

Her accent was German. A meal was in progress in the middle of a haphazard renovation project with sacks of plaster, timber stacked against the wall and tools scattered along a bench in a corner of the room.

'Sit down, Jack. Are you hungry?' she said.

I was hungry. I was ravenous. There were men, women, children, bottles of wine, loaves, bowls of rice and vegetable stews. Almost everyone wore dungarees, and most of the men had unruly beards. A kind of Woodstock in Stoke Newington. A young couple with fierce eyeliner, leather jackets and ripped jeans stared intently at a tall house of playing cards. Punk defiance radiating among a swamp of hippies.

'Can you fix our plumbing?' asked a small girl at my side. 'I want to have a bath tonight.'

The cast iron bath stood in the centre of the sitting room next door, except there was no wall remaining between the two rooms, so it was one large, dilapidated space within which life carried on. I looked at the plumbing.

'I don't think so,' I said. 'I can solder pipes, though.'

She smiled, not at all disappointed. She cocked her head. 'How old are you?'

'Twenty-six. How old are you?'

'Seven.' She ran her fingers along the graceful curves of the bath and looked over her shoulder.

'Where you from, Jack?'

'The Midlands.'

'Like Nottingham?'

'Near there.'

'My name is Rosa,' she said, and sauntered off.

Nobody else asked who I was, but Birgit leant over with a shower of curls that she held over her shoulder.

'Jack. Can you mix us a dressing for the salad? I started it when you two rang the bell, so all the makings are there.'

'You mean, like a salad cream?'

'Here, come with me,' said a man wearing nothing *but* dungarees. 'Are you the new guy?'

I guessed he was Australian.

'No. I came with my friend Rick.'

'Yeah. Rick said he had a new bloke for this place. This is the interview, mate. Made a salad dressing before?'

'No. What do you mean? What are you talking about?'

'S'alright. It's not part of the interview. Watch me. Me name's Pat.'

'Thanks, Pat. What interview? I'm not here for a room, if that's what you're saying.'

'No problem.'

I watched him crush garlic under his palm, pour oil, throw leaves, salt, and pepper into a thick glass, squeeze a lemon, and thrash the whole thing about with a fork.

'There you go,' he said, handing me the tumbler. I took it to the table where Birgit beamed.

'Thank you, Jack.'

I'd been smoking a fragrant roll-up Pat had asked me to hold while he spun the fork through the salad dressing. It must have been strong grass. The making of the dressing had become extraordinarily glorious and Birgit appeared to be so much more beautiful than I remembered from only minutes ago. Looking around the rooms I was struck by the companionship, the joy, the happiness of it all and I felt a broad grin escape across my face.

'The dressing, it wasn't me. It was Pat.'

'I know, Jack. But do you know how to make salad dressing?' asked Birgit.

'I do now.'

'Then all is good. Eat up.'

I ate, helped to wash up, walked around the bath, considering with ignorance the plumbing implications, and danced with everybody to the sound of Jefferson Airplane. Things just happened.

'You're in, mate,' said Pat.

I watched a child knock a bottle from a corner of the table, but a man passing by casually caught it. As the pyramid of cards collapsed, a flashbulb popped, the light ricocheting around the room. I must be stoned, I thought.

'Is there a phone I can use?' I asked Birgit.

'Sure. It's in the conservatory, over there. Watch out, Jack. We think the pigs are listening.'

She saw my expression. I was thinking, that only happened in films. We call the police *the filth*.

'The police, Jack. Be careful.'

'I will,' I said.

I had nothing to be careful about and punched in my mum's number.

'Mam,' I said, when I got through.

She knew it was me, but still said carefully: 'Sellerby, five, one, two.'

'It's me, Mam. I'm okay. How are you?'

We talked for half an hour, for the first time in months, but at last I realised my filter was off. The one that stopped me from telling Mam anything important. What had I said? I had to ring off. I don't know whether sadness or the dope took hold. Unable to think, I lay back in a giant chair in the darkness of the glass lean-to and watched aircraft lights pierce the night sky until I felt a tugging on my sleeve. It was Rosa, the girl who had asked me about plumbing the bath.

'I've got to go to bed, Jack. Goodnight.'

'Goodnight, Rosa. It was great to meet you.'

'I think you're a good person, Jack. I'm sorry I made you look at the bath.'

'It's a good-looking bath.'

'Yes, but the pipes all work, too. If you want a bath in the morning, there's plenty of hot water. Rick put a new boiler in.'

'And it's all connected up?'

'Of course. Don't be silly.'

'But Rosa. There's no walls anywhere. It's in the middle of the living room.'

'That's all right. Nobody minds. You can always put a screen round you.'

'Thank you, Rosa.'

'Goodnight.'

I could hear her doing the rounds, chatting with everyone before she went upstairs. My eyes felt heavy in their sockets.

Birgit came by and stood next to me as the house quietened and seemed to settle. I looked up as she held out a thick blanket.

'Best stay over,' she said. 'You look exhausted.'

'I've never slept on a chaise-longue.'

'Lots of people have slept on this one. It's more comfortable than my bed.'

She laughed so easily.

'Pat said I'd passed the interview. What for? I've got a flat. I don't need a room thanks and,' I paused, thinking with excitement, 'I've got my job back again.'

She smiled.

'Ah. Rick's not told you? There *are* rooms from time to time. Just depends. We're all just friends. Some of us live here. Rosa and me and others. Some just come round to eat. Everybody helps out.'

'Birgit. What is this place?'

She chuckled with a little embarrassment, glancing over her shoulder.

'We don't have a name for it. Not a proper one. Rick calls it *The Wrong Horse Club* because we're all sorts here. It's a kind of drop-in place for square pegs, and it works for us.'

'A sort of commune? Is it a squat?' I said.

'We're just friends, Jack. It is a house of friendship. The important things for us are kindness, music and food. We like having lots of people around. Just sharing things, you know? You get invited. And if you like it, you can come by any time.'

'Why an interview?'

'It's no big deal. We just like to see what people are like. We take it in turns to check out guests, and to say yes or no.'

'Oh. Interesting. Who was it deciding my case?'

She looked at me and her full lips spread into an enormous grin.

'You didn't guess? It was Rosa, my daughter. She has a fine eye for character.'

'Rosa? But what if she's wrong about me? Supposing she's backed the wrong horse?'

Birgit pulled a face.

'Then Rosa will have to ask you to leave. For a joke like that, maybe.'

The house might have been slumbering, but the flashing lights of aircraft still swept over, and the traffic noise never quietened. I fell asleep for the first time there, in a rambling, book-filled place that felt like home, surfacing once or twice as the last people left, shouting their goodbyes, being hushed for the late hour, for Rosa being asleep and for 'Jack, over there.'

'Goodnight, Jack Over There,' whispered someone. It was the last thing I can recall before I awoke in the early hours, something warm and soft alongside me and the scent of frangipani.

* * *

I must have been out for the count. Shielded from the early morning sunshine by my solitary blanket. How Maddy stole in and tucked herself alongside without waking me, I'll never know. There she was, her head in the crook of her arm, breathing softly. Sound asleep despite the thumping beat of my heart. I wanted to hold her, but not wake her, so instead just kissed her forehead. Her lips began to move, silently framing words, her face tensing in the middle of some mystery conversation until, at once, she awoke. In that instant she looked puzzled, then a smile spread across her face.

'It's you,' I said, still surprised.

'It's me,' she agreed and put a hand to my cheek. 'I've missed you.'

'You were talking in your sleep.'

'Oh. I don't want to think about it. Stupid stuff.'

'They say you dream it to get rid of it.'

'I'm sorry. Sorry to turn up like this. Sorry for everything,' she said.

'I don't know how you slept there, perched on the edge.'

'You get used to it. Did I tell you I climb? Always have. You get used to sleeping in the strangest of places. On ledges halfway up a cliff.'

'Aren't you terrified? Of falling off, I mean.'

She sat up. A hand on my shoulder.

'We clip on. A harness, a rope. I didn't need to last night, though.'

'Finding you here. Finding you asleep with me. It was like that hidden room we found. It'll all be gone now. Heaps of rubble. I wanted to take something. Anything, to remember it all.'

I tried to hold the memory of that night in my mind. 'It's great to see you.'

Maddy stood, wearing black jeans and a green vest.

'I need to wash before everyone comes down,' she said.

'You've been here before?'

'Loads,' she said, looking around the shelves near the bath and finding a beach-towel draped over a basket. She turned the taps, and after a sharp kick to the pipes, water finally arrived.

'I love it here,' she continued, pulling off her clothes, at ease with her nakedness, stepping into the tub cautiously, then pulling up the shower head to wet her tangled hair.

'There's a big Chinese screen over there,' I said, pointing. 'I can put it round you if you want.'

She was soaping herself, shuddering a little, for the water was obviously cold. No steam, and lots of goosebumps. Shook her head.

'I'll be out soon enough. No one will be down for a while.' Stepping out, she patted herself dry, her eyes glistening. She put her arms around me.

'I'll make you all damp.'

'I don't mind.'

I closed my eyes to the smell of wet hair, the lemon soap, and her own scent. I could find Maddy blindfolded.

'Why are you here?' I said. 'Was it an accident, or did you know I was here?'

'Birgit called me. She told me you were here. That Rick brought you.'

'He did, but he was a bit mysterious about it all. In fact, I'm still a bit puzzled about what this place is all about. It's a bit of a mess, isn't it?'

She looked around.

'I guess so, but it'll soon get sorted. It always is.'

'By who? Birgit?'

'By everyone. There's always someone coming through who has some skills. You don't need much experience to carry sacks of cement around. It started out as a massive squat years ago. Then it became legal with the GLC amnesty for squatters last year. Birgit and four others have a secure tenancy now.'

'So, you came to see me.'

'I had to see you,' she said, buckling up her jeans. Her green top was damp, and clinging to her. She pulled a heavy old sweater over her head, pausing for a moment with just her eyes peeping over the ribbed neck.

'I feel so awful about that note I left. Just going off like that. I'm still not sure why I did. But Tim has been wonderful. He says all the right things. He does all the right things. He's forgiven me.'

She searched my eyes. A hard little laugh. 'Forgiven me.'

'Well,' I said. 'I guess that's a good thing?'

'Yes. A good thing, I suppose. But you see, he *is* wonderful. I know that. I've been with him for years and we have been happy. It's just that...'

'Tell me.'

'It's how you make me feel. I can't let that go.'

I knew that everything Maddy was saying was true. True for her now, but at once, also a kind of lie. She must have an idea about Tim's sexuality. Surely? And she was here because she was sorry for that letter? I still had no idea where I stood. Or what I felt now. Had she slept with Tim? I felt submerged and needed to surface.

There were footfalls on the wooden stairs. Rosa, followed by Birgit and others, chattering, carrying towels. Birgit hugging Maddy, looking at me as she did so.

'Hello, Jack-Over-There.'

'Thank you for last night. I think I need to skip breakfast. I have things to do.'

I did. I had lots to do.

'Please stay,' said Maddy. A questioning look. Birgit just shrugged her shoulders.

'Let me get you a sandwich,' Birgit said amid the rising clamour in the kitchen with pans crashing on the stove and Rosa, on tiptoe, pulling out plates and bowls.

'I'll just use the phone,' I said. 'I'll leave some money.'

'Ten pence in the tin,' said Birgit. Maddy was already at the table, slicing bread for toast.

It took a long time for the phone at Cossington Street to be answered. Rose had just got in. I left a message for her to tell Kate to meet me at the Dolomites Café at lunchtime. With luck I might catch Gregory too. I put a hand on Maddy's shoulder and said how good it was to meet again, hugged Birgit because I wanted to and because I'd never slept so well. It was a mistake to pick Rosa up. She let out a mock scream.

'Everybody does it!' she complained but wriggled with giggles and fruitless attempts to wipe peanut butter from her mouth. The smell of toast was enough to delay me.

'Bye, Jack,' she called as I left. I'll be back, I thought.

* * *

I liked the Wrong Horse. I liked it a lot. For now, I had other things on my mind. Already the pavement was warm. I could feel the heat radiating from the walls I passed. People stood back from the bus stops, gathering in the shadows of awnings.

At my flat I put the kettle on.

Shit. The sink was full of dirty crockery, empty bottles jostling for space in the corner. A teabag had missed the bin and split open on the floor, dried out but easy to clear up. Was there bread? In the fridge? The cooler the temperature, the less reactions going off. Oh, the cheese had hair. Blue hair. It *was* Stilton, and maybe if I cut it all off? Then, there, in the little freezer coil at the top, enough space for frozen peas; half a loaf. Half a sliced granary lump of bread. Two slices in the toaster, two spoons of Gold Blend in the cup with freshly boiled water, and all was well.

In half an hour I had the place looking tidy and clean. Except that huge wall I'd painted a florid purple. A red and brown purple. Reminded me of a cow's backside. I needed to paint that over. Not now, but this weekend.

Then the phone rang. It was such an old-fashioned ring it had. Another promise to myself. Get onto the GPO and order a Trimphone. That's what they had at the Wrong Horse. It had a great sound. Like crickets in the deep south.

It was Kate.

'You want to meet?' she said. 'At the Dolomites?'

'Can we? At one o'clock?'

'Where *were* you last night? Rick came in at midnight.'

'The Wrong Horse.'

'Was he with Birgit?' she said without a trace of worry.

'I don't think so.'

'I've never been. Someone said it's a knocking shop.'

'Kate. I need to see you. Will you be at the Dolomites?'

'What's it about?'

'Rick said you'd been working on it. Special Schools.'

'That's right. Education are marking black kids down as subnormal and bussing them off miles away. Parents say they've been conned.'

'That's why I want to see you. For Frankie. Frankie and his mum.'

'Was that the boy you hit, Jack?'

'Listen, Kate. I didn't hit him. I did call him names. You know that. Come on. I promised his mum I'd look into it.'

'I'll see you there.'

Next, I needed to fix Nigel. My need to put him up against the wall again had lifted. For his loathsome attitude and what sounded like serious crimes, I wanted him banged up. In Pentonville, where I could visit him.

I still had an hour or two. Time to get to the launderette and make some plans while my washing swam round. The bin bag filled up quickly, and I was heading for the door when the phone rang again.

It was Birgit.

'How did you get my number?'

'I've got Maddy with me. She's been upset since you left. She wants to talk to you. Can you come round?'

I had to think about it for a while.

'I've got your number there, Birgit. I'll ring later. If Maddy's not there, I'll ring her at home. I'm busy right now.'

25
Subnormal

Keerat's launderette, when all the drums were rumbling, felt like a stainless-steel subterranean train. Waiting for a washing machine to become free, I stared at my black bag of clothes. The same kind of bin bag that kids in care like Gregory filled with all he had when I moved him to his first flat. I thought of how he complained about everything in his life being *functional*. No suitcases for the likes of them. Gregory once announced to me 'we are the bin-bag-boys'.

I didn't ring Maddy. I needed to get my head straight first. There was something about that night at the Wrong Horse that had shifted my orbit. I felt unsettled and more. Something nameless. A fleeting sense of joy?

I stretched out my arms wide, grabbed tumble dryer handles, feeling my muscles tense, and swayed a little as if on the midnight train home.

* * *

I dropped my stuff at home, drove south under a railway bridge painted with the slogan *G.Davis is innocent OK* and marched up Church Market. I was early and at last I felt comfortable here. What was it Rick had said at the Greek restaurant when I arrived here? Think of it as your manor. Make the place personal. Listen to people. Hold the gaze. Give something if you can, never ask for favours and always ask permission not forgiveness.

I remember asking Maddy what Rick was going on about, and she just said, 'Think of the opposites. Think of all those shifty-eyed blokes on the make. Just don't be like them.'

At last, others knew I hadn't failed Theo. I could laugh about Linda too, up in that room round the corner. A slight breeze fluttered the pennants strung along the stalls. Ten minutes to spare and time for a feast for the brain at Dimos's.

More than a corner-shop, Dimos's was a *librairie* of all things writing and reading from exercise books with graph paper, to water-damaged copies of *Love On The Dole*, that socialist, sexy book of the 1940s. Behind the counter he still had copies of *The Pearl*, a Victorian pornographic romp, with stickers suggesting that, at *Five Shillings*, it might be *returned if in clean condition, for Two and Six.*

The ranks of magazines filled me with a child's excitement. Glossy and pulp. He stocked hundreds, perhaps a thousand titles, along each side of the shop and in the entrance on towering carousels. More than a museum or library, here was unlimited learning and pleasure, from the keeping of tropical fish to adventures in the Atlas Mountains.

I think Dimos oiled the mechanisms, as the stands span round under my fingertips in a blur of colour, images and beautiful fonts. I flicked from the *Engineering Feats of Ancient Persia*, past the *Time* cover of *Charles, The Man Who Will Be King*, and spotted Jimmy Carter, the President, staring out from *The American.* He looked anxious. Everything on earth and beyond was within my grasp. A swipe of the hand and the spinning distractions settled on *Omni* with views of red planets, science news, science-fiction and stories from the likes of Joyce Carol Oates. What was not to like? I grabbed the last copy and paid Dimos, holding the slippery cover to my nose to catch that sharp nip of ink.

Who needs books? I just wanted facts. Information. Dimos catered for the likes of me who never went to university. Ex-prisoners and prisoners of dead-end jobs. We're always looking for knowledge. In the end, we want to know how to do the right thing. With *Omni* tucked under my arm, I would know more stuff.

* * *

The Dolomites Café hadn't changed much. It seemed a long time since I was last there, drowsy and tired of everything. A giant photograph had been wallpapered over the far wall. A milk-maid's meadow overshadowed by snow-capped peaks.

The place was packed. Ilaria flicked and snapped the giant Gaggia machine as Gregory threaded his way past tables and cubicles cluttered with extra chairs. He beckoned me over. I couldn't see Kate in the throng.

Gregory and I stood at the centre of the crowd, two still figures in a pond threshing with life. Even there I caught his scent of starch and a trace of cologne. Gregory had changed. He was pin-sharp. I blurted it out, with a grin.

'You look good, Greg. You smell great.'

He took a step back and let slip a little chuckle. Put his head to one side.

'"*Signor Vivara*" by Pucci,' he said. 'Ilaria gave it to me. We's a thing, you know, me and her.'

He looked back at her and she saw his gaze, as lovers do. Connected, even in this maelstrom of shouts, waving arms and the clatter of china.

'Where's Kate?'

Gregory set down a tray with coffees and cake about which an elderly couple had been frantically signalling. He soothed their irritations with grace and kind smiles.

'I'm sorry, so sorry. This is my old friend, Mr Jack. He's very important to me,' and looking round, he nodded towards the corner. A small table squeezed behind a plywood screen. A woman with a woolly hat and cropped hair sat hunched in the corner.

'No,' I said. 'That's not Kate. You know Kate?'

He must, I thought. Everyone knew Kate. Tall, an explosion of blond hair, arched brows and pearlescent lips.

'That's Kate,' he said. And he was right. She gave me a half smile. The slightest recognition. Her face had no trace of makeup. A cardigan buttoned to the neck.

'Kate,' I said, sliding in alongside her. 'You're incognito!'

'Fuck off, Jack,' she hissed. 'It's all about appearances to you, isn't it? I wouldn't talk to you normally. Not anymore. '

'Why not?'

'Because you are a man. You're the enemy, Jack. This last week, with everything that's happened. The way you treated Maddy. The way Rick treats me. It's over. I've had enough. Women are rising up. I won't be a collaborator anymore. Last night we marched to reclaim the night from men like you.'

'A collaborator?'

She ignored my question and continued. 'You do realise there's a rapist out there, a killer, the Yorkshire Ripper, they call him. And because of that, they want to keep us all inside. A curfew on women. Why? Why not a curfew on men?'

I just about gathered it was a rhetorical question. Gregory set down a big, fat black coffee in front of me. No amount of scrubbing could remove Kate's cornflower-blue eyes, or that groove in her top lip. Her hair, awkwardly hacked off, just added to an unexpected desire I began to feel.

'I haven't got the time to fuck men anymore,' she went on. 'It's all about control. Keeps us where we are. A class all of our own at the bottom of the heap.'

'So you don't like screwing anymore?'

'I'm a lesbian,' said Kate, exasperated. 'I am a political lesbian, and I'm taking control of my life.'

And that seemed it. The end of that conversation. Her look said it all, as well as the tin badges pinned to her hat, but I had to ask.

'What about Rick?' Their relationship had always seemed *casual*.

'I'm here to talk about your Frankie,' she said, so I waved to Gregory, indicating another coffee was needed.

* * *

The cafe had filled at lunchtime but by two o'clock the tide receded, so we moved to a larger table where Kate could spread out her papers. She took off her hat and macintosh, her short hair spiky and her face different. She was herself, whatever that was. Sensual in a way I hadn't known Kate before. She saw through me, understood and sighed.

'That thing that happened to Frankie,' she began. 'It's been going on for years. For a decade. In Birmingham they're bussing black kids around from school to school to keep the numbers in any one school down to thirty per cent. Here in London, they're completely obsessed with intelligence tests. White parents are complaining black kids are keeping their children back. The test results appear to support that, but they are rubbish. There's no accounting for culture and language, different names for things, and when you do take account of those factors...'

Kate stabbed a set of papers with her flat-trimmed nails. The pink varnish had gone.

'...then there's no difference at all. White kids and black kids have the same abilities.'

'But they are still sent to special schools?'

'It's systematic racism. Black kids are called names. They say they are slow, dull and backward and give them no help. And when the children are frustrated and bored and angry, they are carted off to these special schools. '

'So that's what happened to Frankie?'

'More or less. I spoke to Pat, the headmistress at his old primary school. She said he was a bright child and not at all challenging. But she did think he had some issues with reading and writing. A sort of word blindness.'

'Dyslexia?'

'That's it. So there's a couple of things we could do. The first is to get Frankie to another psychologist in Education.'

'I thought that was part of the problem.'

'It is, but not Waveney Bushell. She's a black psychologist and understands what's going on.'

'And Frankie's dyslexia?'

'We need to get him assessed, and there's a new clinic at Barts Hospital. We could refer him there.'

'Kate. You're fantastic. You've done so much.'

I put my hand on her forearm. The sleeve of her cardigan. She flinched and looked irritated. I wanted to hug her.

'I'll go and see Frankie's mum,' I said.

'Don't take over. Don't do that rescuing thing. Just give Frankie's mum the information. The connections. She'll be fine. Waveney can do the referral to Barts. Here's all the information about the Caribbean Community Education Group. They're parents helping parents. What Frankie needs is to get himself to supplementary school. There's one less than a mile away. Volunteer teachers help Caribbean kids evenings and weekends. They learn about their own history, too. Black history.'

'Kate, this is brilliant. How did you put it all together?'

She was tapping her forehead and halfway through saying 'not just a pretty...' when she caught herself, pursed her soft lips and went on. 'It wasn't hard to find. There's a book about it, and it's a bloody scandal. The point is, we didn't know about it. Do you know why? Why do you think? '

I hadn't seen Kate like this before. Her eyes were alight. Anyone could see she was on fire. A group of schoolgirls skipping afternoon school were open-mouthed. I guess it was embarrassing, but I didn't think so.

'Our whole team is white. All of us. Even our volunteers are white. We're not interested, we don't listen and there's no-one among us to tell us. That's why I've got to change. Why I have changed. Collaboration is not just about fucking men, it's about thinking and behaving like them. Selfish fucking arseholes.'

Kate's voice had been rising and having made her point, she stood up abruptly, pushed all the papers over to me, grabbed her coat and strode out the door.

Gregory ambled over and started clearing the table.

'I like Kate,' he said. 'But she do have a cowboy mouth.'

'Sorry?'

'She loud. Is Kate okay?'

'Just upset, I think, Gregory. Thanks. She'll be fine.'

He gave me a look. A look that suggested he thought otherwise.

'I catch you later,' he said and went into the kitchen at the back.

* * *

I went straight back to Dimos's.

'There's a book,' I said. 'It's about black kids in special schools. Have you got a copy?'

Dimos turned round and surveyed his stock in the shadows. He held himself upright with one hand on the counter and a stick in his other, knuckle-white fist.

Mike had told me that Dimos had escaped torture by troops of the fascist general's government in Greece, landed in England and taken over the shop in 1970. A good, old-fashioned communist.

He leaned awkwardly around a pile of newspaper and placed a book on the counter.

How The West Indian Child Is Made Educationally Subnormal

'Bernard,' said Dimos, 'left me a pile here to sell. I had one in the window but it went yellow. I cannot abide that. He wrote this book, and he made me pay for all of them, too. I usually get my books on account.'

There was a beautiful line drawing on the cover.

'I'll take two,' I said, to grunts from Dimos as he reached for another copy.

'One for you?' he said.

'The other's for…'

'A mother?'

'Yes.'

'Then take it,' he said. 'I just charge you for the one, eh?'

I waited while he carefully wrapped each book in brown paper, and then leaned forward.

'The fathers,' he said. 'Many don't want to understand. So you tell the mother, yes? If the child needs any books, any exercise books, pens, whatever. You tell her to come to me. No charge, all right?'

I nodded. I muttered my thanks and turned quickly towards the door. I had to, for tears were streaming down my cheeks. Dimos was kind to Frankie without even knowing him, and I knew Frankie but had called him all the worst names possible. It was something I would never forget in my whole life.

* * *

I stopped by at Frankie's and sat outside admiring the design of their flat. Tim was right. The council architects had learned from the sixties rush to throw up tower blocks. Taken breath when the slums had been cleared. Listened to the tenants. This was a low-rise arrangement of solid buildings with walkways, trees and awkward angles here and there. Windows and doors were set well into the structure to avoid the rain and frost, to keep maintenance costs down.

I met Frankie's mum as I came up to her door. I could barely see her for the mountain of laundry she was carrying. Frankie must have been watching and opened the door.

'I just been to see my friend Grace,' she said over her shoulder. 'She not listening to me. She do all her cooking and her washing in big pans on the stove and she ask me why she got the damp and the mould. It the condensation, but she won't listen to me.'

'So you're doing her washing?'

'I got a washing machine and we have a bet that if she cook for a week in the oven and I do her washing, the damp go away. Frankie going round tonight with the bleach to get the stains off the ceiling.'

Frankie shot me a grin. I put a hand on his shoulder. Should I have done that? It felt right.

'Mix it with water, Frankie,' I said, 'and please watch out for your eyes.'

I explained to both of them everything that Kate had shown me, gave them Bernard Coard's book and explained how it was a present from Dimos.

'I know him,' she said, pointing at the book. 'Bernard from Victoria in Grenada, like me, but I did not know he write a book. Here, now. Frankie want to show you something.'

He did have something to share, drawing me to a table at the back. It was magnificent.

'Is it a motorcycle, Frankie?'

A model of a futuristic vehicle covered most of the table. Frankie showed me how two out-rigged wheels extended out by cantilevers. The front was long and slim with a single small wheel at the front. Frankie was excitedly explaining.

'It's an electric town car,' he began, 'with a battery here, behind the driver, one in each of the outside wheels for stability and one here right at the front. The front wheel is for steering and has no power, but it's fitted with a dynamo, so it helps to charge the batteries.'

'That really is amazing, Frankie. But what's incredible is the detail. How on earth did you make it look so perfect?'

He took my sleeve and pulled me up half a dozen steps and into his bedroom. It was crammed with models and kits. Aeroplanes hanging from the ceiling, destroyers and racing cars.

'I got the idea from the *Star Wars* film,' he explained. 'All them spacecraft in the film, the fighters? They made from bits from these kits, just like my city car.'

I was uncertain as to how best to celebrate Frankie's impressive imagination, so I awkwardly shook his hand, and after finalising plans with his mum, he showed me to the door.

'Thank you,' he said.

'No. Thank you,' I said. It was all so stupidly normal.

* * *

I dropped by The Wrong Horse on the way home. I wanted to see Birgit and Rosa. Because. Just because.

On the walls at the end of the road were more slogans. In white, was scrawled *REDS GO HOME, NF,* and opposite, *NF OUT,* daubed in red paint. A black van wobbled round the corner at the other end of the road, followed by a white saloon car. Maddy was in the doorway, clinging to the door. She saw me on the pavement and wailed.

'There was no-one else in. Just me and Birgit. The police have taken Rosa.'

'They can't.'

'They did. Birgit's gone with her but they will send her home. They know she's not Rosa's mum.'

'Did they have an order?'

'I checked it,' said Maddy through a tangle of wet hair and tears. 'A Place of Safety Order, signed by Kingsley, the Magistrate.'

'But someone must have applied. Who asked the Magistrate for the order? Why?'

'It was Nigel,' she screamed with both her hands in tight fists. 'Fucking Nigel came with the cops.'

'I don't understand. Why? I saw Rosa. She was fine.'

'They found some drugs. Some dope. That will go down well with the court. But the main reason is that they will say she's been abandoned here by her mum.'

'What do you mean? Who is Rosa's mum?'

Maddy had slumped down to the doorstep now. Her head in her hands.

'Rosa is Annika Petersen's daughter.'

'I know the name, from somewhere.'

'Baader Meinhof gang. The Red Army Faction. She's been on the run for years. Lives round Vicky Park.'

'A terrorist?'

'Not anymore. She's a welder. Goes by the name Anna Parkinson.'

'And now Nigel's got her daughter.'

Maddy could only nod. It seemed obvious that I should get down, kneel with her and put my arms about her, but I didn't. I pushed past her to view the carnage caused by the police search. We had to get Rosa home where she was safe.

26

The annexe

I pushed through the splintered front door, crunching broken glass. There was a thick dust cloud, still swirling and hiding the furthest end of the room. Everything was tossed or turned over. A nine-foot length of timber by the Georgian door had smashed through the pink glass of the fanlight. What kind of a search was this? They must have enjoyed their work.

There was a heavy, dry smell, like a presence in the room. It choked me as it hit my throat.

As my eyes began to open up the shadows, I saw a venerable armchair had been stabbed, its white guts squirming out in rolls. The bath was on its side, a little water licking the floor. Thankfully someone had turned off the main.

In the kitchen, among jumbled pans and plates, was the Coronation mug I knew had contained their dope. It was stained with the black dust used to reveal fingerprints. The police did not have to look far. There was a lingering pressure like the lost echo of a bomb. Then I heard footsteps in the debris, and suddenly she was there.

'You didn't ring me!'

I froze. Maddy came at me like a tornado, punching and pulling at me. My mouth fell open.

'I, I...I can't.'

'Why? Why not?'

I knew at that moment that something had changed, but I couldn't say it. I didn't even know.

'You love me!' Her eyes searched mine.

I knew I did, perhaps I always would, but it was different. I felt like someone else.

'How can you? I need you.'

'You don't need me. I'm what you want. What you need is Tim. It's Tim you love.'

'Jack! Come back!'

I had to say it, 'No, I can't do this. On, off. Up, down. Never for me.'

She stayed silent.

'Anyway, you know he's gay.' I had said it and I could not stop, 'Tim and Matt are lovers. You know they are…'

Her face shrunk and she looked away. I couldn't stop.

'You are going to marry him, aren't you?'

She looked up at me as if I knew everything she needed to know. There was a long silence. Her voice was weak. 'He's not gay, he's bi.'

'But you know something else, don't you?'

She staggered back a little. 'No I don't. What else?''

'None of this matters. Tim wants children.' I should have stopped there, but I went on, wishing I hadn't, 'And anyway, you should know…'

She turned back on me fiercely. 'What? Know what?'

'I think it's your money he wants.'

Her eyes opened wide, blazing, 'You are so wrong!'

I tried to hold her gaze.

'At thirty there'll be a fund settled on him. £350,000.'

'What?'

'Then when his mother dies, he'll inherit even more.'

'So he's playing poor?'

'He really is poor at the moment.'

'Who cares? You're made.' I could not stop myself smiling. 'You'll be the happy family, married with kids, nice house. You'll be rich.'

She was crying now, murmuring, 'So you were never mine?'

I was shaking my head. 'I warned you, I won't be anybody's bit on the side.'

I knew what I had done, and I tried to hug her, but she was stiff and cold. She moved away, then crept back to me, and I began to say quietly I was sorry, but there was a noise in the big room. Footsteps were crunching across the floor.

'Maddy!' It was Birgit, released by the police because she knew nothing.

* * *

We were sitting in a row on the chaise longue, Maddy, Birgit and me. Planes wound slowly over the skylight. This was the bed we had slept in, and I could still smell Frangipani. Maddy was there but I was sitting next to Birgit, and did not want to move. It felt nice. Tim and love were deferred. It was about Rosa now, where she might be and how to get her back. Nigel must be in with the police. The dusty trimphone was on the floor, its receiver in Maddy's hand.

'How could I know that, Nina? Police just took her...'

I kept quiet, left it to Maddy.

'No, it was a friend who looks after Rosa, and no, her mother Annike dumped her two years ago, couldn't cope... So now you know it all, Nina.'

Birgit looked at me. We should get going.

'... No, it's a *Place of Safety* order. Hostel somewhere, the police will know but who have we got in there? ... Oh Mike! Of course. Well then, Nina, we're coming over.'

On the way up Church Street Market, wading with Maddy through drifts of rubbish at the end of a market day, everything had changed. How I had longed to be alone with her, and now I was, with a mile between us. I went first up the stairs and heard her feet behind me, as if in an endless dream, walking and walking, never getting closer. What was I doing, going mad? On the second flight Mike and Rick were coming down with Moira, who as the clerk had found Nigel's address. We had to reverse and stumble down again, sounding like a herd in the Serengeti. 'Where to now?' Well, it was obvious. Nigel's.

We were all in the old green Commer van, all we had at Cossington Street, and so noisy we could not hear each other. Backs against the sides, we were like a bunch of drunks on the way to the nick. Mike was driving, he knew his way to Hackney. Nigel's flat was ground floor, with no lights on.

'Gas?' Rick asked.

I sniffed, 'As usual.'

We had all done this before, saying we smelled gas as a cover for unlawful entry, then Mike did an expert cutting of the front door glass, a neat circle near the lock.

'Where d'you learn that?' I asked, but I needn't. Coppers make good burglars.

There was a strange atmosphere inside, dark and dirty, smell of rotting vegetables, nobody could have been there for some time. Dead flies under the windows. It looked as if he had been moving. There was something sad about a few scattered clothes and a ravaged drum kit with two broken skins and no side drum. An *NF* poster was starting to curl from the wall, with another of Phuket already on the floor.

Mike remembered something in the office long ago. 'Nigel made odd phone calls when he thought he was alone in the office, "No, two of them, girls, eleven and thirteen. Nice clean girls. Came from the police." He clammed up when I came into the room.'

There was an envelope with the receipt for an air ticket to Bangkok. 'It's tomorrow,' said Mike. Rosa must be his last deal, and she'd be going with him. She must be with him now, in whatever children's home had accepted them. Who knew the children's homes? Only Gregory. He'd grown up in one. We were back in the Commer.

It was a soft evening, and coming around the back of Gregory's we smelled weed. He looked as clean and smart as ever, he and Ilaria smiling profusely as he replied, 'In a safe house? Yeah, I do know a hostel, massive place. Some kids go in there and don't come out.' Smiling with Ilaria, Gregory made no more sense but for one thing.

'The place you want is Dougie's.'

* * *

Rick drove this time, avoiding dumped cars under a bridge and firemen putting out a rubbish fire filling the street with acrid smoke, and Mike produced an impressive radiophone, which he plugged into the cigar-lighter. 'Police issue,' he whispered.

Rick slowed the van and Maddy said, 'Wait a moment, Mike! Is this a police raid?' and as the van stopped everyone was ready to get out.

'What's going on?' said Rick.

Mike was laughing. 'Got you there, kiddos. We'd never find it without this.' From then on he was constantly calling and getting almost unintelligible replies. We knew we'd arrived when we passed two parked police vans. We crept by slowly, looking up at the four-floored corner building, with an imposing porch near the corner, its elegant Corinthian cornice now cemented over, and an entrance down into the basement area on the long side. At the far end three topstorey windows were blind and the brickwork blackened by a fire. A sharp black and gold tower block thrust up over the roof, cutting the skyline, with windows glowing in the evening light. Another the same appeared further back. The rounded street corner and the wall under the roof showed faded names of a builder's merchant and a hairdresser. The house must have been nearly a hundred yards long.

There was no response at the grand entrance, and we could see that it had not been opened in years. Maddy had already started the few yards towards worn steps to the basement when a bald head appeared, and Maddy shouted, 'Mr McDougal?'

'Aye, who wants him?'

But he had retreated before she could reply. We started down the dished and cracked stone stairs into a dustbin area below. A thin rat hurried past us on the way out. Inside there were several long bare tables with benches and a huge gas stove among stainless steel kitchen tables. A dim fluorescent light glowed above enamel shades over the tables, all switched off. We could hardly see the far end of the darkened room as we heard hollow footsteps approaching, 'Ye'll be the Welfare, no doubt. I dinnae ken why ye's here, 'cos the police've been here an hour now.'

'It's a lost child.' Maddy had taken control.

'Oh aye, and d'ye ken this building's full o' lost children?'

'It's one named Rosa...' but he had turned his back on us and was on his way up a wide staircase at the back. We turned and followed.

We emerged into a vast hall, the ceiling twenty feet up in darkness, and a few small lights at a mahogany reception desk. McDougal was already turning over the stiff pages of a large register. 'Rosa...would that be Rosemary?' I could see on Maddy's face that she knew this would be a long haul, and we had little time. A desultory man with an arched back droned back and forth with a Hoover, making it hard to hear anything.

At that moment a heavy rumble on the stairs announced six coppers, followed by their superintendent, telling the last one, 'NFPA. We'll be going back.' I could hear the squawk and crackle of radio-phones surrounding them. Mike stepped aside from the noise with the senior policeman, who nodded and shook his head indulgently as Mike tried to negotiate. The interview ended with Mike frowning and the super shaking his head with a broad smile as they came back to us.

'Don't know him. There's nobody from Acton police here. D'you mean Ashford?'

Mike mumbled, 'So who are you then?'

'Superintendent Dent, Kent Police,' he grunted. 'Maybe you thought we were from the Met. We've been drafted in for the demo tomorrow, and we were twiddling our thumbs. Commissioner is a college friend of mine and I said I'd come and help if it's a child abduction.'

Rick looked confused, but Maddy rose to the challenge. 'So can you help?'

'We've done our searches, been all over. Five dormitories full of sleeping children. This place is enormous. We've found nothing so we'll be on our way. My boys need some sleep before six AM tomorrow.'

That was it. They had searched but had not found. Maddy turned away with Mike, 'What time is the flight tomorrow?'

'Ten twenty but Nigel would have to be there with her by eight.' Maddy and I looked at each other, then Maddy sidled away with Superintendent Dent to discuss nothing, playing for a bit of time.

Just then the vacuum cleaner stopped and the bent man started winding in the cable, but the silence showed up something else. I could hear distant coughing, and I searched the vast room. It was a child's cough. There was only one possible place. 'Mr McDougal?'

'Aye, can I help?'

'What's that door over there—the thin one?'

The bent man had just opened it and was laboriously lugging the Hoover up a long flight of stairs. Douggie turned to me. 'You'll no be wantin' to go up there.'

'I heard a child.'

'Mebbe you did 'cos that's also the quarantine. But it's where Archie keeps his cleaning stuff. There's a thousand loo rolls up there. Follow Archie if you have to. Mind the stair, 'tis steep.'

I was up the precipitous stairs following Archie, and he cursed as the Hoover crashed against every step. On the top landing he kicked the machine into a corner, and waited for me, then pushed the door ajar. 'I wouldn't go in there!'

'Just need to see. Excuse me.'

There was a column of tins of Gumption, a wall of cartons of Izal Germicide, an open carton with a jumble of boxes of Flash and Vim, some huge packets of Tide, and a clutter in the corner of brooms and mops. I looked around the door and there was a little cot with an angry looking face sitting up in bed. It was a boy, perhaps nine years old, in faded pyjamas. He glowered at me then turned away and crashed onto the squeaky bed springs, muttering, 'Just leave me alone!'

I shut the door and headed down again, but looking up on

the landing, a few feet from the dim bulb in the ceiling, there was a tall, thin window, letting in darkness from outside. I stood on a heavy box from opposite and I could see the garden, the dark jungle now far below, and out beyond that there was a long building on two floors, what must have been the original stables and rooms for the staff. No window was lit, and several had been broken. Douggie was waiting below to close the door behind me, and I asked him, 'What's that big building out there at the end?'

'You mean the annexe? There's nae thing in there. Not been used for ten year.'

'So what's it for?'

'For? It's for demolition.'

'Can we have a look?'

'If you must, but you'll no get in there. Sealed. There's a hoarding round it.'

But that was it and we conferred with Inspector Dent, who divided his small force between the garden and the street beyond the stable building, and the squawking radio phones began again. Maddy and Moira went out with three coppers and found the site entrance in Down Close, while I and the others thrust through the brambles to the end of the garden. There we split up as they were looking for a door, but I went back and soon found a sash window and to my surprise it lifted. There was a moist and warm human smell inside. I hesitated, wondering if I were breaking and entering, but I had used no force. I climbed in and immediately heard a crunch where my foot had landed in loose debris, but I edged towards a sound I could hear, and I knew it instantly. It was Rosa's voice, chattering away unstoppably, and it even covered the sound I made creeping along the corridor. The door was slightly open. I pushed it. It creaked and I froze. There he was, the old Nigel, looking gaunt and uneasy, fiddling with a camping gas stove and a tin of soup. Rosa sat beside him, apparently telling him a story. I took a breath ready to talk to him. He froze, 'Jack! Who let you in?' and Rosa shrieked. A crash opposite threw everything into chaos.

The door opposite me burst open with a splitting sound, and a trio of policemen stood gawping. Inspector Dent pushed past into the room. Then a figure broke the light from outside and stood, almost filling the empty doorway. It was Rick, huge and heavy, in baggy trousers and a seaman's cream jumper, and he stood there, great paladin of a man, gazing into the dark room.

Nigel approached Inspector Dent, who amiably took his elbow. 'I think we should be getting along now, sir.'

'No, no, no! We have a deal with you guys.'

'Not with us you don't. We are Kent Police.'

The explosive entry had shaken Nigel. 'Hang on guys... where's Nina?' He jerked away awkwardly, his back and legs still bent, he scanned the three other walls of the room, then he launched at Rick as if from a catapult. Rick did not shift an inch. Everyone else had started to move, but Nigel had a march on them, and he flung himself at Rick, who remained filling the doorway. Nigel pushed past the massive Rick, who dropped his shoulders and subsided onto the floor with a ghastly belch and gurgle. I could hear the coppers outside shouting and I knew they had caught Nigel. Rosa screamed. Another commotion turned out later to be Theo's 'uncles'. I knelt beside Rick, holding his head and shoulders, and I heard his faint voice.

'Pull it...out!' I looked down at his hands, one holding the handle of a carving knife, wobbling weakly, the other clutching a squirming gut in a swamp of gore in his white jumper. I shook my head. His eyes opened again. 'I think he wanted to get you, Jack. But he missed.' He smiled. 'Don't worry, what more can I lose?'

There was a mad torrent of movement, and both Moira and Maddy rushed into the room, Maddy scooping up the screeching Rosa in her arms. Police were everywhere, I don't know what they were doing, but I knew they would want to interview me. I asked them if they had sent for an ambulance, and Inspector Dent nodded. I was still holding Rick in my arms. Then the room went quiet as they realised what was happening, and they circled round him. His eyes flickered and wandered. He no longer knew where he was, then they came to rest on me.

'Breathe, Rick,' I said to him. His lips parted to say something, but I couldn't hear. Then his eyes closed again, and I laid him gently down. I was still looking at him when everybody else had left the room. He was breathing short and shallow breaths. Then the ambulance crew arrived.

27

Aftercare

In the gentle hug of the Wrong Horse, after weeks on the beach, I was out in London streets again. Monday was the hearing for cuts, and I needed to know what had happened. The great sighs of passing buses left my feet hard on the ground. I had not even heard from the Cossington Street team. As I approached the town hall, the murmur of crowds rose, with the hollow rattle of horses' hooves and shouts in chorus, 'Stop the cuts. Stop the cuts.' Rounding the bend I saw it all, a field of battle.

Groups with placards and banners converged. *Cut the iron lady not our jobs. Firemen going cheap. 10% more or war. Fight Welfare cuts.*

The town hall looked patiently down, high above the street, new rain shining on its marble stairs. There were several groups, one of them firemen, with a grey bunch of dustmen emerging around a corner. Some groups were all men, one all women. In another line further back, blue-uniformed men on horses from the Met stared over them, waiting for trouble.

Then the crowds coalesced, and by now I was among them. They were laughing and chatting, a party feeling, and small groups hugged and chanted. The police were kettling, and the pressure mounted, until the crowd swayed and lurched, and my feet lost hold. Among packed unsteady people I nearly went down. It felt like a heaving sea swell, and for a moment again I felt the helplessness of Theo, swept out by the sea that even a strong swimmer like him could not oppose. The crowd surged, dragging me off balance, stealing my will, until I felt the ground, like a beach, the marble steps of the town hall beneath me.

I was on my feet again, standing above them, watching

them sway. Theo was in my head, out there waving, the water swirling and pulling him away, like the crowds below me. One day, after weeks on a Spanish beach, there had been a rip tide—and that was the day I knew. I had been watching for weeks. Two lifeguards were helping someone, but they couldn't. The wave was six feet high. It crashed over them and they went under. The man they were helping had gone under too, then he came up again but I saw and I knew. Nobody could beat a wave like that. Theo was not waving. With a dry throat I shouted into the howling crowds.

I felt a firm hand on my shoulder. 'Steady, Jack,' and I spun around. I was eye to eye with Greg. Ilaria chuckled behind him.

'What's been going on?' I asked him. I felt starved of news.

'Don't ask me. It's all ending. We've got the iron lady and her stiffs now. Everybody else is out.'

'What about the Welfare, then?'

'Asking the wrong man, Jack. They're all in there,' thumbing the town hall meeting over his shoulder. 'Tina, Liza, Kate, Maddy. Tim's making a big speech. He's their best hope for your lot. I can't bear it in there, staying outdoors so I can have a smoke. Some of them already left, they say it's a foregone conclusion.'

'Are they coming out here?'

'Nah. Going to the Butcher's. Get on down there. I'll be with you in a gasp.' Ilaria giggled on. His wan dope smile was a benediction. I turned to go.

* * *

They sat around the biggest pub table. It was an important assembly; even Moira and Rose were in their places. The autumn sun crowned their hair. Kate, changed again into someone I had never known, sat in the corner with a tall, svelte woman with French flares and a beret. She still did not acknowledge me but her companion gave me a crooked smile as if she knew our past. Lefty saw me come in and reached me a glass. Bass, he knew mine. They surrounded me. 'Where've you been?' 'You got your job back?' 'Is it you and Maddy now?' 'Are you leaving the country?'

I gasped, 'Sitges ... Yes ... No ... Wait a minute.'

Nigel? McDougal? I wanted them to tell me. Gradually it came out. Inspector Dent from Kent Police had supervised charges for Nigel and the two uncles, *cruelty, child abduction, attempted murder, corruption of police*. We wouldn't see them in a while. McDougal had been suspended after the Home Office had instigated a surprise inspection by the Department of Health Social Work team. What had happened had raised a storm about child abductions with the likelihood of there being more to come out. It was being handled by a new Metropolitan Police unit for corruption, named Unit A10, but known in the force as *Rubber Heels*.

In the silence following those revelations, I looked out towards the door of the Butcher's Arms, and there, silhouetted against the dazzling sun, was a large figure in a wheelchair, hesitating before coming in. Nobody knew him but something about his body was familiar, which resolved as he glided across the floor to our table. His presence was massive. 'So I've come to the right place.'

It wasn't funny but everyone laughed because now everyone knew him. This giant-on-wheels was our own Rick, back from the dead. 'It'd take more than Nigel to kill me.'

'But you were...'

'Bit of nerve damage and some organ punctures. It'll take time, but I'm mobile. Anyone for a drink?'

Now I could complete the picture, but Rick said that nobody had seen Mike. Without a social work job he must have been re-absorbed into The Force. I hoped it was A10 Corruption Unit rather than as undercover police spy. Rick wondered if life was easier without Mike, but he was alone with that one. I said that he had answered all our questions and he always got us there. Rick smiled. 'Yes, that's what I mean.'

With another pint in my hand I started to tell Rick my story. 'Nina sent me off to sort myself out. Passed the hat around and stuffed my pockets with pesetas. "Come back when you know who you are." I told her I would go to Spain, to see what happened to Theo, and where. "Well, don't go alone. You'll go off your head."'

* * *

Birgit was the last person I had to ask. She brightened, 'A holiday? Where is it?'

'Costa del Sol. Fish and chips and cheap plonk.'

'Rosa, what d'you think?'

'Pistachio ice cream?'

'And honey-nut nougat.'

I didn't try to talk her out of it. Birgit was someone it was possible to just be with and say nothing. No difficult questions. I didn't know anybody else like that. I booked two rooms with balconies facing the sea, and a week later we were in Sitges.

I never even thought of a relationship. We were neighbors, occasionally raising a glass to each other on the balconies. I watched them sometimes, Birgit writing with Rosa a story of what happened to her real mum Astrid, who had changed from a violent activist all over Europe into a welder working in a car repair workshop near Victoria Park, in working clothes almost unrecognizable even as a woman. 'Is she coming here to Spain?'

'No, Rosa, she won't.'

'Are you my mum now?'

Birgit smiled. Rosa looked up at her.

'Are you going to find me a dad?'

'We'll see.'

Not my business. I was there to see where Theo died, put it all to rest. She saw a little of me at my best, teaching Rosa to swim. For my worst, leaving the beach, a bunch of rowdies lurched towards us, not just Brits but NF. I knew their walk and swagger. 'Hippies, dippies, chop them into chippies.' Rosa steered me away, but I strode back and had to crash through the middle of them. My fist was already formed, I was just choosing the first one to take my swing. Somehow I burst through the middle of them, all jostling me and jeering, and they didn't come after us. Looking down, there was my right fist, still pounding my left palm. I hadn't hit anyone.

Three weeks later I tapped on Birgit's door after Rosa had gone to sleep. I invited Birgit to help me finish a bottle of wine. We went to Sitges as friends and came home as family.

I treated Rosa to a ride on the Seaspeed hovercraft from Calais to Dover. Birgit and I with our tall rucksacks, Rosa with her little leatherette suitcase with fairies and rabbits. Rosa said, 'There's spray in his face and Jack's laughing.' I liked sea spray. Later grubby trains and tubes showed me the truth of London streets. Centuries of betrayals, triumphs, loves and lies ground between the cracked pavements. We landed at night.

The Wrong Horse had waited in the dark as we came in, the lights came on and we were surrounded by friends, cheering and singing, and the table was loaded with stews, bean salads, wine, lentil soup, and amazingly for a vegetarian house, a small but nicely roasted chicken. I wanted to be nowhere else.

* * *

After the town hall vote, at the Butcher's Arms entrance, a sturdy group squeezed in, spreading towards us. Liza and Maddy clung to Tim, with Greg and Ilaria hovering behind. There was awkward competition amongst the advance party and a hum of admiration arose from the table, and two people stood up to give a seat to Tim, clearly the man of the moment after his speech. Three staggered from the bar with drinks, and every word of Tim's was greeted with fawning chuckles.

Glasses were swung across the table with a lot of cheers. As the arrivals settled, I saw that I was the only one without another drink. Laughing sourly at myself, I stood to make room for more chairs. I was no longer at the table or in the crowd. They were all toasting Tim, and his chest seemed swollen to bursting.

Moira tinkled a glass and started to announce the results of the council vote: 'Opposed to savings and proposed cuts—twenty-three.' Several cheered. 'In favour of cuts—thirty-one.'

A silence came over the whole company.

Gradually a conciliatory murmur arose. 'Bastards! Not listening...' 'Should have been a pushover...' 'Councillors not present...' 'Should be voted again...'

The whole group seemed to shrink towards Tim, as if he had been the total opposition to the reductionist measures. He sat there surveying his troops. I stood beyond the table, empty glass in my hand, and never had I felt so detached. My friends, my colleagues, the soldiers who had fought with me for the result that was not ours, they could not be further from me. The battle had been fought and lost without me. Why was I even here? I turned away and my eyes found the door.

That was when I saw Maddy. She was beside Tim, just touching him, but she too seemed scarcely present. Her eyes were not on the company, not even in the Butcher's Arms. She was in herself, and everything around her was her own. She had all she wanted. Still interrogating her private face, I suddenly knew everything about her in that moment. She was with the man in her life, he was hers, and she must be pregnant. Mine? Who could know? She had captured the castle.

All this was in a second or two. Now it was over. I had loved and lost, and now I should leave. In that moment, as I made a first step towards the door, she saw me, her face changed, and she must have seen just where I was.

In a second she was with me, clinging to my arm, walking with me. She was talking to me but I didn't hear any of what she said. And then we were at the door. I stepped in front of her and was outside.

I didn't say goodbye. I just looked at her. I must have smiled, I don't know. Then I walked away towards Church Market. I stopped after a long way and turned, there was the Butcher's Arms and she still stood there, looking at me. Now I smiled but she probably did not see me, and I walked away around the corner.

* * *

'Birgit! How d'you spell *crystal*? "K - R – I – S...?"

A voice called out from the kitchen, 'That's German, Rosa. "C – R – Y..."'

On the long table at the Wrong Horse, with abandoned breakfasts thinly scattered, at the end, leaning over and concentrating, Rosa crouched with two drawing books, her right hand with a huge pencil wobbling in her fist, her left hand with two coloured felt pens clutched ready over the other book. Cornflakes and fruit elbowed away.

Rosa wanted answers. 'Ja-ack. Why do we only have five fingers on each hand?'

'Isn't that plenty?'

'One more and you could point while you're holding something.'

I was about to take Rosa to school but she couldn't wait. Rosa was an innovator. She was proving she could write two stories at the same time, one with each hand. And Rosa's questions: she asked every person in the Wrong Horse. Ten minutes skipping beside me to the school gate were crammed with questions. If I took too long she jumped to the next one.

When I came back it was on to mixing cement on a huge, dirty sheet of plywood. I was soon good at that, judging the mixture colour by the grey cement with the orange sand, then slopping water and shovelling quick before it breached its walls and went all over. Work went on every day, with whoever was there. Somebody knew the plan.

The house was at its best later on. The steaming kitchen, the peeling and chopping, with no two plates the same pattern and odd glasses. Always wine, I don't know how. The house itself seemed to laugh. I suppose it was stoned.

The trimphone chirped while I held the other end of a moulding high above my head, the drill dangling from my other hand. 'Jack! For you-oo.'

'Where have you been?' Nina in her severity. First time since she sent me off to sort myself out, and I ended up in Sitges, along with Birgit and Rosa, following her warning, 'You're not going on your own? In your state? No, Jack.'

The present rose in me, 'I was about to phone you…'

'I hoped you'd be on top of the jobs by now.'

I felt bullied. 'Been a bit busy.'

'Well, you know I spoke for you. Oh, don't worry. I gave you a good notice at County Hall. The one of all of us with the most heart. Not bullshitting, Jack. Don't let me down. You know what you put me through. So for the interview on Tuesday, stay calm. You'll be fine, you come across well.'

I was spluttering a little, 'Tuesday?'

'Jack! You got my letters? That was over a week ago. First board next Tuesday. Tell me, Jack!'

'Of course, Nina.'

That did it. I had told a lie.

I saw straight away. I had come back days before, my head still on the beach in Sitges, with the smiling faces in the Wrong Horse, and I had not even been home.

The mail.

Dropping the cement shovel, 'Pat, can you take over?' I legged it to my flat.

Dusty smell when I pushed my door open, heaving the pile of post. Dishes dry and hard in the sink. Bottles on the floor, tea bags crisp among them. A pile of dirty washing still smelled a bit locker-room. Beautiful smiling purple mould whiskers in the fridge seemed to move on their own.

Then the letters. Sort in three piles: serious, not sure and promotions, which went straight in the bin. Nina's stood out. Used envelope and decorative Edwardian bordered label, my name big and black. Three separate interviews. She'd put a lot into my future. Her note was a pep-talk but severe, be professional, smile if they knew about what I did with my fists, less said the better. Nothing about Nina and where *she* was going. This was my first job interview for years and I needed a lesson. Should I go in a suit?

Church Market smiled at me from both sides, Sandra in Triangle Travel, Bob the Antiques, Cohen's furs, then onions, pans, light bulbs, flash jackets. My back yard. My feet would take me to Cossington Street if I was asleep.

The Welfare was closed. Why was I going? I did not have much time, had to be back here at four. Birgit and I were taking Rosa to a puppet show. She'd been talking about it for a week.

There was Cossington Street. Of course I was going. My manor.

Thirteen, the small Georgian door with the dark glimpse of the basement. Home for two years, now big padlocks gripping the door jamb.

Cossington Street opened in front of me like a stage set, and the show was about to begin. A company of distant figures: away over there that might be Raymond. The two dodgy boys must be Chas and Pete. There, holding his hat on, surely that was Dr Hope. It was cool and misty, late September, and suddenly I wasn't sure. I blinked and slapped my face. I was not even drunk. Over the road a few men with hollow eyes smoked outside the betting shop. They all fitted into something I could not be sure about. An ending. The spirits were leaving.

Wraiths.

I turned away. My reflection in the window of Bob's Antiques, dark enough to hide itself. What I saw in shapeless jacket and straggled hair was me. I was now the ghost. I left, scared of myself.

I must have run through the market. Never before. The costers gone, the street seemed wide and empty. I dodged people with nothing to do, until I saw them, bottom of the street, wheeling around each other as Rosa always was, and her voice rattled down the empty street, 'Jack, d'you know, puppets can be as tiny as my little finger, or as big as an elephant?'

'Better not tell me, Rosa, I think I'm scared.'

'No, you aren't. I'll look after you.'

'Look after yourself, I'm a giant puppet, and I eat little girls.' I grabbed her hand and swung her round until she shrieked.

We stepped out, three in a row, Birgit and I, each holding a hand.

'Giant steps, Jack!' She dragged back a little and Birgit and I threw her forward between us and she stuck her feet together for the next giant step. Every pace rippled with her chuckling laughter. Strangers watched and smiled.

When Birgit bored of swinging Rosa, she was mine in the evening sun. I pirouetted, swinging her by the arms, up and down and round and round. Then into the air, ducking my head and she was riding my shoulders, a screech shrinking into a sigh. She squinted at the blinding sun, peeking through the cracks between her fingers. I squinted through half-closed eyes to see the same.

I was blind again, Rosa mumbling into my ear, Birgit singing a Black Forest song, I saw nothing of the dirt and dull faces of hopeless people, the sad eyes of the homeless and the girls out for their first tricks, the telling clothes in holes of those who had not worked in weeks, nor the old men dragging cardboard suitcases.

I saw the Autumn sun, burning a way ahead down roads I had walked for two years.

Rosa squeaked into my ear, 'Do you know where we're going, Jack?' I nodded.

'Have you ever got lost?'

I nodded again. 'If I hadn't been lost, I would never have found you.'

I heard her chuckle above my head, 'Don't be scared, Jack.'

Afterword:
a note from the author

Nothing prepared me for London, but when you are young, you adapt quickly. Arriving in the city in 1977, I found somewhere to live, in a commune in Stroud Green, and joined a neighbourhood social work office. My previous job, in a market town, had been stifling and lonely. Soon, I got used to the city streets and London life.

The scope of the team was extraordinary. We intervened in mental health emergencies, protected abused children, organised support for the disabled and found residential home places for the elderly. The basement of our office hosted parenting groups, mutual support groups, a cooking club and a youth crime intervention project.

The day ended when the day's work ended and that could be very late indeed. There was no idea of work–life balance, but the mutual support, pride in our work, and the creative drive to do things differently carried us along. Looking back after many decades, I see how special those years were for me.

I fell into writing this book by accident. I wrote a short story about my time on the Welfare team, and my writers' group seemed to enjoy it. And then the tales started pouring out, the characters took on lives of their own, and instead of a private memoir, I ended up with this novel. That is the beauty of writing. Out of old stuff, something new and different is created. In this case, a time-machine. Welcome to London in the 1970s.

About the Author

Robert (Harry) Harrison was active for 50 years in social work, specialising in child protection. He arrived in London in 1977 and worked for North London boroughs until 1999, when he moved to Kent and worked for Medway Social Services. In later years he established a practice as an independent child protection trainer.

He was winner of the BBC Radio 4 Ticket to Write competition in 1989, reading his account of sailing across the Atlantic for broadcast. More recently he joined a writers' group and had two short stories published in *Saxon Shore*.

Harry was married with three adult children and lived on the south coast.

He died of leukaemia aged 71, in November 2023.

www.ingramcontent.com/pod-product-compliance
Ingram Content Group UK Ltd.
Pitfield, Milton Keynes, MK11 3LW, UK
UKHW020438140225
455017UK00010B/103

9 781849 212601